# RED AS ROYAL BLOOD

# Red as Royal Blood

ELIZABETH HART

HARPER
*An Imprint of* HarperCollins*Publishers*

HarperCollins Children's Books, a division of HarperCollins Publishers, 195 Broadway, New York, NY 10007

HarperCollins Publishers, Macken House, 39/40 Mayor Street Upper, Dublin 1, D01 C9W8, Ireland

Red as Royal Blood


harpercollins.com

ISBN 978-0-06-344111-8

Typography by Chris Kwon
25 26 27 28 29 LBC 5 4 3 2 1

FIRST EDITION

TO ALL THE WOMEN WHOSE HARD WORK GOES UNSEEN AND UNRECOGNIZED.

I SEE YOU.

# ONE

A TORN SLIP OF PAPER skates under my door as the last stub of my candle gutters.

I close my book and scurry to the door, my bare feet chilled by the cold stone. Only one word is scribbled and ink-smudged on the paper—*stables*. I've just read it when the last flicker of the candle dies.

With a little grin, I swap my long woolen nightgown for my gray maid's uniform, the routine so ingrained I can easily tie my apron strings in the dark. By feel, I shove under my pillow the book I . . . let's call it *borrowed* from the royal library. Then I pull on my work boots and hurry to the stables as the last stars burn in the slowly lightening sky, grateful that the wind streaming in from the river has kept its late summer warmth.

When I reach the giant, white-washed stable doors, a hand reaches out and yanks me around the corner into a deeper pocket of darkness.

I yelp, my fingers going to my apron pocket, but when I hear the low, familiar chuckle behind me, I leave my knife where it is. "Rowan!"

"Sorry," he says, sounding the opposite. "You were about to give us away."

I twist to face him just as he adds, "Come on!" and pulls me down the side of the stables to a smaller door at the back.

An empty stall glows with the light of one small candle, set carefully on the newly swept floor. Next to it rests a polished wooden chessboard.

My eyes light up. I scramble to the far side of the stall and sit down beside the black-painted set of figures. "I've only got an hour before morning rounds."

It won't be the first night I've missed sleep entirely, between reading and meeting Rowan.

"Plenty of time for me to beat you," he replies, dropping to the floor behind the ivory set.

There's enough light to see him now—his untidy blond hair, the dark shadow of stubble along his jaw, his full lips curled into a challenging smile. And, of course, his sparkling blue eyes, full of what Mellie calls "the devil's mischief" but which have always seemed harmless to me. Any royal who's willing to be friends with a maid can't be that bad.

His clothes are rumpled, his shirt falling open at his throat, which should make him look more mess than prince, but instead gives him a disheveled charm. It's obvious he's been up—or at least busy—all night.

"So," I say, arching a brow, "who—I mean, what—were *you* doing? You've obviously not been to bed."

Rowan turns his attention to the board, agonizing over his first move, and doesn't answer. But his ears turn pink.

"Shameless."

He shrugs. "What else am I supposed to do? Cedric's off in

his own world, Belle barely talks to me, Asher's busy being commander of the guard or whatever bullshit Father set him to, and Sorren—"

He cuts himself off abruptly. But I know what comes next.

*And Sorren is dead.*

It's been six months since Prince Sorren fell—or, if the rumors are true, jumped—from the Old Tower. My heart aches for Rowan. He wasn't close to his eldest brother—as heir, Sorren was busy learning the business of the kingdom—but he looked up to him.

Everyone did.

Prince Sorren was the golden son of the kingdom of Lumaria: handsome, confident, kind. His death rocked the entire kingdom, and that made it even harder for Rowan. It wasn't just his grief he had to deal with—it was everyone's. It also doesn't help that they look—*looked*—so similar. For a while, Rowan said he could barely stand his own reflection.

As I play my first turn, I ask, "How's the king feeling?"

King Octavius has been seen little since Sorren died. No one knows exactly what his ailment is, but it's clear Sorren's death has taken a toll on his health.

"I haven't talked to him in a couple days. He hasn't wanted visitors." Rowan plays a pawn. "But I hope he's building his strength, because there was another protest yesterday. He has to respond."

"I thought Prince Asher sent troops . . ."

Rowan rakes a hand through his light hair. "He did, but that's all he can do without Father's approval. And who says troops are the answer anyway? It's not as if we want actual violence. The protests have been peaceful so far . . . if the soldiers attacked, it would be a disaster. I think—well, it doesn't matter what I think." He looks suddenly weary. "It's not as if anyone will ask me. Asher, of course, wants the show of force."

"Lately he's been really good at those," I say, not bothering to hide my distaste. Ever since Sorren's death, Asher has become so angry, short-tempered, and exacting. He's fired at least three of his valets and two of his betrothed's maids. He's always sending troops out for extra training or to intimidate protesters. But he wasn't always like this. I hate how much it bothers me that he's changed. Like it makes any difference to *me* at all.

Rowan rolls his eyes. He, on the other hand, hasn't seemed to change at all. He's always been warm, engaging, and mischievous. He was the prince who played pranks on his nanny and snuck out to learn card games from the stablehands.

"Ruby," he says reprovingly, "I did not sneak you out of the castle to talk politics. Don't you be boring too."

"Excuse me, *I* snuck myself out of the castle."

His hand hovers over his knight. "True. Your craftiness is one of my favorite qualities. But it does have its limits."

"That was the bird's fault, not mine, and you know it."

He laughs.

Five or six years ago, an owl flew into a tree at the edge of the castle gardens—the tree I happened to be hiding in. When I shrieked and lost my grip, I fell to the ground at Rowan's feet, giving away that I'd been spying on him. He chose not to punish me for my transgression. Instead, he asked me to sneak him an extra batch of Mellie's famous peach tarts from the kitchen.

My life of crime was short-lived, but our friendship has lasted.

"So which book had you up all night this time?" he asks. "One of Mother's romances?"

I shake my head, wishing my hair was loose so I could hide my blush. I should never have told him about the book I found nestled in a dusty corner of the library near some of the queen's old journals. Calling it a romance is kind. I've never read anything, before or since, that was so . . . explicit. He, of course, demanded I hand it over to him instead of returning it to the library. I have no doubt that he made use of whatever he learned in its pages.

Before he can tease me further, I tell him about the book I was reading before I met up with him, about a lost princess and her quest to stop the evil queen who stole her kingdom. Our game passes with the story, until the sun tilts a small, friendly beam into our stall, and I tip his king on its side.

"All right, that's it," Rowan says. "I refuse to play with you anymore. You're too brilliant."

I grin. "Actually admitting defeat this time? No claim of 'letting' me win or insisting it was the spirit of the Great Betrayer moving your hand?"

He flops back onto the packed dirt floor and stretches out, hands behind his head. "The night's wearing off. Why's the sun so bright?" he groans.

I climb to my feet. "Go pour yourself into bed. Some of us have to work."

He grabs my ankle as I pass. "Don't let any evil queens steal you away."

"Let's hope your mother doesn't find us, then," I return.

He guffaws. "Did you just call my mother evil?" Before I can backtrack, he adds with a snicker, "Actually, fair. Do you know she had me kissing babies yesterday? Actual babies, Ruby. Some foreign dignitary's progeny. Disgusting little things, covered in drool."

There are few limits placed on the royal family of Lumaria, but Queen Narissa does, on occasion, give Rowan what he considers punishment: royal duties.

The horror.

He releases me with a theatrical shudder, his knee scattering the pieces of our game.

"Hush," I admonish. "It's not just the queen we have to worry about. If the master of the horse catches me again, he said he'd make me clean stalls after my usual duties."

*Not* something I want to do after a night of no sleep. Or at all.

Rowan sobers. He knows as well as I do that I'm the one taking the risks here. Queen Narissa might give him a slap on the wrist or make him kiss a baby, but his livelihood isn't on the line.

Rowan and I murmur our goodbyes, and then I hurry to the stable door and slip out into the first cheerful rays of morning. It's much brighter—and later—than I thought. Shit.

The kitchen yard's the fastest route back to the servants' entrance and hopefully, if there's time, my breakfast, before I begin my duties.

As I approach, my stomach sinks. The gate's ajar. That means—

I rush into the yard, but it's too late.

There's blood everywhere.

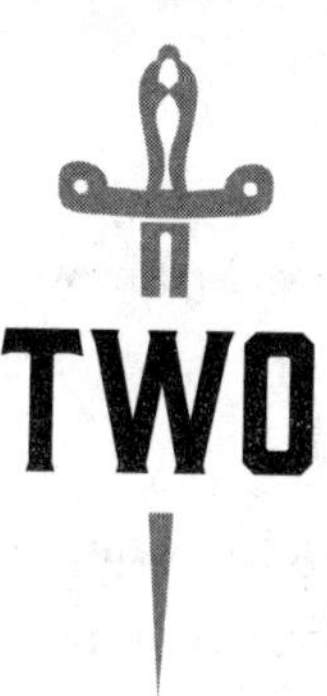

# TWO

IN THE CENTER OF THE mess of blood and torn flesh, a coyote snarls, its muzzle dripping red. My shout does nothing to distract it from its feast. I scramble for the small knife I keep in my apron pocket and throw it as hard as I can. I manage to nick the animal, which finally scares it off, but the damage it did remains.

Prince Asher's favorite dog knows how to unlatch the gate, and once open, the kitchen yard is prey to all manner of vermin—snakes, rats, badgers. Last week it was a family of foxes. We lost half the royal chickens that day.

Today it's our best mouser and her babies, tiny kittens only a few weeks old. My hands shake with rage as I clean up the carnage.

There's a small squeak, a shift in the pile of bloody fur. One kitten is still alive. It's impossible to see the extent of its injuries—there's too much blood—but I pick it up and carry it to the well to clean it off. *Keep breathing, little one. Keep breathing.*

"Come off it, Ruby," Hessa calls. "There's nothing you can do but put her out of her misery."

I stare down at the small body, streaked with its mother's blood, and imagine another baby, left alone in the wreckage of a war-torn home. If the stranger who found me crying in the arms of my dead mother had done me the same mercy—

Yeah, well. Hessa's new. Mellie would have known that the kitten would be coming with me, "mercy" be damned.

Death is never a mercy.

"I guess we'll see," I say, elbowing past her. I've got about three minutes to change my apron, find some goat's milk for the kitten, and get up to the royal family's library to start my work, or I'll be behind all day.

No time for breakfast. Damn.

The kitten mews hungrily in my arms.

"Don't you be feeding that yard cat my porridge," Hessa grouses from behind me.

"I'll keep her out of the porridge, don't worry." I grab a clean washcloth and dip it into the pitcher of milk on the table. Hessa huffs angrily as I give the kitten the wet cloth to suck on.

"She's going to break your heart, girl. Kittens that young die without their mamas. You know that." Hessa heads toward the massive cooking hearth, her arms full of herbs from the garden.

"What kitten?" Sara asks, swooping in to grab a tray of food for the main hall. Her thick brown hair has already pulled free of her braid to curl around her face. As one of Hessa's minions, her day begins even earlier than mine.

I hold up the calico fluff in my hands. "Prince Asher's dog let in a coyote this time. I could only save one kitten."

"You better hide her. Bryson's on a tear this morning." Sara raises a brow. "The king had a bad night."

Bryson, the king's steward, is *always* on a tear. His hair perpetually sticks up because his nervous hands pull it every which way, and his eyes are always bloodshot from the wine he sneaks to keep his anger in check.

Gareth, the royal food taster, nods to Hessa from the long table. "Delicious. Nothing amiss here."

Hessa grabs the tray of food. "Sara, take this to the king's chambers," she calls, but Sara's already left the kitchen.

"I can do it." I tuck the kitten into my apron pocket and take the tray from her.

I make my way up the servant stairs to the first floor, hurry along the Great Hall and down the hallway that runs the length of the castle, between its two tall, round towers. The North Tower holds bedchambers for the nobility, while the Old Tower is largely empty, with storage and several little-used rooms for those the king wishes to punish. This central section, near the Great Hall, houses the royal family. King Octavius's bedchamber sits at the center, overlooking the road leading to Ryvin, Lumaria's busiest port, and beyond it, the sparkle of the Talas River.

When I reach the main hallway, a chill wind sweeps along the back of my neck. I pause for a moment as the faint sound of a giggle echoes in the distance.

With a shiver, I glance around, but no windows are open and the giant door to the king's chambers is, as always, closed tight. Today, Drake is on duty, standing at attention in his leather armor.

I shake off my nerves and approach him.

"Morning," I say, handing him the tray. "Bad night?"

Drake shrugs. He's not much of a talker. The younger guards are bigger gossips.

With a knock, he slips inside the king's chambers, and I head back down the narrow corridor to where the royal library waits, dim in the faint glow of predawn.

The large room, designed as a private gathering place for the royal family, is quiet and empty, save for the faint memory of pipe smoke. King Octavius has always insisted this room be cleaned first each day. I settle the kitten into one of the tall-backed chairs by the hearth. She protests the separation from my warm body, but soon enough she's back to nursing the milk-soaked cloth.

Quickly, I build a fire, dust the bookshelves, and swish a broom across the cold stone floor and thin carpets, imported from some far-off country, their colors vibrant even after all these years.

I wait to dust the table by the fire until last, my heart beating a quickening tattoo in my chest.

Finally, I pause and stare at the game sitting on its polished surface.

Someone has moved the obsidian rook and taken the marble knight.

*My* knight.

*What are you playing at? You've exposed your queen.*

I stare at the board, imagining all the possible moves, teasing out every potential outcome.

And then, finally, I see it.

*Ah. Clever.*

But not clever enough.

I avoid the trap easily.

*Check.*

Rowan swears he's not my mysterious chess partner in the royal library, and I'm inclined to believe him. Seeing as we play together all the time, there's no reason for the secrecy, and he's also not as good as the person who's been playing with me, on this specific board, since I was a child. But Rowan's also always told me he doesn't know who it is, and that I'm less sure about. Whenever this particular game comes up, his eyes flick away and he usually changes the subject.

Suddenly, a thud echoes through the room. Before I have time to move, Prince Asher staggers through the doorway. He shudders to a stop when he sees me standing by the fire. I pause a moment too long, shocked myself.

Lord, he looks terrible.

His hair is a messy, chestnut whorl, much darker and longer than Rowan's, his velvet jacket singed and unbuttoned, the white shirt beneath hanging open at the collar, exposing his velvety tan skin. Okay, actually, he doesn't look *bad*. Just terrifying. His half-open eyes stare at me, dark through the firelight.

For a moment I'm caught in his gaze, surprise curling through me. He never looks at me. Why would he? I'm the broom that invisibly sweeps the floor, the magical spark that starts the fire in the hearth, the rag that disappears the dust.

I'm invisible.

I'd be lying if I said it didn't bother me. If I didn't spend nights imagining his eyes on me like a physical touch. Now, for the first time, I have his attention . . . and I don't have the first clue what to do with myself. Is this a dream?

A feminine voice sounds behind him.

"I don't think you need a book at this hour, Your Highness." A thin, pale arm shoots out to hook his elbow, followed by an ethereal face with the perfect frame of heavy, red-blond hair. "Maybe just some sleep?"

Lady Rosaline, his betrothed, doesn't notice me.

But it's obvious now that I've interrupted a private moment between them, and my frozen body thaws immediately. No wonder he's staring at me. I need to get out of here now, before he does more than stare.

I drop into a hurried curtsy, stuff the broom into the small closet behind the fallen-knight tapestry, and scoop up the kitten.

"Pardon me," I murmur, my head down. "The room is ready for your use."

"Oh! A kitten!" Rosaline's lilting voice is far too loud in the quiet. And the arms reaching toward me far too demanding. "How *precious*."

I jerk away from her grabbing hands. The kitten squeaks in protest.

"Oh, please let me see her," Rosaline says, smiling prettily. Her cheeks carry a smattering of freckles—since Sorren's death, some of the other noblewomen have taken to dotting on fake freckles with makeup now that Lady Rosaline is marrying the new heir to the throne. "I've always wanted a pet. Asher, wouldn't you like me with a little fur kitten around my neck? Like a stole that purrs! I can just—"

"No." My voice bursts out of me, shocking Rosaline into silence. I've always thought she was superficial, changing into multiple different gowns every day, making her lady's maid redo her hair over and over, but a kitten as a *fashion statement*?

"What?" Prince Asher's voice snaps across the room, sharp as a whip.

Shit. Now I've really got his attention.

"She's mine," I blurt, and then curse myself. I'm a maid. *Nothing* is mine. "I mean, I'm sorry, Your Highness. She's a mouser in training. Her mother was killed. By your dog." *No. Don't say that, don't accuse. You'll make it worse.* "I—I mean—the kitchen needs her."

I back away, toward the door. I'm in so much trouble. He's going to snatch the kitten right out of my hands. He's going to have me whipped for my impertinence. He's going to fire me—

Oh hell.

I don't wait to find out what Prince Asher will do. I turn and flee down the hall, the kitten clinging to my chest with her tiny claws.

I've just made it to the Great Hall when the lilting, haunting sound of the fife fills the room.

I stop short, dread unfurling through my body. The music is odd this early. I haven't heard it since . . .

Since Prince Sorren's death.

Across the room, Bryson bows his head as servants drape black fabric across the long windows at the far end of the hall.

Sara slips up next to me and whispers, "Did you hear?"

I shake my head, the dread now sitting like a boulder in my stomach. "What happened?"

Her hands clench into fists. "King Octavius is dead."

# THREE

IT TAKES A FEW MOMENTS for the words to sink in. The king is . . . dead? I was at his door less than an hour ago. Rowan was just saying he hoped his father was getting his strength back.

"Drake found him dead in bed when he brought him his breakfast," Sara whispers while Lissa comes up on my other side. She's holding an armful of linens, as if she was interrupted mid-task.

"So it'll be King Asher then," she says quietly, tension tightening the corners of her mouth. "Like that's any better."

"I quite liked Sorren," Sara murmurs. "He always left out sweets for us on winter solstice. He might have been different as king."

Lissa shakes her head. "They're all the same. Until they're all gone, nothing will change."

I nudge her with my elbow and hiss under my breath, "You can't say that. Not here, Lissa."

My gaze sweeps the quiet room. Like us, there are other clumps of servants standing around, with several of the older maids huddled in the corner openly weeping. I don't see any guards or anyone else paying attention to us. But that doesn't make me feel safer. If anyone overheard and reported back to Bryson . . .

Lissa hates the royal family, and she's got good reason to. Her parents died in the brutal, short-lived war with Castella, after their brazen attack on her border village. It was brutal in that many

Lumarians died, and short-lived because King Octavius paid Castella off with a chunk of our southern countryside, including the village they destroyed. A reward for their slaughter, Lissa calls it.

Lissa feels safe saying things like this around me because she assumes I hate the monarchy too. My parents were also killed in the war, after all. But she doesn't know about my friendship with Rowan. Or the books I've read on the history of our kingdom. I've never quite been able to blame King Octavius. It's not as if *he* started the war. It was his closest advisor, Lord Garrick Donahue, who sold Lumaria's secrets to Castella. Garrick, the "Great Betrayer" who gave them the troop movements and numbers they needed to successfully attack our southern border. King Octavius acted quickly to imprison his friend and end the bloodshed.

And it's true that Garrick is the most hated man in all of Lumaria. But there are those who also feel the king was too lenient . . . and too weak. Lumaria has struggled since—so much of our farmland was burned or annexed by Castella—there is real suffering. I can't deny that.

I didn't know the king personally, of course, but he always struck me as even-handed and kind. As someone who carried the weight of his country on his shoulders. Rowan has stories of his father being gentle and attentive with his children when they were young, actually spending time with them despite Queen Narissa's insistence that the king's presence wasn't necessary. And the few times I came upon him in the library, he always asked after my health. A king who notices a maid, let alone speaks to her . . . Well, it's hardly the norm.

Plus, the royal family allowed me to be raised within the castle.

I could have been sent to an orphanage. I could have been left to die as a baby.

So while I know why Lissa hates the royal family, I just . . . can't.

Across the room, Bryson clears his throat.

"As many of you have heard," he starts, his voice hovering on the jagged edge between reverent and stricken, "King Octavius succumbed to his illness this morning. There will be much to do in the coming days as we prepare for his funeral and the new king's coronation. The royal family has granted you the next several hours to mourn this incalculable loss. Please return to your rooms. You have until fifth bell to gather yourselves for your evening duties."

At the clap of his hands, we disperse.

I try to stifle a yawn, but Sara notices.

"You better use your time to sleep, Ruby," she says, nudging my arm. "You look tired as a bear in winter. I'm sorry for the king, truly am, but I can't say I'm sorry we have a little time to ourselves."

Lissa sighs heavily. "Doubt I'll get any rest at all. Can't just leave these linens, now, can I?"

She trudges off, making no effort to keep the linens from dragging on the floor. Sara and I head for our rooms.

"So," she murmurs, checking to see that we're alone in the corridor. "Another rendezvous with your prince? Don't think I didn't notice you coming into the kitchen from the yard."

My lip quirks. "You make it sound so tawdry."

Sara's the only one who knows about me and Rowan. She's

my best friend—and it's not as if I haven't covered for her a time or two for her own secret rendezvous.

"He'd make it tawdry if you'd only let him. That man has slept through half the women in this castle, noble and commoner alike." She waggles her eyebrows at me but stops suddenly when a valet turns the corner and strides down the hall toward us.

We're silent until he passes.

"It's not like that," I say when we're alone again. "We're friends. Like you and me."

Sara pauses outside my bedroom door. "Ruby, you and *Prince* Rowan are *not* friends like you and me."

I roll my eyes. "Oh, go on, Sara."

This isn't the first time we've had this conversation. And it's not like I'm entirely immune to Rowan's charms. But he's never made a move—and I've never invited him to.

I remember the way he grabbed my ankle, so casually. And so casually let me go.

I shake my head with a little smile. Sara's seeing something that isn't there.

Once in my room, I let the kitten out of my pocket. She curls up in the blanket on my cot and goes to sleep, her mottled fur sticking up like dandelion fluff. I stare at her for a moment, weighing the impossibility of us both being here, alive within the castle.

My hand slips under my collar to squeeze the small pendant hidden there, the ruby-red stone warm against my skin.

It was Mellie, the old cook, who named me, when the stranger who saved me brought me here for safekeeping. She who ensured no one took my necklace, the one piece of my past life I brought with me to my new one. I don't know what my real first name was or who my parents were. Only that they died in Castella's invasion, that I was saved by a stranger, that I was brought here, and that I was wearing this pendant when I was found.

The kitten squeaks in her sleep. She's a survivor, all right. We both are. And, like me, she needs a name. My gaze drifts to the corner of the book hidden under my pillow.

Princess. It's a frivolous name, but the lost princess in the story defied all the odds, and I'm determined that this kitten will too.

"Princess," I murmur, stroking a finger along her soft fur. Vibrations tickle my fingertip as she starts to purr. "Well. That settles it."

I tuck my necklace back under my collar and snuggle beside her on the cot. I haven't had a day off in five years, and despite the circumstances, it's luxurious to think about having seven whole hours to myself. I consider picking up *The Lost Princess of Lennox* again, but the sleepless night is catching up with me. I've almost drifted off when a loud knock shakes my door.

Groggy and a little confused, I get to my feet, smooth my apron, and straighten my shoulders. Guess our grieving period is over already.

I open the door and let out a strangled gasp.

Bryson is standing before me, a guard flanking him on either side. He has never once come to my door.

His face, drawn with exhaustion, looks especially grim. "Come now, Ruby."

"Excuse me, sir?"

"Don't make a fuss," he says wearily. "It won't look good for you."

With a quick, furtive look back at Princess, who's thankfully still asleep, I follow him into the hall.

"What's going on, sir?" I dare to ask, my heart suddenly pounding.

He doesn't reply. The guards fall into formation in front of and behind me, as if I'm a prisoner they're marching off to trial.

Is that what this is? Am I in trouble?

It's obvious Bryson won't answer my questions, and I'm certainly not about to ask the guards. They're not among the handful I know, and their faces are drawn into severe frowns.

By the time we re-enter the Great Hall, my pulse is shuddering in my throat and my hands are slicked with sweat. There's only a handful of things I could be in trouble for, but the most recent is my behavior toward Prince Asher and Lady Rosaline this morning.

He's going to fire me. I'll be out on the streets, my meager candle money too little to find shelter for more than a night or two. I might find another job, but I've heard he likes to blacklist those he lets go. I'll have to leave Ryvin altogether.

Tears well in my eyes. *Shit.*

We don't stop in the Great Hall, and I nearly lose it completely when Bryson leads our little entourage straight for the ornate, gilded door to the throne room. We can't be going in there.

We *can't.*

The only maid even *allowed* in that room is Miriam, and that's because she's so ancient she can't hear anymore.

Oh God, I'm in for it. This is going to be worse than a firing. He must be *really* pissed.

The throne room glows with opulence. Low lamps hang from the ceiling, burnished and beautifully bright. Sharp, shining swords hang from the walls, a line of soldiers in front of them. A royal blue carpet leads from the doorway straight down to the dais, where two golden thrones loom, draped in blue velvet.

One, of course, is empty.

Queen Narissa sits on the other, her golden hair pulled in a twisting sweep to the shining crown at her forehead. King Octavius's children stand on either side of the dais. My gaze finds Rowan immediately. His eyes ask a question I can't answer . . . and make it clear he doesn't know why I'm here either. I move my shoulders in a tiny shrug. He looks just as worried and confused as I feel, but more than that, there's an uncharacteristic heaviness to his features. To lose his eldest brother and his father in less than a year . . . my heart breaks for him.

Sometime in the hours since dawn, Rowan has changed into a black jacket and brushed his hair. Prince Asher, on the other hand, is still in his singed velvet coat, looking even worse for wear than when I saw him last. Dark shadows crowd under his eyes, and there's a twist to his mouth that makes the breath freeze in my chest.

Rowan's twin sister, Princess Belle, stands rigidly straight on Rowan's other side, her eyes glassy, her thin body tight as a bowstring. Their youngest brother, Prince Cedric, stands off on his own, still in his dressing gown. He's my age but has always seemed a lot younger. He stares at the swords on the wall and appears to be ignoring the rest of us.

Aside from the soldiers flanking the thrones, King Octavius's three advisors are the only other people in the room.

"Your Highnesses," Bryson says, bowing to the royal family. "Ruby, housemaid."

I curtsy a little awkwardly under the weight of their stares, and Queen Narissa raises a brow, her mouth twisted suspiciously. "Lord Hayes, why is a maid here? I don't understand."

Oh good. I'm not the only one.

Lord Tareth Hayes, one of the king's three senior advisors, clears his throat. "Upon his death, King Octavius left an edict, written in his own hand, witnessed by his youngest son."

I look up, surprised at the words. Lord Hayes rubs at the craggy line between his brows. His neat beard hides most of his face, but it's clear he's frowning. The other two advisors, Lords Simon Rutherford and Liam Stone, Lady Rosaline's father, stand beside him.

Prince Cedric remains fixated on the swords.

"An edict? Really, Tareth. I'm certain my husband's latest education crusade or pay-the-maids-more scheme can be handled tomorrow." Queen Narissa settles back in her throne, looking exhausted even as her voice shows fangs.

I catch Prince Rowan's eyes again. Did his father discover our friendship? Is this decree something to do with us?

Lord Hayes clears his throat. "Your Highness. I assure you, this matter must be handled expeditiously." He pinches his lips, like what he's about to say is as distasteful as Hessa's first attempt at liver pie. "King Octavius has . . . ahem . . . named Ruby, a housemaid, his heir. Our queen."

When he finishes his pronouncement, he stares at me, waiting.

I blink.

Wait, *what*?

# FOUR

THERE'S A MOMENT OF ABSOLUTE, deadly silence.

Then Queen Narissa yells a violent, "*What?*"

Rowan lets out an incredulous laugh. Princess Belle's eyes go wide. The soldiers shift, their swords clanking. Prince Cedric continues to stare at the wall as if he hasn't heard.

Before I can do more than gape, an "excuse me?" half-formed on my lips, Prince Asher lunges for me, his hand encircling my throat.

"What are you?" he growls. "A spy? A whore?"

I try to shake my head. Panic pounds in my chest. In moments, spots are dancing before my eyes. He's trying to kill me.

He's *going* to kill me.

"Asher, stop!" Rowan cries, rushing toward us.

Lord Stone grabs Lord Hayes's arm, his many rings clinking. "Tareth, you should have told us first," he hisses. "We could have prevented this scene."

*This scene* meaning my murder.

Prince Asher glances at the men, his grip relaxing the slightest bit as his brother reaches his side.

Just enough for my hand to shoot out from my apron pocket holding my hidden knife. The blade presses against his throat.

I can't hurt the prince. Obviously.

But neither am I prepared to die.

"Prince Asher, stand down." Lord Rutherford's voice rings out over the chaos. It's the first time the eldest statesman has spoken. "You there, maid, you too."

Like hell.

For a long moment, Asher and I stare at each other, barely a breath between us. Our lives reduced to the grip of a hand, the sharpened edge of a blade. His forest-green eyes glint with unapologetic, murderous intent.

Ever since he was sixteen, Prince Asher's been training to lead the king's army. As second-born, that was his birthright. But after Sorren's death, he was set to inherit the throne.

A throne the king has left . . . to *me*.

A shiver chases down my spine. If this man doesn't kill me now, he has every reason to try again, without the audience next time.

I try to lift my chin. I'll die before I let him see my fear.

"Asher." Lord Hayes speaks to him like a parent warning a child. It's wildly inappropriate, but maybe that's why it works.

After another breathless, razor-edged moment, the prince lets me go.

I drop my hand to my side, still white-knuckling my knife, and cough as air rushes into my lungs. My throat aches. Tomorrow I'll have bruises.

"Is she . . . is she our sister?" Rowan asks, his face pale, his expression unreadable.

"Of course not. She's not the king's bastard. She can't be," Queen Narissa spits out, disgust coating her words.

Before I can even begin to consider the implications, Lord Hayes shakes his head. "No. She doesn't share the royal bloodline. The king states explicitly that she has no birthright claim to the throne."

"Then we'll have the edict dissolved," Lord Stone says. "Blood claims supersede whatever this drivel is. Our country can't be given to a *maid*."

Honestly, I'm sort of offended now? Even though I agree with him. There's obviously been a mistake, with four children of the king still living.

But Lord Hayes shakes his head. "The edict was witnessed, written in the king's hand with his personal seal. This is now the law of the land. You know that, Liam."

"But," I say, my voice hoarse and far too hesitant, "did he say *why*?"

Lord Hayes's expression eases. He looks truly regretful as he says, "I'm afraid not. Only that it had to be you, and that you're not of royal blood. Perhaps his reasoning will become clear in time."

Cedric abandons his contemplation of the wall and shuffles to my side. He pats me on the shoulder. "'Ruby's history is Lumaria's history. She will be our kingdom's future too.' That's what Father said." His green eyes, so similar to Asher's, seem to look through me, his skin chalky white in the flickering light.

"This is absolute horseshit," Prince Asher breaks out. He looks like he wants to strangle me again.

It's hard to blame him, given what was taken from him. But

I'm not up for another murder attempt. I take a wobbly step backward.

"I . . . I need a minute," I say softly. "Can I take a minute?"

Lord Hayes draws my arm through his, as if I'm a lady to his gentleman. "Of course, Your Majesty. You should rest. Tomorrow will be a very complicated day. We'll have to announce the king's edict, start to prepare you for the coronation. It will take some time, a few weeks perhaps, to organize everything—"

"You can't be serious, Tareth. Are you telling me we're not going to even try to fight this?" Queen Narissa stands up, looking as fierce and terrible as any mythical dragon.

The advisor's jaw tightens. "There is nothing to be done. The king's word is unto God's."

"But what about Asher?" Princess Belle breaks her silence.

Her question hangs in the air, unanswered. I try to catch Rowan's eye, but he's looking at his sister.

Lord Hayes turns me around and leads me out of the throne room with his final words, *the king's word is unto God's*, ringing in my ears.

I'm so dazed, so utterly disoriented, I don't notice where we're going until Lord Hayes stops before a massive door, Drake waiting beside it.

I balk. *No.*

"This isn't my room," I say, my voice a jagged memory of itself.

"It is now." Lord Hayes ushers me inside a vast suite: velvet chairs, roaring fire beneath a massive marble mantel, an arched doorway leading to a four-poster bed that is itself bigger than my entire bedroom. This is another room I've never had permission to clean.

"My lord, I can't sleep here. These . . . chambers . . . are not mine. I belong in the servants' quarters. I have a room. My room—" My tiny room with one candle per week, one low cot, one blanket. The same room I've slept in every single night since I came to the castle as a baby.

Princess is there now, alone.

Panic seizes me, the words spilling faster and faster. Away from the royal family, away from the surreal shock of the throne room, reality is starting to set in.

Except this is absolutely *not* reality.

The king's advisor lays a heavy hand on my shoulder. "I know you've had a shock. Hell, we all have. I had no inkling the king intended to make you his heir and, frankly, I would have counseled him otherwise. It's to your credit that you're grappling with this . . . well . . . let's call it a gift. I pray, Ruby, you'll use your newfound power wisely."

His words are meant to be a comfort, but the weight of his hand feels like a warning.

He gestures to the soldier standing in the hallway. "Drake will be one of your personal guards, as he was the king's."

"I don't need—"

He silences me with a look. "You have no conception, dear, of how many people now want you dead."

I swallow down the breath caught in my throat, along with the memory of the murderous glint in Prince Asher's eyes.

"Good day, Your Majesty," Lord Hayes says, bowing his head. And with that, he leaves, closing the door behind him.

As soon as I'm truly, utterly, alone, I sink into one of the chairs by the fire and begin to cry.

# FIVE

WHEN MY TEARS FINALLY DRY, I look around the velvet-draped room, trying not to gaze through the arched doorway at the empty bed in the other room.

The bed where the king died. Just the thought sends a shiver through me.

I force myself to focus on the cobweb clinging to the ornately carved leg of a desk in the corner. The smudge on the decorative silver plate on the mantel. A small stain at the edge of the carpet under my feet.

I stand up and run a finger along the shelf next to the mantel. Sir Miller, the king's valet, is responsible for cleaning his chambers, but the king sometimes called for Lissa to help. Now I can see why.

My hands itch to dust the shelf, to scrub the carpet, to wipe away the cobweb, to polish out the smudge. I've never been idle a day in my life. I've wished for time to relax, with no tables to dust or sweat-stained linens to shuttle downstairs. I've fantasized about reading a whole book sitting in a chair in the sunlight of the garden, as I see the nobles occasionally do.

But I have never wished to be a queen.

*Never.*

A soft knock startles me, my whole body freezing like I've been caught stealing. I wait for a second, but of course the king isn't going to open the door. *Get it together, Ruby.*

Sara is waiting on the other side, Princess in her arms.

"Oh Sara, thank God it's you." I grab her in a tight but awkward embrace, trying not to squish the kitten, and pull her into the room.

The tension in my shoulders immediately loosens. It takes me a moment to notice how rigidly Sara is holding herself, in contrast. I release her slowly.

"This little terror was roaring like a bloody panther in your room," she says. "I figured you'd want her with you." She hands me Princess.

"You're an angel. Thank you."

With a single demure mew, the kitten starts licking my ear. "I guess you really are a princess now," I murmur, comforted by her presence.

"Is there anything else you need, Your Majesty?" Sara asks with a strange edge to her voice. She curtsies stiffly.

"Oh no, don't do that. It's *me*, Sara. Please," I burst out. Today has been the most surreal day of my life. The last thing I need is Sara curtsying to me.

For a sickening second, I think she's going to do the "Your Majesty" thing again.

But, instead, her stiffness breaks, and she rushes to my side. "Okay, Ruby, spill. Were you having an affair with the king? That's what everyone's saying. That he was madly in love with you, mad enough to make you queen. How could you not tell me? I could shake you!"

"Uh, Sara, you kind of *are* shaking me."

She loosens her grip on my arms. "Oh. Sorry! But seriously, tell me what the hell is going on."

My shoulders sag. "I honestly don't know. I was definitely *not* having an affair. If I had been, believe me, you'd know. I've never even kissed anyone aside from Milo, and remember how many hours we spent on that disaster?"

She opens her mouth, closes it, then arches a brow. "So was he your dad? Are you a secret love child or something?"

"Not according to Lord Hayes. Everyone seemed very insistent that I have no connection to the king. It has to be a mistake." I slump into one of the stupidly opulent burgundy chairs. "I meant less than nothing to King Octavius. I think he once asked me if I was having a good morning. I didn't even realize he knew my name."

And yet he chose *me*?

Sara sinks into the chair across from me. "What does Prince Rowan think?"

"There was no time to talk," I say. "But he seemed as mystified as everyone else."

"I guess you won't have to keep your friendship a secret anymore."

I haven't had time to think through any of the implications yet. But that does seem like a not-terrible thing. "True. But I . . . I don't know how any of this is going to work. It doesn't seem real."

Sara gestures at Princess, who's gnawing on the end of my apron strings, and says, "I guess she won't have to be a secret either."

"I need to find her some food." I rub my hands over my face. I probably should eat something too. But it's not like I can pop into the kitchen and pinch some of Hessa's fresh-baked bread, like I usually do.

"I'll bring you something," Sara says, moving to stand.

"Wait, Sara. Will you stay up here with me?" I ask. "You can be, well, I guess my maid? Or something." The question feels strange in my mouth. My brain refuses to accept that we're on such different footing so suddenly. But I can't do this without her. She's my best friend.

After a moment, she shakes her head. "I'd like to, but I don't think that's a good idea. How would it look if, first chance you get, you promote your friend to one of the most prestigious jobs in the castle?"

"Like I'm smart to keep my friends close?"

"Or like you're doling out favors. And it's not like I can really help, anyway. I work in the kitchens and deliver food. What do I know about makeup and gowns? I'd have you looking like Lady Fordham after she fell into the punch bowl."

"But Sara," I protest, even though she's probably right.

She stands over me and touches my head, briefly, fleeting as a benediction. "I'll still be here in the castle. Send for me anytime you need me. And don't be a shitty queen, all right? You know what it's like for the rest of us. Don't forget."

As she turns away, her usual grin slips, revealing the barest hint of envy. I don't blame her, just as I know she wouldn't believe me if I said I didn't want any of this.

"I won't forget," I call as she slips from the room.

As I sit alone, the silence grows teeth. What did they sound like, the gasps of the king's final breaths?

Do I hear them now?

And what are the servants and nobility saying about me? That I was sleeping with the king? That I'm some kind of bad actor, stealing the throne?

I can imagine their whispers, cruel and dismissive.

I try to focus on Princess's quiet purr, the snap of the fire. My own breath, fast but reassuringly steady. I try to imagine my future.

But hell if all I can see before me is the smudge on the stupid silver plate on the mantel. I let my face drop into my hands. I'm sitting here, supposedly the fucking *queen*, and all I want is to clean away that stupid smudge like the maid I actually am.

I can't help myself. I take the edge of my apron and rub savagely at the mark. It disappears long before I'm satisfied, and I rub and rub and rub.

When at last my arm is tired, I move to put the plate back. That's when I see the small box hidden behind the plate. It, too, is smudged.

It's small and silver, with a strange indentation on its lid. And a single word, engraved:

*Ruby.*

My heart flips in my chest, and a faint buzzing sounds in my ears.

I try to open the box, but it's locked. I try pressing the indentation with my fingertip, but that does nothing. Only . . . the shape seems weirdly familiar, almost as if it's the impression of something . . . something I've seen before.

My hand goes to my necklace.

No. It can't be . . .

Almost as if compelled, I remove the pendant from my neck. I place the ruby stone into the indentation. A little shift, a roll, and *there.*

I press, and the lid clicks.

My breath stops. Just completely stops. A hidden box with my name on it, and the key is the necklace I've had all my life.

My hands tremble as I open it. Inside, a scrap of parchment. And beneath it, a thin band of gold. I unravel the parchment to find a note written in the king's hand, the same stark, aggressive penmanship that marks all the king's edicts, hung in the Great Hall. Will the one declaring me queen be hung as well?

*Ruby,*

*If you have found this letter, it means I am dead and you are queen. I know I can trust you, as I could not trust anyone within my circle.*

*Because if I am dead, then I have been murdered. And by someone close enough to strike. A viper dressed in royal clothing.*

*You are now in danger too. Find my killer, for your own safety and for the safety of Lumaria.*

*The answer lies in history.*

*King Reginald Octavius*

# SIX

MURDERED. THE KING WAS MURDERED.

I sleep restlessly, awakening often to turn the king's words over in my head. All I can think is: It has to be a joke. A cruel joke. Or a nightmare, one that I would really love to wake up from. But the hours pass, with the deep onyx night giving way to the butter yellow of dawn, and I'm still here, in the sitting room, with the parchment bearing the king's seal in my hand.

I've committed the words to memory, but I can't tease out their true meaning. *The answer lies in history.* Lumaria's history? Or my history? The history of an orphaned girl who doesn't know her last name? I don't even know where to start.

Outside, the church bells sound out the hour. Eight in the morning. Hours after the first of the castle staff have awakened to begin the day—stoke the fires, feed the chickens, clean up whatever messes the royals made during the night.

That is my true history, my birthright. I should be down there right now, listening to Lissa grumble about the royals, teasing Sara for eyeing the new maid. Not up here, trying to solve a murder. But just as I landed on Mellie's doorstep twenty years ago with nothing but a ruby necklace, this is how my board's been set.

Which means it's time for me to make my opening move.

I have to go see the king himself.

King Octavius lies in state in the Great Hall. The room is dim, lit only by a ring of candles around the body and a faint glow filtering through the black curtains. The doors will be open to the public tomorrow, after the edict is read and the line of succession announced, but for now only the royal family is allowed. Which includes me, I guess.

So, for now, I'm alone.

Me and the king.

The king who was killed. The king who chose me as his successor. Who tasked me with solving his murder.

Oh God.

I'm so out of my depth I might as well be tangled in the reeds at the bottom of the Talas River.

My slippers whisper against the stone floor as I approach the ring of candles. It feels indecent to be here, by myself, staring down at the king's face.

A giant golden pendant rests on the chest of his blue velvet coat, and a crown dotted with rubies has been set on his artfully arranged hair, which began showing streaks of gray a few years ago. Despite the makeup and massive ermine fur draped around his shoulders, his skin has a bruised, bluish tint to it. His lips are closed but his mouth looks strange, as if he died gritting his teeth.

As if his death—his murder—was painful.

Did he see the end coming? Was he face-to-face with his killer? Or did he die in the dark, aware of the blow about to fall but not aware of the hand that dealt it? And what was the manner of death? What could kill a man without leaving a mark?

I could fill a kingdom with all my questions. And it's selfish, so selfish, I know. But all I want, more than anything in the world, is to ask him *why*. Why me? Why did he think I, of all people, could do this?

"Why?" I whisper into the silence, reaching out a tentative hand toward the king's waxy, bluish-pale hand.

"He owes us all answers."

I nearly jump out of my skin. Looking wildly around, I finally see him, deep in the shadows beyond the circle of candlelight.

Slowly, Prince Asher comes to join me. He looks more put together than the last time I saw him, and deadly sober. His dark green eyes glint gold in the firelight, and my heartbeat quickens. He's so close I can smell his woodsmoke scent, see the strain of his muscles beneath his jacket. The hard edges of his beauty are terrifying. He's changed so much in the past six months. It's no wonder my fascination has turned to fear.

I take a step back.

"Are you here to grieve?" I ask, forcing my voice to remain steady.

If someone killed the king, my money's on the newly violent son with the most to gain.

"I could ask you the same," Prince Asher says.

Mellie once told me, *Sometimes the lords will talk while you're in the room and you'll think they're talking* to *you. But to them, we're not real people. Say nothing, and they'll work it out soon enough.*

So I stay quiet, my eyes trained on him, waiting him out. The move here is his to make.

He steps forward, resting his hand on the polished mahogany

table his father lies on, and growls, "My father was born in this castle, like his father before him. Our family has led Lumaria for generations. Do you really think my family's legacy will be yours?"

I shrug as casually as I can, ignoring the frantic beat of my heart. "Your father did."

He makes a noise in this throat. "My father was ill and heartbroken. Susceptible to influence. What did you say—or do—to him?"

He steps closer, and suddenly I'm excruciatingly aware that we're alone. Drake is waiting for me outside the hall . . . If I scream, will he reach me in time?

Trying to keep my voice even, I say, "I don't think you're giving your father enough credit."

Fury breaks across Asher's face, his eyes burning like green flames.

"Good day, Prince Asher," I say, before he can try to kill me with his bare hands again.

"You're wanted on the terrace," he grinds out, as if the words cost him something. "For breakfast."

"Breakfast?" I echo, blinking at his sudden apparent attempt at civility.

His eyes take in my clothing, the maid's uniform I have yet to change out of. "I hope you have other clothes. If we are all to play this foolish game, then dress for the part"—he casts me a cutting glance—"while you still have it."

I bristle. I may be "just a maid" but I know what disrespect sounds like. And I've never been good at keeping my mouth shut.

"Your Majesty," I say sweetly.

"Excuse me?"

I tilt my head, my gaze as steady as Asher's. "You forgot to say 'Your Majesty.' You can thank your father for that."

With a last little smile for the prince and the king lying in state behind him, I spin and head for the doors.

It's no doubt a trick of the light but, for one brief moment, I could swear that the dead king smiled back.

# SEVEN

WHEN I WALK OUT ONTO the terrace, the nobles taking their breakfast fall silent. Absolutely silent. Every face turns to me, except for Rowan's. He's staring fixedly at the table. I raise my chin, thinking of the king's note. Any one of the people eyeing me could be the killer.

Lord Hayes leads me to an empty chair at the head table, with Prince Cedric to my right and Rowan on my left. Rowan is the only one who stands as I approach.

"Welcome, Your Majesty," he says, loud enough for everyone to hear. "You look beautiful."

I glance down at my dress. After I returned to the king's—*my*—rooms, Lords Hayes and Stone arrived, along with Beatrice, the head seamstress, who came laden with Princess Belle's old gowns and an army of assistants. Even though Lord Stone sniffed disdainfully at the choice, I ended up in a sky-blue gown with puffed sleeves and no corset.

My first win as queen, I guess.

I cut my eyes to Asher, whose lips are pursed in a tight line. I raise a brow in his direction, my message clear. *Did I get it right?*

Rowan takes my hand and draws me close enough to kiss my cheeks, enveloping me in his warm, peppery scent, like bourbon and pipe smoke. "They expect you to act like a maid," he murmurs. "Surprise them." He pulls away, blue eyes glinting. His words are encouraging, but there's tension in his body and little warmth in his eyes. Is it because he doesn't want anyone to guess our history?

Or because he begrudges me my new title?

I sit down, my back straight. It hasn't escaped me that Prince Asher is seated at the center of the U-shaped table, his mother at his right hand, Lady Rosaline at his left. Rosaline's thick red-gold hair is braided into a crown, and with her lovely green dress and regal bearing, she looks the part of a future monarch. For the past couple of years, there's been speculation about why they haven't set a date yet. Asher doesn't seem like he's in any hurry, though Lord Stone's impatience is palpable.

I could lay claim to the seat of honor, but it feels prudent to wait until after the actual coronation to assert myself. Letting them all think I'm a submissive, pliable maid, way out of my depth, could be helpful. In all the mysteries I've read, the murderers are caught by their own hubris. And, in chess, overconfidence will kill you every time.

Let them underestimate me.

Prince Asher catches me looking at him. His glare could blister the skin off a tomato. There was a time when I would have welcomed the attention. But now I hold his gaze with effort, secretly relieved when a server appears beside me, blocking my line of sight. Once the food is in front of me, I can't look at anything else. I haven't eaten since yesterday morning, and it smells *incredible.* Hessa's been working on perfecting these quail-egg salads for months and it shows.

"Will you be needing a lesson in table etiquette, *Your Majesty*?" Prince Asher asks, his voice as hard as stone. "I can't imagine that's a traditional part of maid training."

Rosaline coughs into her napkin while Queen Narissa doesn't bother hiding a low chuckle.

"I don't require any assistance, thank you, Your Highness," I reply, forcing myself to meet his flinty gaze once more. "I was just admiring the splendor of this meal. I've never seen quail eggs arranged in such a way. The sugar nests are truly inspired."

For a split second, he looks flummoxed. I smile beatifically and take a delicate bite—with the correct utensil. I wonder how Asher would feel if he knew his childhood tutor taught me the alphabet *and* table manners. Mellie had insisted on the lessons after finding me up a tree for the dozenth time, spying on the young princes during their sparring lessons—and . . . other pursuits—declaring that it might make me less of a menace if I had something to do.

Not that it stopped me from climbing trees, as Rowan can attest.

As I eat, I take inventory of the table. Princess Belle sits across from me, with Lords Hayes, Stone, and Rutherford spread out beside her. She doesn't acknowledge me. Then again, she isn't really acknowledging her meal either. She just sits, spine like a wooden rod, her ice-blue eyes unreadable. Her blond hair's been bound in a smooth, severe bun, and she's so still it's almost as if she's carved of marble. The effect is unsettling. I've never met anyone who revealed so little of what they were thinking and feeling. Rowan is always trying to convince me that he and Belle can read each other's minds, but it's hard to imagine Belle tipping her hand to anyone, even her twin.

The conversation resumes around us as everyone begins eating. I hear comments about the weather, a recent joust, and an upcoming theater performance from a traveling group—everything but the fact that the king died and named an interloper as heir. Throughout it all, Asher's glare singes me; it's easy to imagine he's restraining himself from throwing a dagger across the table straight into my heart. I feel for the knife I tucked into my reticule, grateful for its familiar weight.

And even though it's Asher's gaze I feel, he's not the only one with murder in his eyes. Queen Narissa looks particularly incensed. But any one of them could have killed the king. Any one of them could want to kill me now.

As if reading my thoughts, Cedric leans in closer beside me. "I'm sorry about my family," he says, speaking for the first time, his voice barely above a whisper.

His brows are a little untidy, his dark hair a bit unkempt, but he has the same craggy good looks as his brothers. He's different, though. Both kinder and yet a little more . . . vacant. Connell, his valet, told me once that he hasn't been the same since Sorren's death. Cedric saw his brother fall off the Old Tower battlements and was the first one to come upon his broken body.

"It's an adjustment for all of us," I say, trying to be charitable. "Prince Asher expected to be king. I imagine any prince would want to be."

"Not me," Cedric says, shuddering slightly. "The decisions a king has to make. . ." He trails off and shakes his head.

"I haven't had much practice making them myself," I say ruefully, and then want to pinch myself for drawing attention to my *extreme* lack of experience.

"How will you do it then? Do you have a plan?" For the first time, Cedric's gaze sharpens, like he's fully focused on my answer.

A plan? It hasn't even been a full day since Lord Hayes declared me queen. Of course I don't have a plan. I barely feel like I have a functioning mind. But to admit that aloud . . .

I glance around the table, but no one appears to be paying us any attention. Princess Belle is locked in conversation with Lord Hayes, and Rowan's still focused on his plate. Even Asher is occupied, responding to a question Rosaline has asked him. "I trust . . . I trust we'll muddle through somehow."

Cedric's expression tightens. "You shouldn't trust anyone here. The castle is a den of vipers. Lies upon lies."

A chill runs down my spine and a thin ribbon of fear curls through my body. *A viper dressed in royal clothing.* Is it a coincidence that Cedric used the exact same word his father did in his note of warning?

"Even you?" I ask with a smile, trying to lighten the mood before one of the other royals notices our conversation. It's dangerous, so dangerous, talking about this here, now. My time as a maid taught me that someone is *always* listening, whether you know it or not. And in court, words are as good as weapons.

Cedric loses focus once more, like he's not really seeing me. "My whole life is a lie."

His words land like a stone. Before I can answer, though, Rowan taps his glass. The silence grows thicker as he raises his goblet toward me, an almost agonized look flitting across his features. "I'd like to propose a toast, to the new queen of Lumaria. May she—"

"This is horseshit." Prince Asher shoves to his feet. "Continue with this absolute joke if you must, but do it without me."

In the stunned silence that follows, he storms off the terrace and into the garden. Every eye lands on me. Rowan is the only one who looks away. Somehow, that makes it so much worse. A flush rises to my cheeks. Suddenly, it's all too much. The edict. The note. The lack of sleep. All of it.

"Um, excuse me for a moment, please," I say, pushing my chair back. I force myself to keep my pace steady until I reach the hallway just inside, where I pause and take deep breaths until my pulse slows. I stare at my reflection in one of the many decorative mirrors hung in the airy hall. Suddenly, it's not just my reflection that stares back.

I gasp.

Princess Belle stands behind me, the pallor of her face heightened by the stark black of her dress.

"You shouldn't have left the table," she says.

"I'm sorry, Your Highness," I say automatically.

"And what exactly are you apologizing for?" she asks mildly, one eyebrow drawing up.

"I just . . . I mean, I'm sorry for—" I trail off, cursing my awkwardness.

"First rule," Princess Belle says, eyeing me narrowly. "Never apologize. Ever. A queen owes nothing to anyone."

"I—"

"And keep your true feelings to yourself. Don't show any fear, or any emotion at all, for that matter. We will be watching you. *Everyone* will be watching you." A shadow crosses Belle's face. "Your time of bowing and compromising and considering others is past. If you show weakness, if you fail to assert yourself now, we will devour you. Do you understand?"

I nod, at a loss for words.

"Good," she says. "Now let's return to the table. And this time, don't flinch."

As we walk out to the terrace, her words of warning ring in my ears, sharp as teeth and ready to swallow me whole.

# EIGHT

EVEN AFTER LOCKING MY CHAMBER door behind me, even with Drake standing guard outside, I can't relax. I pace in front of the fire, Princess chasing after me.

Cedric said everyone in his family lies. Belle told me her family would devour me. Earlier today, Asher flat-out attacked me. Queen Narissa was openly hostile. And Rowan . . . well, he stood up for me, but he also acted strange. Tense. He wouldn't meet my eyes.

Is a member of the royal family a murderer?

*Think, Ruby. If you were playing chess, what would be your next move?*

I pause, focusing on that. Chess strategy. That's something I know.

What do I need? More information. Okay . . . so I've got to use my pawns, a knight, maybe, to explore the board.

I ring for Sara.

By the time she arrives, I've settled slightly. Princess is curled in my lap, her tiny body warm and relaxed. She purrs loudly. The fire crackles. It's too hot in here, but I don't want to open the windows and risk someone overhearing our conversation.

"Ru—Your Majesty." Sara stands awkwardly by the door, looking like she can't decide whether to serve me or hug me.

"Come sit down, Sara. You know you don't have to do that queen stuff with me." I gesture to the velvet chair across from me.

She makes a face. "Bryson gave us all a lecture about how we're supposed to treat you now. He said no 'fraternizing' or 'familiar airs'—"

"I don't give a fuck what he said." She doesn't flinch. My anger's not for her, and she knows it. "Please, Sara. I need to talk to you."

As soon as she hits the chair, she sighs and melts into the soft cushions. Princess stands up, arching her back, before she turns in a little circle and resettles.

"I need your help," I say quietly. "And your discretion."

Sara's brow rises. "You know you already have both, right?"

I take a deep breath. "I think King Octavius was murdered."

At that, she sits up straight and her eyes open wide. She stares at me. *"What?"*

"He left me a note. It explains nothing, of course. Maybe he was afraid the wrong person would find it. But he did say that if *I* found it, it meant he was murdered."

"Ruby," she breathes. "But that . . . that's . . ."

"I know." I lean toward her. "What are they saying in the kitchens? Are there any rumors going around about his death?"

She shakes her head, her eyes wide. "Just that he'd been ill, and he died in his sleep. Nothing beyond what we heard before."

Okay, died in his sleep. That's what the advisors reported to me too. So, what kind of murder looks like someone falling asleep? I shift another pawn and study the board.

"Smothering someone would be hard to prove. Or poison," I muse out loud. "Or . . ."

"Or he was a delusional old man?" Sara suggests. "You know Octavius wasn't in his right mind. Can you really take him at his word?"

"I don't know." I sit back in my chair, mind racing. "Delusional or not, the fact remains that he's dead, and he changed his line of succession. There has to be a reason, Sara."

"Fair," she says. "So. Let's say he was murdered. Maybe he was smothered. Poison would leave too much of a mark, no? Bloat, foam at the mouth . . . that's what happens to the rats and snakes in the cellar."

I grimace at the mental image. But she's not wrong.

"Okay, then it had to be someone who was physically in the room with him. Smothering . . . that'd have to be done face-to-face." She looks torn between fascination and disgust. I think I'm leaning more toward disgust, personally.

"We need to know who visited him that night. And I wonder if Drake was the first one in his room that morning. Wouldn't Sir Miller have stoked the fire?" My stomach is heavy as a rock. Someone close to the king, someone he trusted—or should have been able to trust—sat beside him on the bed, took his pillow, and shoved it into his face until he died.

Is that really what we're suggesting?

Sara tilts her head. "Wait, I think I heard Sir Miller was ill that night. He was off wailing about how he failed his king, then immediately retired. He's already left the castle."

"Was he really ill? And did he leave in disgrace, or was it so he couldn't be questioned?" I ask.

Sara shrugs. "Impossible to say."

"Can you ask around? See what you can find out?" I can't go around interrogating people myself, though I might get away with asking Drake a few questions. Maybe Sir Henry Locke, the castle's physician, too. But Sara, she's always been a gossip. Her digging for information won't strike a single soul in the kitchens as odd.

"Do you really think the king was murdered?" Sara asks, still grappling with the possibilities.

I shrug, my heart jumping like a frightened rabbit. "I don't know. But if he *was* . . ."

"Then you're in danger, too," Sara finishes grimly.

I don't get a chance to speak to Drake until the next morning. And even then, I'm not sure how to broach the topic. In the end, I just have to ask.

"What is your usual shift, Drake? It seems you're always here." I push today's ridiculous gown through the doorway and into the hall.

"I work from twelfth bell at night to ninth bell in the morning, Your Majesty," he says stiffly. Drake was the king's personal guard for over a decade. He's a tall, muscular man with a close crop of silver-gray hair and deep frown lines.

"A night shift! Every night? Do you ever see the sun?" I try a smile, but as usual, Drake doesn't reciprocate.

He does answer my question, though, which is a change. Whenever I tried to make conversation as a maid, he ignored me. "I do."

Well, I guess it's an answer.

"I saw you the morning the king died," I say, more seriously, because he's giving me nothing. "Had you worked all night?"

He nods, his mouth tensing.

"Did you see King Octavius when you started your shift? Did he . . . did he look like he was about to die?" I've gone way beyond polite conversation now—I can only hope my questions sound like morbid curiosity rather than an interrogation. As the incoming queen, of course, I can interrogate all I like—but if it gets around that I suspect foul play, I'll have made myself an even bigger target. In chess, you never want to telegraph your next move.

"I saw him," Drake allows. "He didn't look any different. But he did ask me to skip my breaks that night."

The thought is jarring. "You stood out here for nine hours without a single break?"

He shrugs. "It can be done."

"Did anyone visit the king that night? Was he alone?"

"It was the middle of the night. No one entered his room until I did. The next morning. With his breakfast."

And that's when he found the king dead. I don't need to ask about that. But I do have one last question. "Sir Miller . . . shouldn't he have been in early to stoke the fire?"

Drake shrugs. "He didn't come."

I nod, letting that sink in.

"You've been working too hard," I say, because it's true. And because I need to have a purpose for this conversation. "I don't want you standing out here for nine hours without a break. I'll speak to Lord Hayes."

Drake bows his head. "Yes, Your Majesty."

As I make my way down the hall, I file away what I've learned. Drake was the last person to see the king alive and the first to see him dead. He didn't hesitate to share that information, so either it's true or he's a very good liar, trusting that his "honesty" will deflect suspicion.

He could have murdered the king himself. Or he could have fallen asleep on the job, allowing someone to slip in and out undetected.

Or, more likely, the king died in his sleep, and his note to me was the paranoid musings of an ill old man.

But if the king *was* murdered, and no one came in or out of his room that night, then there's only one other possible explanation: poison.

# NINE

IT'S BEEN AT LEAST A year since I've visited Sir Henry's workshop, but I was here quite a bit as a child, during my somewhat calamitous falling-out-of-trees phase. The room hasn't changed much. There's still a small rack of potted herbs by the single window, a long, low table covered with a blanket for his patients, and shelf after shelf of vials and bottles and other ingredients for his tinctures and salves.

The room's warmer than the cool damp of the Great Hall, almost stuffy, with a roaring fire in the hearth.

As I enter, I notice Belle sitting by the fire. Sir Henry is at his worktable, grinding something with a mortar and pestle.

"Excuse me." I stop myself from apologizing for interrupting them. I already know how Belle feels about a queen apologizing.

She looks up, obviously surprised to see me.

Sir Henry abandons his work and hurries over to me. "Your Majesty. Are you all right? What can I do for you?"

Most of the maids have had a crush on Sir Henry at one time or another—more than one girl has even made herself sick just to have an excuse to be treated by him. He's uncomfortably handsome, his silky blond hair touched with a distinguished gray at the temples. He's got the kind of eyes that stare straight into you, right under your skin. Maybe that's on account of his profession, but it's hard to look at him when it feels like he's reading every intimate thought you've ever had.

"I'm fine. I need to speak with you for a moment. Is now a good time?"

Abruptly, Belle stands and heads for the door. "Thank you, Sir Henry. I'll be back for that sleeping draught this afternoon." She curtsies briefly to me. "Your Majesty."

"No need. I'll have it sent to your room," Sir Henry replies, bowing gently.

With a nod, she disappears into the hall.

Sir Henry turns his attention back to me. "What can I do for you, Your Majesty? It was my impression you would be attending the public reading of the edict."

"Yes, I only have a little while, but that's what I wanted to talk to you about," I say. "The king's decree has everyone on edge, and I certainly wasn't expecting this . . . honor. In your opinion as the king's physician, what was he like in his final days? Did you have cause for concern?"

Sir Henry moves back to his table and begins grinding the herbs in his mortar. "I didn't see him in his final days. He refused my services. Which, yes, was cause for concern."

That's odd. Why wouldn't King Octavius want his physician there? "Did anything happen around that time? Did it appear his illness was progressing?"

Sir Henry's hands still. He stares at the table, unfocused, as he thinks back. "The last time I saw him, he was complaining of stomach pain, so I gave him a tincture. It should have helped, but he refused to see me the next day. I could hear him roaring in his room. He sounded in pain, or perhaps angry. I begged him to let me help, but he refused." He turns his gaze to me, his eyes full of regret. "If I may be frank, it has haunted me."

"Had he ever refused your services before?" I watch him closely. If the king thought he was in danger . . . would he suspect his physician?

Sir Henry shakes his head. "Never."

"Sir Henry, the whole castle knew the king was ill, but I don't remember anyone talking about what his illness actually was. Were you able to come to any conclusions?"

Sir Henry leans against the table with a sigh. "Truthfully? I thought he was heartsick. Stomach pains, fatigue, an aversion to light . . . they were all classic signs and began just after Sorren's fall. I've never seen a case so extreme as to lead to death, but I've read that it can happen."

I study him closely. "Could poison cause the same symptoms?"

His gaze flies to mine. "Poison?"

I don't blink.

Slowly, he shrugs. "I suppose. But I would expect more extreme effects, were the amount sufficient for death. There would have been discoloration of the skin, endless vomiting, an altered consciousness . . . I can't say for certain, but I don't believe the king's symptoms were consistent with a poisoning."

For a moment, I consider the possibility that he could be lying. That he slipped the king something in his tincture that, far from healing his stomach, slowly poisoned him.

But as I study Sir Henry, his brilliant, sad eyes and the collection of medications he's handling so carefully, I can't see it. He's been a trusted physician in the castle for twenty years, far longer than most physicians last. He's cared for the servants in the castle as carefully and studiously as he has the royal family.

"Thank you, Sir Henry," I say.

"May I ask, Your Majesty, the reason for this inquiry?" Sir Henry looks troubled. "Do you have evidence that the king might have been—"

"Of course not," I said hurriedly. I've moved too quickly across the board and made him suspicious. "It's just that everything has happened so fast. I have a lot of questions, just as we all do. And naturally, I want to take measures to ensure my own safety."

He nods. "I understand. I hope I've eased your mind."

"You have. Thank you," I say, smiling to hide the lie.

I step into the hall to find Lord Hayes striding toward me.

"Your Majesty, there you are," he says, breathless and disgruntled. "The council has called a meeting. We need to speak with you before the reading of the edict."

"We have a problem," Lord Stone says as soon as I enter the throne room. The royal family is here, as well as Lady Rosaline, who stands close to her father. She's perfectly dressed, as usual, but there's a subtle tension in her features and the way she holds her shoulders.

Narissa is wearing a gorgeous deep purple mourning dress with her gray-blond hair twisted intricately into a knot, and her eyes are staring daggers into my forehead.

Lord Rutherford sits at a polished table off to the side, buried in several old books and sheaves of parchment.

"Your Majesty," Lord Hayes says, ushering me to the throne.

There's something incredibly awkward about walking past Prince Asher to sit in the golden seat that we all assumed would be his. My stomach turns over. I seek out Rowan, hoping for a reassuring smile or some indication that he's happy to see me, but he's studying the edge of one fingernail, a frown flitting across his face.

It bothers me that we haven't had a chance to talk, and if I'm being honest, it's even worse that he's pretending we have no history together. If anything, my new position should make our friendship easier to maintain, and yet he can't seem to even look at me.

Belle and Cedric stand off to the side, murmuring quietly to one another. Belle keeps running a hand down his arm and squeezing his hand. Cedric looks younger today, less vacant and more uncertain.

Worried.

Lord Stone gestures to the books and papers in front of Lord Rutherford. "There hasn't been a female monarch since the days of Queen Cora, nor a break in the royal bloodline. According to the historical record and laws of the land, queens must have a prince consort upon coronation."

"What does that mean?" I ask, though my stomach is already sinking. I'm pretty sure I know, but I really, really want to be wrong.

Almost gently, Lord Hayes says, "It means you have to be married, or at the least betrothed, by the time you are crowned queen."

With an effort, I keep my jaw from visibly tensing. I have even less interest in an arranged marriage than I did in becoming queen.

"The coronation isn't for several weeks. Why are we discussing this now, before the edict is even read to the public? The people need to know what's going on."

Narissa makes a noise in her throat.

Lord Hayes draws himself up. "Are you aware, Your Majesty, that the current royal family will be utterly deposed upon your coronation? Dowager Queen Narissa is afforded certain comforts, but there are no such protections for her children once they're removed from the line of succession. Prince Asher will cease to be commander of the Lumarian military; Princess Belle's marriage prospects will evaporate. If you don't award Prince Rowan and Prince Cedric a lordship or financial support, they will be entirely excluded from the society to which they've belonged their whole lives."

I swallow back my shock. I hadn't even considered that their position in the castle would change. Suddenly, Rowan's wariness—and Asher's anger—make a lot more sense. "No," I say, trying to keep my voice steady, "I was not aware."

"In the king's edict, he makes no provisions for them. He merely names you his successor."

Each of Lord Hayes's words strike me like blades. How could the king do that to his own children? Did he truly trust them so little?

And what am I going to do about it? Obviously, I won't push them out on the streets with no status or money.

Another question rises in my mind, a confusion I can't quite unravel. "Why are you telling me this now? What does it have to do with my marriage status?"

Narissa's jaw works before she manages a barbed smile. "Surely it's obvious. A marriage to one of my sons is the only possible way forward."

Lord Hayes adds, "Marriage into the former royal family will legitimize your position as queen and show that the king's family—and the nobility—support you. We can announce the betrothal today, along with the edict, to help smooth the transition. As family to the prince consort, this will also protect King Octavius's children and preserve their place in Lumaria and in this castle."

My mind turns over his words. *Marriage into the former royal family. Protect King Octavius's children.*

*Marriage.*

"Who?" I ask, as Rowan finally raises his gaze.

"Prince Rowan makes the most sense." Lord Stone says it so casually, like he's negotiating the price for a new horse. "It would be Prince Asher, as eldest, but he's already betrothed to my daughter."

I ignore him. I ignore everyone but Rowan.

He meets my eyes, but I can't read his expression. What does he think of this arrangement? What do *I* think? I'm being dragged into this new life, whether I like it or not. At least Rowan's not a stranger, but marriage, on top of everything else?

My heart pounds in my chest. My throat tightens. Shadows crowd my vision. The flickering candlelight dims. I grip the slick gold arm of the throne as the room dips sickeningly. I'm going to faint. I'm going to collapse right here in this golden chair. I can't—

"Ruby," Rowan says, moving to kneel at my feet. He doesn't touch me, but something like understanding softens his mouth.

He knows me. He knows I'm coming undone. His voice, so familiar, steadies me. "Ruby, will you marry me?"

I take a deep, slow breath. In all the years we've been friends, I never imagined—could not even conceive—that Rowan and I would ever be in this position. But somehow, knowing that it's him, seeing his warm blue eyes staring up at me, I have the strength to say "Yes."

I don't want him to lose his position in the castle. I don't want any of them to.

And I definitely don't want Prince Asher, commander of the Lumarian military, to have a reason to test whether the army is loyal to the crown—or to him.

In chess, when your hand is forced, you have to regroup, make sacrifices . . . anything to keep your queen in play.

Lord Hayes claps his hands. "Excellent. Lord Stone, draw up the papers. Your Majesty, Prince Rowan, you come with me. We must read the edict and announce your betrothal. The rest of you, please join us as well. A united front will calm the people."

Narissa looks as if she'd like to object—Asher too—but when Rowan stands and offers his arm to me, the moment passes without argument. As a group, we head to the royal balcony, from which the king always gave his proclamations.

My heart flutters in my throat. Awkwardly, as Lord Hayes opens the doors and the roar of the waiting crowd washes over us, I take Rowan's hand.

# TEN

LORD HAYES DOES ALL THE talking, thank God. My job is to stand and wave. The warm pressure of Rowan's hand grounds me, even as everything around me feels like a dream. Once the announcement is over, so is my patience.

"Prince Rowan, I must speak with you," I say with as much authority as I can.

With a nod, he accompanies me back to the throne room. I dismiss my advisors, until at last we're alone.

And now, of course, I don't know where to start.

Finally, I blurt, "We're getting married."

A corner of his mouth quirks. He leans against the table, his legs crossed at the ankles. His relaxed pose is the opposite of the electricity running through me. I feel as if I'm about to shiver out of my skin.

"What's really going on, Ruby? I thought you were a maid," he says, and it's suddenly clear that he's not as relaxed as he looks. Tension is humming through him too.

"I *was* a maid," I say. "I have no idea why your father chose me."

The smile drops from his face. "I find that hard to believe."

"Rowan, you know me," I say, taking a step closer. "I have never lied to you."

He stares at me for a long time. Then he blows out a breath

and rubs his hands over his face. "I don't have a clue what's going on, but I believe you. It does make things more difficult, though. You're not my secret rebellion anymore. My *wife* . . . What a way to take the fun out of it."

Without thinking, I punch him in the arm.

He gives a theatrical moan.

It's the same noise he makes when I beat him at chess. A wave of nostalgia breaks over me. In just two days, my entire future—my entire *life*—has changed into something I don't recognize. My knees threaten to buckle. It's just so much.

"This isn't what you want, is it?" I mutter, trying to keep it together. "I'm so sorry, Rowan. Your plan was to wait as long as possible to get married—"

"Ruby," he puts a hand on my arm. "I have always been a shit, you know that. I was always going to get married. At least, this way . . . well . . . maybe it won't be so bad, right?"

He ducks his head so he can meet my eyes. In his gaze, I find warmth, familiarity, and maybe something else, something I don't have a name for. On impulse, I reach up and touch his cheek, warming my chilled fingers against his skin.

"If it had to be someone, I'm glad it's you," I admit. For an instant, the air between us thins. His pupils start to swallow the blue of his eyes. I start to feel—

I drop my hand and step away.

My heart flutters in my throat. Awkwardly, I take his hand. "Come on."

I lead him to the thrones.

In silence, we sit down on the blue velvet cushions, our hands splayed across the golden armrests.

"Are we ready for this?" I ask, my voice a husky whisper. I'm not even sure the question is for him. Maybe I'm asking myself. Or the ghost of King Octavius. Or, hell, the universe itself.

But, of course, it's Rowan who answers. "Ready to get married and become the rulers of Lumaria? Absolutely not."

Preparations for my coronation are unlike anything I've experienced. Instead of getting up early to sweep the library and haul linens to the wash house on the other side of the kitchen yard, I'm standing for hours as Beatrice and her minions poke and prod me. Rather than gossiping with Sara about the latest noblewoman to show up in Rowan's bed, I'm listening to Governess Blake lecturing me on etiquette . . . and thinking about how *I'll* be expected to join Rowan in bed. Rather than rolling my eyes at Bryson's newest rule over burnt pork ends and gravy in the kitchen, I'm trying to ignore Prince Asher's suspicious glares as I eat my candied pork and roasted potatoes in the awkward silence of the Great Hall.

Not once do Rowan and I have the time or the opportunity to sneak away to the stables and play chess. Not that we would have to sneak around anymore. I still read, sometimes late into the night, but now I don't need to pay out of my meager savings for more candles. Lissa has become my lady's maid, and while she used to gripe about the royal family to me, now she keeps her mouth shut and her face smooth and hard as a rock.

Neither do I have much time to do what the king tasked me

with: solving his murder. And truth be told, I'm not sure there is much to do. Drake says no one visited the king the night he died, and Sir Henry said it was unlikely the king was poisoned. Sara's heard few rumors, and the ones she has heard name me as the killer. I've debated sending a message to Sir Miller, but I'm not sure how to approach that without giving away my suspicions. The more time passes, the more I'm convinced the king was mistaken.

But even if he did die in his sleep, that doesn't mean there wasn't someone in his inner circle who wished him ill. All I can do is watch and listen and wait. For now, anyway.

Lord Rutherford has apparently chosen to focus on the logistics of the ceremony itself, while Lords Hayes and Stone take it upon themselves to oversee my transformation from maid to queen.

Lord Stone proves to be quite helpful with all my fashion decisions, though I could do with fewer withering looks and less whining about how his daughter would have made a more beautiful queen. It's clear Asher believes he should be in my shoes, but Rosaline herself doesn't appear all that upset. She smiles at me at luncheon sometimes, though we don't have a chance to talk.

Belle makes little effort to speak with me, but I notice her watching me often. Assessing.

*We will devour you.*

I also learn about the coronation itself, which is, of course, more than just a single ceremony. First, a week after the reading of the edict, there will be a parade to formally present me—and my prince consort—to the people. Then, a week after that, a ball to shore up the support of the nobility. Finally, two weeks after the ball, we'll travel to the Towered Arches for the actual ceremony.

Lord Hayes has concluded that it's enough for me to be betrothed at the time of the crowning, so Rowan and I will have a slight reprieve before we say our vows.

Despite Asher's little speech about his father in the state room, my ascension as queen will not be the first to break a bloodline succession—in the last week Governess Blake has taught me a lot about Lumaria's history, including the story of Mad Queen Mildred, who named her favorite horse her heir, and the ensuing war between her four lovers, two of whom were women. Queen Cora won that time, and the kings ever since have been her direct descendants. I believe the governess told me the story to underscore how rare and ridiculous it was for King Octavius to name me heir, but my takeaway is that there's precedent.

And hey. At least I'm not a horse.

On the morning of the parade, I still feel like a maid, but even I can see I no longer look like one.

The first of the three ceremonial gowns Beatrice made has transformed me. I stand before the mirror, swathed in red and gold, and don't recognize myself.

I force myself to take slow, deep breaths as my stomach bottoms out. The ring the king hid in the box with his letter is on my finger, a thin, cool band of gold I twist around and around. I still can't believe this is happening.

"Are you ready?" Lord Stone asks, bustling through the door, his own clothes resplendent, his strands of gold necklace clinking.

I turn away from the mirror to face him. "Yes," I reply as my heart pounds the frantic echo of Rowan's *absolutely not.*

The royal family and I ride in an opulent open carriage near the end of the parade. Lord Hayes said it was important that we all ride together, overruling Lord Stone's assertion that it should be just myself and Rowan—or else his daughter should be included with the group, which was what he was really after. But Prince Asher said something about the size of the carriage and safety concerns, so Lady Rosaline is riding with her father.

It's a bit of a tight squeeze, even without her. Narissa, Belle, and Cedric are seated together, their backs to the carriage driver, and I'm squished between Rowan and Asher. Which is not at all ideal.

"Can't you keep your hands still?" Prince Asher snaps. He doesn't touch me, but I can tell he wishes he could physically hold my hands down in my lap to keep them from tapping my knees and twisting up in one another.

"Let her be," Rowan grumbles. "She's nervous."

"Your Highness, I'm not—" I start. The *Your Highness* pops out automatically. I can't remember whether I'm supposed to call him that now. Governess Blake has a tendency to drone on, and I have a tendency to stop listening after a while.

"It's distracting," Prince Asher says shortly.

"You should have ridden with the troops if you were concerned," Rowan replies, a line appearing between his brows. "Have there been more protests?"

Asher surveys the streets around us. Most of the crowd is waiting along the road into Ryvin's main square, but there are a few stragglers here. "There are always protests."

"What are you going to do about them?" I blurt, remembering

what Rowan said before the king's death, about the question of force.

Asher turns his piercing green gaze on me, sending bolts of self-consciousness through me like lightning. "I believe, *Your Majesty*, that's up to you."

Shame curls in my belly, and my mouth goes ashy dry. I've had meeting after meeting with Lord Hayes, I've received Lord Stone's opinions on dozens of gowns, but no one's talked to me yet about the business of running the country.

"I—"

"Don't put her on the spot like that," Rowan says. "We all know it's Lord Hayes's call until the coronation, as the most senior council member. You're just trying to make her feel bad."

I appreciate Rowan's support, but it bothers me that he didn't give me a chance to defend myself first. I put my hand on his arm as a subtle *stand down*.

Asher tracks the movement. "I see you two are taking the arranged marriage well."

Literally every word out of this man's mouth is incendiary, and I can feel the angry response rising in me. But there's a split second, just as he turns away, where another expression flickers across his face. Was that . . . envy? Or suspicion?

"Boys, we're about reach the parade route," Narissa interjects, giving her sons a reproachful glare. She doesn't deign to look at me. "Let's focus on that, shall we?"

Rowan redirects his attention, but his hand slides over mine for a moment, cocooning my trembling fingers.

"Look, Belle!" Cedric says, pointing toward a fountain festooned with greenery.

Cedric is the only one of us who looks like he actually wants to be here. The childlike excitement on his face makes me wonder how long it's been since he's left the castle grounds.

There's certainly a lot to look at. Colorful squares of fabric and bright greenery are strung from windows above the streets, and bright fall leaves decorate the cobblestones. We finally reach the bulk of the spectators, and many of them are waving more of the colorful squares as flags.

Our royal carriage is the grand finale of the parade; just in front of us is another carriage carrying the three advisors and their families, including Lady Rosaline, who's waving prettily.

I should probably be doing that.

In front of us marches a line of drummers, followed by soldiers carrying the red-and-gold flag of Lumaria, with a black stripe to mourn King Octavius. Their footfalls echo in rhythm with the drums. Even the carriage horses are stepping in time. Another, smaller formation of soldiers marches behind us. The noise of the crowd is building, and it's not sounding entirely joyful.

I clench my hands into fists to keep them still. Wouldn't want to distract Prince Asher.

The people waiting on either side of the cobblestoned streets are divided pretty clearly into two camps. There are those who are cheering, waving their flags and smiling up at me. But there's a smaller, nastier group that jeers and screams. A few rotten pieces of fruit hit the ground near the carriage—no one dares throw anything at the carriage itself.

It's unclear whether these are the usual antiroyalist protestors or a new faction upset with *me* being the one to wear the crown. After all, I'm queen without a single drop of royal blood.

An older woman lunges for the carriage, throwing a tomato at the wheels. Asher tenses beside me, but a soldier escorts the woman away.

What can I do, beyond smiling and trying not to look like I'm about to pass out? I don't want the soldiers to hurt the protestors. Like Rowan, I don't think violence is the answer.

I try a little Lady Rosaline wave, but it feels weird and awkward, so I stop. Prince Rowan squeezes my arm encouragingly, but I can tell he's unsettled, too. This isn't a full protest, but it might as well be.

"Smile," Narissa says. "A queen must smile upon her subjects."

"Even the ones who scream that I should rot in hell?" I ask, smiling extra sweetly at her.

"Especially them," she counters. "You must convince them you are legitimate. You must *look* like you belong—"

A sudden shriek drowns the cheers of the crowd. There's a shadow behind me—I turn just as the carriage rocks violently to one side. Many hands reach into the carriage, clawing at my sleeves, my hair, my crown.

The crowd surges, roaring louder than the pounding of my heart. Someone grabs my wrist and *yanks*. I brace myself against the seat, struggling to pull back, but the force is too strong.

"Ruby!" Rowan's shout barely cuts through the chaos.

My other hand fumbles at my dress, searching for the knife I'd be carrying if I was still a maid. But there's nothing—only heavy brocade, useless against the wave of bodies crashing against the carriage. It all happens so fast.

We lurch again, tilting sharply as a person pulls me halfway out of the carriage. My shoe catches on the frame, and I scream as I lose my balance.

Prince Asher is suddenly there, his arm locking around my waist. "Hold on!" he commands, and I'm so shocked that he's helping me, I nearly do the opposite and let go.

Rowan is shoving at the hands that reach for me, his fine black coat catching on sharp fingers. Drake, off to the side on a horse, shouts something, his voice nearly drowned out by the roaring crowd.

Suddenly, something whistles by my head, and then Narissa and Belle are screaming too. I turn to look, and my eyes catch on the quivering shaft of an arrow embedded in the carriage wall.

"Get us out of here!" Asher growls at the driver. The horses jolt forward, just as a new wave of soldiers peels off from the parade and starts shoving people back.

I'm trembling, shaking so hard I can barely cling to Asher's arm. My hands are scraped and red from clawing at the wooden frame, my cheeks stinging where someone's nails raked across them. Or maybe it was the arrow grazing me. I put my hand to my cheek; it comes away streaked with blood.

"Are you hurt, Ruby?" Rowan asks from my other side. His golden hair is disheveled, his blue eyes bright with concern. He looks ready, maybe even eager, for a fight.

"My face," I whisper.

He examines me, his fingers gently cradling my jaw. "It's just a scratch. You're okay."

The carriage picks up speed, weaving through the lines of soldiers flanking us on the way back to the castle. Prince Asher releases me and focuses his energy on shouting orders to the driver. Cedric looks near tears; Narissa tries to comfort him, but all the color has left her face. The hem of her black dress is ripped. Belle sits rigidly on the bench, looking as if she might shatter.

"We'll get you to safety, Ruby," Rowan says, putting his arm around me. "You'll be okay."

But will I?

"That arrow," I say, staring at it. "That was meant for me. Someone in that crowd was trying to kill me."

Narissa says something, her tone cutting, but I don't hear. The king's words are echoing too loudly in my mind.

*You are now in danger too.*

# ELEVEN

BY THE TIME THE CARRIAGE sweeps into the castle's stable yard, I can mostly breathe, and my hands have stopped shaking. Narissa has gotten Cedric calmed down, but his face is still pale.

Rowan helps me down from the carriage. I can't help leaning into him; he's so warm and solid, so steady and familiar. We've never really hugged or touched much—our friendship wasn't like that—but I find myself holding him tightly now. Within the circle of his arms, I feel safe.

For an instant, he tenses, but then he draws me against his chest, and we stand like that, just breathing.

Behind me, someone clears their throat.

"Give us a minute, Asher," Rowan says, but he gently pulls away.

Asher's glaring at us, and Drake isn't the only guard watching.

"You two act as if you've always known each other," Asher says lightly, but his gaze is shrewd. "How sweet."

Lord Hayes hurries up and ushers us inside. Asher takes my arm, but I pull out of his grip.

"You don't need to touch me," I say. "I'm coming."

"Sorry . . . Your Majesty," he says, but it doesn't sound like he really means it.

Why didn't he just let the crowd have me? Isn't that what he wants . . . me out of the way? I can still feel his arm pulling me close to his body, protecting me . . . and the violence of his hand around my throat that first day in the throne room.

Rowan pushes up between us, and I'm grateful. I can't look at Asher right now.

"So what do we do now?" I ask, directing my question to Lord Hayes. "What happened back there?"

Lord Hayes slows as we approach the library. "As you know, there's been a growing faction unhappy with the crown's rule. I doubt it was an organized attack by antiroyalists, but we'll investigate who incited the mob and how they got through our defenses. In the meantime . . ." He shuttles me into the quiet, deserted room, leaving Drake, Asher, and Rowan in the doorway. "Your Majesty, please stay here a moment. I think it's time we develop a more . . . robust . . . plan to protect you. I'll return shortly."

"Shouldn't I be part of that discussion?" I ask, remembering what Belle said about standing my ground.

Lord Hayes pauses. "Of course you may, Your Majesty, if you wish. But, with due respect, what do you know about security measures?"

Fair enough.

Rowan moves to step into the room. "Would you like me to stay with you?"

"I'm okay by myself, thank you," I say. The quiet of the library is what I need right now. A moment to wrap my head around what just happened.

"I'll see if Sir Henry has a salve for that scratch," he says, nodding toward my cheek.

And with the quiet thud of the door closing behind the men, I'm alone in the king's library.

My favorite room in the whole castle.

A fire crackles cheerfully in the hearth, and the curtains are open, letting in the last golden streaks of the day. For a moment, I stand in the sunlight and close my eyes, breathing in the smell of pipe smoke and old books.

*The answer lies in history.*

It's the one line of the king's letter that feels like a true clue. But *history* is so broad . . . I haven't come up with a good way to follow the thread. As I stare at the shelves, I wonder if the answer is somewhere in this room, among these books. My interest has always been in fiction—fairy tales and romance—but I've read a few history books too.

I run my fingertips along spine after spine. There's no real organization that I can see. A history book about the ancient people of Tartula is mixed in with several books of Argan folktales. But eventually my hand catches on something interesting: a thick brick-red tome called *The Seven Weeks War: A History*. Its spine has been damaged, a large V-shaped nick taken out of the leather at the top. It looks like someone took a knife to it. I glance along the other shelves; no other books are marked in this way.

Hmm.

The Seven Weeks War is my history too, the war that killed my parents, that gave us the Great Betrayer and the rise of antiroyalist sentiment. Maybe this is the history the king wanted me to find.

I pull the book off the shelf and flip to the first page.

> The Seven Weeks War began not with an explosion or even a call to arms. No, the deadliest war on Lumarian soil in at least a hundred years began with a weakness of character and a betrayal of values, morals, and integrity. It began with treachery and hubris.

Deadly boring and the author has a gift for the dramatic. But that's not what catches my attention.

There are letters underlined.

L-O-O-K-B-E-L-O-W

*Look below.*

Look below what? I flip the page, but there are no other letters underlined. I run my hand along the bottom edge of the book, fan the pages. Nothing. Okay, look below. Below the book itself? I move closer to the bookshelf and run my hand along the empty space where the book rested. My fingers come away with the fine grit of dust, nothing more.

*Below.*

I move books around, press my fingers into the back of the shelf. Then move to the shelf below. The books directly below are nondescript, tomes in dark leather about commercial fishing techniques and farming. Except, wait—

I pull the books directly below the history book off the shelf. There, tucked behind, flat against the back wall of the shelf so you'd never see it if you didn't know to look . . .

I draw a slim leather volume out from the darkness. There's no title pressed into the spine, and the pages are thin. I open it gingerly to find words written in the king's own hand.

A journal.

The king's own journal, hidden here in the library. Was this what he meant for me to find?

I head for the chair by the fireplace, the book cradled in my arms. There must be something here, maybe the reason he chose me. Here's where I'll find answers.

Automatically, I glance at the chess table as I pass and stop short, distracted.

My partner has played.

I bend to examine the board. Hmm. Interesting move, but also—

Ha. I knock my opponent's king on its side.

Checkmate.

Very quickly, my smile of triumph fades. I study the board more closely, work through all the possible moves my unknown partner could have made.

There are at least three moves that would have thwarted me. How did they not see them? I've never won so easily before.

It's almost . . . almost as if they let me win.

I stare at the board like it's a deck of fortune teller's cards, trying to divine meaning out of the small marble figurines. The king on its side. A wall of pawns and bishops. The queen's triumph, in the spot where the king once stood.

My arms tighten around King Octavius's journal.

Suddenly, I have no idea what game I'm actually playing.

And I'm not sure I've won at all.

# TWELVE

"YOUR MAJESTY, RESPECTFULLY, THAT'S NOT the way to hold a dagger." Lieutenant Gaynor waits for my nod before reaching for my hand to adjust my grip.

Prince Asher is leaning against the wall a yard away, watching us closely, clad in leather armor and a sneer. I feel his scrutiny like a hand on the back of my neck, which makes me want to turn this knife on *him*.

Lord Hayes spoke to him about my protection because he's the head of the military. Together with Drake, they came up with the plan to teach me self-defense. Rowan was skeptical, and honestly, I am too. How will knife skills save me from an arrow to the head? But it's *something* I can do, a piece of my protection within my own control. So I agreed.

But it's not exactly going well.

Now, I almost wish I'd flounced off to my chambers and just . . . stayed there. No need to protect myself if I never leave my room. No need to see the prince and his body-hugging armor either.

And yet.

Here I am, locked in the armory with Lieutenant Gaynor and Asher, who, heroics at the parade aside, tried to *kill me*. Truly, I'm feeling so very safe and confident in these lessons.

"Your Majesty."

I force my attention back to Lieutenant Gaynor.

"You see? You have more control this way, more leverage." He shows me where to aim on the straw dummy to do the most damage.

I try to thrust the knife the way he shows me, but it feels weird, different from how I used to hold the smaller, lighter knife I carried in my apron. When the point of the dagger hits the straw, I lose my grip and the dagger tumbles to the ground.

Asher makes a small noise that sounds suspiciously like a snort of impatience.

"Excuse me for not being perfect at something I've literally never tried before," I snap.

"Never? You held *me* at knifepoint just fine." Asher pushes away from the wall and stalks toward me, his armored leathers creaking faintly. His dark hair falls forward to hide his eyes as he picks up the knife.

I flinch before I realize he's holding it out to me, hilt first.

"Again." As he turns away, his jaw tenses.

With more effort than I should need, I refocus on Lieutenant Gaynor and the straw dummy.

I try again.

And again.

And again.

The complaints are endless: I don't pierce the straw deeply enough. I don't hold the blade tightly enough.

The angle is wrong.

I dropped it again.

I stood too far away from the target.

I flinched.

There is nothing I want more than to drive the fucking thing through the prince's cold, sneering heart. Rowan once joked that his father should have put Asher in charge of the library, not the army. I remember that thoughtful version of Asher, the one who would stretch out in the garden on a sunny day with a book and a sweet, forgotten smile on his face. I have never admitted to Rowan that my love of reading was sparked by his brother.

Back then, Asher could be exacting, but he was never cruel. Not until after Sorren died. It always seemed to bother Rowan that he and Asher weren't closer. He blamed his father for putting so much responsibility, so much violence, on Asher's shoulders.

But I don't know. Maybe we just didn't see it. Maybe the violence was always there.

"Enough," Asher says at last. A moment later, he's in my space, his hands on my hands, his smoky scent pressing against me. "You can't *truly* be this bad with a dagger."

"Let me use my own knife," I say in exasperation. "Or try another move. Something else. *Anything* else."

Asher looks at me for a long moment, his hand still locked around my wrist, twisting it into what he considers the correct angle. His green eyes flash, and suddenly, all I can think about is the moment he tried to kill me. How close we were then. How close we are now.

How a blade hovers in the air between us.

He steps back, releasing my wrist, and my arm drops like a stone. The knife clatters to the floor.

I heave in a breath.

"Come with me," he says, and I follow before he can think about grabbing my arm. Soon we're hurrying down the chilled stone corridors of the castle.

"Your Majesty," I remind him. "Where are we going?"

He doesn't bother answering.

When we get to the narrow, twisting staircase of the Old Tower, he orders, "Follow me, *Your Majesty.*"

"Do I have to?" I challenge, bristling. Even when I was a maid, I didn't like being ordered around with so little civility.

He doesn't dignify this, and despite how it rankles me, he doesn't really have to. I'm not even officially queen yet. I don't have much practice being the one in charge.

That doesn't mean I like it. Glaring at his back, I climb the narrow, twisting stairs.

It doesn't take long for me to lose my breath and regret every life choice that has led to this moment.

Actually, you know what? That's wrong. I regret everyone *else's* life choices, namely the king's. Far as I can see, the decisions I've made have had very little bearing on how I came to be here, soon to be coronated queen, climbing this endless stone staircase for all eternity.

That's what Asher doesn't seem to understand. *I* wasn't the one who made myself queen. Who made myself a target of antiroyalists and of a would-be murderer.

Our current predicament is *not my fault.*

I'm gasping and shaking when we finally reach the very top of the tower.

Prince Asher shoves the heavy wooden door open, fighting the wind that swoops down the stairs with a wail. Oh, this isn't ominous at all.

Reluctantly, I follow him out into the open air. The Old Tower overlooks the city and, farther, the wide farmland of Lumaria, dotted with small villages. The Talas River flashes to our left, and the wide blue sky arcs above.

"What are we doing up here?" My hair, once neatly pulled into a bun, immediately becomes writhing black shadows around my face.

For a moment Prince Asher stands in the howling wind with his head tipped back, his eyes closed, and his hands fisted at his sides. His body tenses, and if he sprouted wings and leapt right off the tower, I honestly couldn't say I'd be surprised.

Instead, he uncoils like a snake and springs in my direction, gripping my arm and pulling me to the low stone parapet. He pushes me against it, his body flush against my back, holding me so tightly with his *whole fucking body* that I can't escape.

"What are you doing?" I ask, my voice a breathless scream. It's impossible not to think of Prince Sorren, who leapt to his death from this very tower only a few short months ago. We're so high up, the ground so small, so hard down below.

"Do you see it?" Asher growls in my ear, his breath a hot contrast to the wind.

"See what? What is wrong with you?" The rolling fields below are making my head spin, and my heart is trying to beat right out of my throat.

I'm shaking. He's going to push me over. Oh God, I'm such a

fool. I followed him all the way up here, straight to my own death. They'll find my body on the cobblestones below. Right where they found Sorren's.

Asher will have the kingdom, and no one will ever know King Octavius was probably murdered.

That *I* was murdered.

"All of that is yours now. All the people out there are living with the shock and uncertainty of an absolute fucking *stranger* taking the throne. They're waiting—no, *expecting* you to make a wrong step. To hurt Lumaria. So you tell me something, *Your Majesty.* If you don't believe in your own self-preservation, why should they believe you'll protect this kingdom? *Why should they?*"

I fight against his grip, twisting until I'm facing him, my heavy skirts tangling around my legs. My chest aches as I gasp, my corset pressing painfully against his armored leathers. His face is so close, his throat just a breath away. I wish I had my kitchen knife so I could leave my mark as I fall. He'd see how "useless" the tools of my former life really are.

His gaze burns across my face, dips to my mouth and back to my eyes. The fire of his anger is too hot. Entirely too much. I shake my head a little, the past pushing at me. I'm not the only one with a former life. I remember who Prince Asher was once.

"What happened to you?" I can't keep the words from escaping. "You didn't used to be like this."

"You don't know me." It's not until he speaks that I realize he's panting too.

"I know you used to hide in the orchard when you were worried about your lessons," I say. "I know you used to care if your dogs behaved badly. You'd work with them personally. And you were kind to the staff. You kept your hands off the maids." My gaze flicks to his hand, still gripping my arm, its heat searing into my skin.

His grip loosens, but he doesn't let go. "How could you—"

"I know you cried when your brother died. When he fell from *this very tower*."

A storm breaks across his face. He lets go fully and steps away from me. "Don't talk about Sorren. Don't talk like you know *anything*."

"Maybe instead of killing me, you should take a minute to wonder why your father thought me necessary. Why would he choose me? Why not you, Asher? Do you really think it's because of *me*?"

As Mellie always said, I'm a make-mistakes-to-learn-from-them kind of person.

And I know soon as the words are out of my mouth that they are absolutely, one hundred percent a mistake.

The storm in Prince Asher's eyes quiets to a dangerous, *ravenous* glint. He pushes up against me, his hands gripping my waist, ready to heave me up and over.

*Shit.* I scrabble at the stones, trying to find purchase.

"Your Highness, that part of the parapet is old. Please take care."

I whip my head to see a soldier approaching. He's in uniform, an array of weaponry strapped to his back. Obviously on duty.

He looks almost . . . embarrassed?

Suddenly, I'm even more aware of the way Asher's holding my

waist, the closeness of our bodies. It's possible the soldier is misinterpreting this little murder attempt.

Do I scream? Tell him to shoot Prince Asher?

Would he even do it? What the hell kind of loyalty can I expect when my coronation is still weeks away? He'd probably cheer if Asher pushed me to my death. They could have a little bond over my crumpled body, share a pint, and reminisce over how they saved Lumaria from the evil maid.

I shove Asher's chest with both hands, as hard as I can.

For a split second, he's a rock. And then, miraculously, he yields.

I make space between myself and the crumbling parapet. Space between myself and the prince. "Thank you, sir," I say, addressing the soldier. "I think you might have just saved my life."

And then, before he can reply—before Asher can put hands on me again—I sweep my heavy dress to the door and descend the narrow stairs.

# THIRTEEN

"ARE YOU READY FOR YOUR evening bath, Your Majesty?" Lissa asks later that night.

"Yes, thank you." I stand up slowly, cradling Princess in my arms. My body creaks, sore from the training with Lieutenant Gaynor, achy from the tension running along my shoulders.

Dinner was exhausting. Asher kept staring at me, Rowan seemed lost in thought and barely spoke, and Lord Hayes couldn't shut up about the new security measures. Narissa gossiped with her noblewomen friends, their frequent glances making it clear who was the subject of their barbs. Belle and Cedric weren't there at all. I hope Cedric isn't too traumatized from the parade, but I'm also kind of jealous. I wish I'd thought to have dinner brought to my rooms.

But now, finally, it's the one time I get to silence everything, even my own mind.

Theia, my other maid, follows Lissa into the bathroom; a moment later the sound of rushing water fills the room. Princess squirms until I set her on the ground. I open the windows, letting in a cool breeze.

In the distance, bells chime. The king's chamber faces the Talas River. All I can see to the horizon is the pinks and purples of sunset reflecting on the water and a small, bright suggestion of sails near the port. I stand in a wedge of fresh air and breathe deeply.

*You'll figure this out, Ruby.*

I've already read the final entries in the king's journal, looking for an explanation of why he chose me. But the last entry was from years ago, long before even Sorren's death. I'll have to start again from the beginning. *Something* in there must be important. Else why all the secrecy?

And then, of course, there's still the mystery of whether the king was murdered at all. If Drake is telling the truth, no one was in the king's room the night he died. And if Sir Henry is right, he wasn't poisoned. But someone tried to kill me at the parade. And the king felt he couldn't trust his own inner circle, maybe his own family.

Who was he afraid of? And why did he choose me? I can't help hoping that . . . somehow . . . *my* history is important. That I might be able to discover answers to the questions I've been asking my whole life. Who were my parents? Why was I taken to the castle instead of an orphanage or another family? What about me or my history made the king think he could trust *me*?

My heart aches with the uncertainty of so many unknowns. I can only stand still for so long before I have to move, before I have to do something.

I grab my small maid's knife from the table beside the chair. The dagger Lieutenant Gaynor used in training is still down in the armory. As frustrating as today's lesson was, I do need to learn to defend myself. Prince Asher made that *very* clear.

I try the moves, holding the smaller knife this time.

*Dodge and jab.*

*Dodge and jab.*

The last rays of daylight flash against the blade as I twist and thrust into empty air. I don't have a straw dummy to practice on, but hell, I do have pillows. It's not like I'm using them to sleep. It's been more than a week, and I still haven't brought myself to lie in the bed where the king died. The chair's just fine. The crick in my neck will ease eventually.

I prop the biggest, firmest pillow against one of the posts at the foot of the bed.

*Dodge and jab.*

The pillow gives under my blade. So much easier with a knife more suited to my hand. I imagine the pillow is Asher and shove the knife in deep.

*Dodge and thrust.* His pretty, hateful green eyes. *Dodge and thrust.* His sharp, unforgiving jaw. *Dodge and thrust.* His naked, heaving chest—

"Your Majesty!"

With a gasp, I whirl.

Theia stands in the bedroom doorway. All around me, clouds of feathers float gently to the ground.

Theia's younger than Lissa and I, thin and wispy, with corn-silk hair that constantly comes free of her braid. Normally, she scurries around like a terrified mouse, which always puts me on edge. Right now, she's staring at me, wide eyed, like she expects me to stab her next. Her voice barely audible, she says, "Your bath is ready, Your Majesty."

At that moment, Lissa appears, jerking to a stop right behind Theia.

Well, this is awkward.

"I'm sorry," I say, hiding the knife behind my back, like a child caught stealing candy.

Lissa bustles into the room. "We've all seen worse, haven't we?"

"Still. I can—"

"Do you need help with your gown?"

I stifle a groan. I do indeed need help getting out of this death trap. "Yes, please," I admit.

"Of course, Your Majesty," she says as she loosens my stays. Theia starts collecting the pillow carcasses. I watch, my cheeks burning with shame.

"Thank you," I say.

When Lissa finishes, and I'm wearing only my chemise, she helps Theia gather the final feathers.

"I'll be right up with fresh pillows," Theia says, her voice muffled by the tower of fluff.

"Please bring them up in the morning," I say quickly. "I don't need them tonight. You two can have the rest of the night off."

"Yes, Your Majesty. Thank you." Lissa curtsies and then helps Theia with the door.

When they are gone, the quiet embraces me.

It isn't until I'm standing next to the steaming bath in my chemise that I realize I'm still holding the pillow-murdering knife. I set it on the decorative table that holds the lotions and soaps.

Delicately, I slip into the hot water. The heat eases into my sore shoulders and wrists. The tension in my neck melts. I unwind my tightly bound hair and dip beneath the water, letting it swirl around me.

Eyes closed, breath held, I'm cocooned with my own thoughts.

Which definitely should be on figuring out who was a threat to the king and what it had to do with history.

But it's Prince Asher's face in my mind. Not the angry, burning face I saw earlier today, when he nearly pushed me over the battlements.

No.

I'm back in the library a few months ago, just after Sorren died. I'm dusting the books and sweeping the floor and looking toward the chess table, eager to play my turn, and jumping, nearly screaming, because there's someone sitting in the chair by the cold hearth. It's Asher, head in his hands, his shoulders shaking. He hears me and looks up, his cheeks wet, his eyes hollow.

For a long moment, we stare at each other, as my heart slowly breaks for him. He is wrecked, wretched with grief, so hurt, so lost he actually notices me, the invisible maid.

I reach for his shoulder, this man I've grown up with from a distance, this man I saw as a boy following his golden older brother like he was the sun. I reach for him automatically, as if I know him, as if he were a friend like Rowan, just as he remembers himself.

He heaves from the chair, knocks over the chess table, and, as the pieces crash across the floor and my hand brushes his arm, he flees the room.

Now I push up through the water, gasping in a breath, trying to break free from the memory. From the ache in my chest that doesn't feel as much like annoyance and frustration as it did an hour ago.

I blink my eyes open.

And that's when I hear it. A *scritch, scritch, scratch.* I pull my hair back, squeezing to stop the dripping so I can listen.

*Scritch, scratch . . .*

The room chills. Goose flesh bumps up along my arms. The silence presses against me.

*Scritch, scratch . . . meow.*

Meow?

And then I see it, a single white paw curling around the partially open door.

*Princess.*

My heart rate slows. I smile, but the spell of the bath has broken. The warm foam of my fancy royal soap has dissipated, leaving my pale knees exposed. Beyond them, a black rope wraps around the plumbing, but it's come partially undone, threatening to fall into the water. That's a weird place for a rope.

I lean forward to rewrap it around the spigot—

Holy *fuck*, that's not a rope. It's a snake.

# FOURTEEN

WITH A SCREAM, I LAUNCH myself out of the bathtub. My wrists and elbows bang against the slick tile floor, knees crunching against the side of the tub. I'll have bruises all over tomorrow. But bruises are better than a snake bite.

I scramble to get my feet under me, glancing back to see the waves I've made have been enough to swing the snake up along the rim. It slithers along for a second and then falls to the ground in a coiled black heap.

Shit.

At that moment, of course, Princess trots in to see what's wrong. The snake sees her and unwinds, weaving quickly across the floor.

"No! Get out of here, Princess!" I scream.

She doesn't listen, not as soon as she sees it moving. Her fluff stands on end, her back arches, and she hisses, standing her ground. If she was full grown, this would be an easy fight.

But she's still a baby, and the snake is most definitely not.

Wildly, I look around the room for something to throw at it, or something heavy to crush it with. My eyes catch on the knife still perched on the delicate table on the other side of the tub. I lunge for the blade.

Behind me, Princess hisses again.

There's no *dodge and jab* this time.

I just hurl my blade at the snake and watch the knife sever the coiled body in two.

At the same moment, a giant crash sounds in the other room, and someone throws themselves through the doorway.

"Drake?" I shout, whirling.

But it's not Drake. Not even close.

It's Rowan.

"What's happened? Are you all right?" he cries, just as I ask, "What are you doing here?"

For a moment, we both freeze, panting. I can't imagine what the scene looks like to him: a puffed-up kitten, a severed snake, a naked girl.

I lunge again, this time for my robe. He coughs, his cheeks reddening, and turns around while I slip the robe on.

The thin silk clings to my still-wet skin, but it's covering the important parts.

"There was a snake in my bath," I say. "An adder."

And with that, reality catches up to me. There was a venomous snake inches from my skin. It could have bitten me. It could have killed Princess. It could have killed *me.*

I take a step back, and my foot hits a wet patch. All of a sudden, my legs slide out from underneath me.

Rowan catches me around the waist before I can fall. "Easy, easy now," he murmurs, his breath warm against my ear, his arms strong around me. "It probably came up through the pipes, looking for food. Did it bite you?"

"No." My teeth chatter, from the chill and from the flimsiness of Rowan's explanation. Do snakes slither up pipes? Because that's not the first explanation I land on.

He pulls me tighter. "Let's get you to the fire, warm you up."

But as we head back to the sitting room, I realize that my door is closed, Drake nowhere to be found. There's no way my guard would have let Rowan come barreling in here and not come to my rescue himself.

Wait . . .

"How did you get in?" I ask, stepping out of the circle of Rowan's arms. His shirt is soaked through, and my robe is plastered to my breasts, leaving very little mystery.

I look wildly around the room, like I can materialize Drake just by thinking of him. But I see something else. A thick shadow behind—*behind*—the tapestry. "Why is there a hole in the wall?"

Rowan's gaze drops for a split second. He clears his throat as he returns his gaze to mine.

"Answer me," I urge more sternly.

"There are secret passages throughout this wing of the castle." He taps his fingers rhythmically along the mantel, a nervous tell. He always does that when he knows I'm beating him in chess. Rather than meet my gaze, he watches Princess twine around my bare ankles. "My room is close. When I heard you scream, well, after the parade . . ."

He thought I was being murdered.

"Why?" I ask, my throat closing on the word.

"I don't want anything bad to happen to you, Ruby. You know

that." He looks so distressed I nearly reach out to comfort *him.* "I couldn't let—I wanted to help."

"No, I know," I say. "I meant, why are there secret passages?"

"Oh. So the royal family can escape in the event of an attack," he explains. "They lead all the way to the cellars, to a tunnel that ends outside the castle walls." Rowan's ears slowly turn pink as a sheepish look steals across his handsome face. "That's not all they've been used for, of course, but you know, primarily they're for our safety."

"I've never heard anything about secret tunnels before." My brain is trying to process a lot right now. "The servants don't know?"

"I should hope not. They're called *secret* passages for a reason." He steps a little closer and brushes a lock of hair out of my face, tucking it behind my ear. "Truthfully, I've wanted to tell you for years. It would have made our rendezvous easier."

"But you couldn't trust me?" A fine tremble has begun behind my knees. I don't know if it's the chill or reaction setting in.

"It wasn't about trust. It was about the lectures from my father." He smiles ruefully. "He was very clear he didn't care what *I* used the passage for, but that under no circumstances was I to let anyone else use it."

Given the sheer number of Rowan's romantic conquests, it's actually quite impressive that he never gave the secret away.

But secret passages can only distract me for so long.

"I think I need to sit down." I take a shaky step toward the chairs. *An adder. In my bath.*

"Ruby, come here," he says softly, like it's the most natural thing to open his arms and draw me against his chest. Like we hug all the time. Like it's normal for his hands to splay across my back and the side of my hip. Like we're betrothed by choice, not duty.

He's so very warm.

Princess winds between our feet, chirping for attention.

Gently, Rowan kisses my forehead. At first, I think he means it as a comforting, brotherly gesture, but he lingers. His hands slide up my wrists, up my arms, to my shoulders, where my thin robe is coming undone. With his thumb, he brushes a drip of water off my cheek. His soft, inviting lips are parted, a breath away from mine.

In the firelight, his eyes are molten, and suddenly I'm aware, so aware, that this man will be my husband.

"Ruby . . ." he murmurs again, and I don't know if I'm ready for what he's about to say, or for the way his chin dips, drawing us closer. A flock of butterflies explodes in my stomach. I don't know—

A knock shatters the moment between us. Before I can even exhale, his arms drop from my shoulders, and he steps away. "Good night, Ruby."

He bows and is gone, the tapestry flat against the wall. Flustered, it takes me a moment to answer the door.

Sara hurries in with a tray.

"Is Drake outside?" I ask, shivering again without Rowan's warmth.

"No," Sara says, frowning. "There was no one there. Why are you all wet?"

I stare out into the hall. The *empty* hall. The advisors have had around-the-clock guards stationed here since the king's edict was read. And suddenly, the night I find a snake in my bath, no one is here?

"Sara, I need you to find Lord Hayes. Drake too. And Sir Henry, just in case."

When I turn to look at her, she's gone pale. "Why? Are you okay?"

"Not really," I say grimly. "I think someone just tried to kill me."

# FIFTEEN

"IT'S DEFINITELY AN ADDER," Sir Henry says, standing over the body of the snake. At his nod, Lissa begins to clean the mess up. "Are you sure it didn't bite you? Do you feel dizzy or short of breath?"

I shake my head. "It wasn't in the bath itself. It was dangling from the spigot. I jumped out as soon as I saw it."

"That's fortunate." He glances at my legs anyway, as if looking for bite marks. I've changed into a longer, heavier dressing gown. Still, I can't help the blush that creeps up my neck.

"How in the world did it get up here?" Lord Stone says, flapping his hands in agitation.

"Someone must have put it here somehow," Lord Hayes says, looking thunderously angry. "Your maids—they'll be arrested at once."

Bent over the body of the snake, Lissa stiffens. I've known her for years—we're friends. Or we were. It's nearly impossible to imagine her planting a venomous snake in my bath. Nearly but not entirely. She's made it clear, time and again, that she has no love lost for the royal family, which now includes me.

Could she have done it? Did she really try to kill me?

As for Theia, she's afraid of everything and everyone—I'm pretty sure she'd faint if she *saw* a snake, let alone touched it. She came with Lissa when I rang for them, but she hasn't ventured into the bathroom, instead working to stoke the fire.

"Wait," I say, before Drake can follow this order. "What about . . . could it have traveled up the pipe?"

Sir Henry inspects the plumbing in a cursory way. "I suppose it's possible. Snakes have been found in other parts of the castle before. Still . . . it strikes me as suspicious."

"The maids should be questioned," Lord Stone insists.

In a split second, looking at Lissa's bent shoulders, I make my decision.

I gesture to the clump of men crowding the doorway to my bathroom, shooing them back into the living room. "You can ask them questions, but they should be allowed to continue with their duties."

"What if one of them is guilty?" Lord Stone asks, incensed.

If Lissa didn't have anything to do with this, I don't want to be one more reason for her to hate and distrust the monarchy. But if she did . . .

I give him a look. "By all means, at that point you should lock my would-be murderer in the tower."

After a pause, he nods. "Of course, Your Majesty."

"And what about you, Drake?" I ask, shifting my attention to him. "You weren't at your post outside my door. Where were you?"

Drake's craggy face twists into a mixture of shame and confusion. "I received a message that Lord Hayes wanted to speak with me in the Great Hall. But when I got there, he was nowhere to be found. By the time I tracked him down, a footman had found us both, explaining only that you were in trouble. And Lord Hayes had no idea about the message. He'd given no such order."

I study the guard closely, looking for a shift of his gaze or a prick of sweat along his brow. "Who gave you the message?"

Drake reddens. "An errand boy. I don't remember which one."

"You don't *remember*?" Lord Hayes practically shouts.

I put a hand on my advisor's arm. "Lord Hayes, please have someone speak to the errand boys. See if we can figure out who gave the message and upon whose authority." I turn to Drake. "I think we need to assume that every deviation from the norm is important at this point."

"Yes, Your Majesty, I'm so sorry. I should never have left my post." He holds himself stiffly, his hand on his sword. Embarrassed, maybe. Exhausted, definitely.

Aren't we all.

"You're right. You shouldn't have." Asher appears behind the gaggle of men standing before the fire. They break away from him, like waves sluicing off the sides of a ship, as he strides to the center of the group. That leaves only Theia, trembling by the hearth.

Rowan follows behind him, looking for all intents and purposes like he just wandered by and poked his head in to see what all the fuss was about. He even gives me a little wink.

My gaze is drawn back to Asher, who's staring at Drake, his eyes burning. The burgundy jacket he's wearing gives his skin a warm glow.

Drake bows his head.

"How many hours have you been on duty?" Prince Asher asks.

"Since first bell," he says.

"That's nearly twelve hours."

"Yes, Your Highness. Garon and I've been on twelve-hour shifts."

"On whose orders?" He turns to look directly at me. "You've worked these men harder than I do in war exercises."

"I didn't, I don't—" My mouth closes on my excuses. I had no idea Drake and Garon were working such ridiculous hours, and they certainly weren't doing it on my order. Drake told me he had the overnight shift for the king. He didn't say he was working more than that for me.

But it doesn't matter. I *should* have known. I should have asked. I got so caught up in everything that I never even went to Lord Hayes to shorten Drake's night shifts like I'd promised.

"Drake, you're on leave for the next forty-eight hours. Tell Reece and Calen they're added to the queen's detail. Eight-hour shifts, overlapping two hours each. Never more than nine hours on duty. A lapse like this could get someone killed."

Asher eyes me again, and it's hard to tell whether his expression is a reproach or a warning.

What I do know is that I've had quite enough of all of this.

"Gentlemen, leave me." I swallow down the *please*. "We'll discuss further action in the morning."

They file out, Asher's expression mutinous, Rowan glancing at me with his brow raised, a subtle check to see if I'm okay. I give him a small nod. Theia scurries out so fast she forgets to curtsy. Lissa brings up the rear, carrying out a blood-soaked bag containing the severed snake. She dares to meet my eyes just once, her expression unreadable.

I don't know whether Lissa let the snake loose in my bath. I don't know whether she had anything to do with the king's death. But I do know, better than anyone, to never underestimate a maid.

The snake has me more shaken than I'm willing to admit to my advisors, but Sara knows. When I beg her to stay with me overnight, she agrees without question.

I check twice that the door's locked before we settle into the king's bed.

"This is the first time I've slept in here," I admit to Sara. In the flickering light of the candles, her eyes widen.

"In the bed?" she asks, sounding scandalized. "Ruby, it's been almost two weeks!"

"The chairs are very comfortable." Princess purrs beside me on the pillow, perfectly happy with the new arrangement.

Sara flops back, her hands behind her head. "Comfortable! This *bed* is the most comfortable thing I've ever felt. I'm going to sleep like an angel on heaven's cloud. You're going to have to shove me out to wake me. Why in the world have you been sleeping in a *chair*?"

She's not wrong. It's divine. Being able to stretch out fully, the soft down of the mattress . . . but . . . "Sara, King Octavius died here, in this bed. I just . . . I couldn't stop thinking about it."

She sits up abruptly. For a moment, she doesn't move, warring with herself.

The bed wins.

She lies back down, facing me. "We'll ward off his ghost together."

I reach for her hands, the way we did when we were younger

and one of us snuck into the other's room after a bad dream. "These past few days, I'd almost convinced myself that the king couldn't have been killed. But now . . . I don't know. What if he was bitten by a snake? He could have died in bed. That's a kind of poison, right? Would Sir Henry have looked for a snake bite? Someone could have let the snake loose any time. Long before Drake began his shift."

"And it was just . . . slithering around? Until it finally bit him? And then waited around to attack you, too?" For a long moment, we stare at each other. Then, as one we throw the covers to the bottom of the bed.

Sara holds up the candle. "Do you see anything?"

"No . . . do you?" My skin crawls at the thought of more snakes sliding through the thick shadows beneath the bed.

"We've got to look everywhere now, don't we? Just to be sure." Sara's brows are drawn together, and she looks just as unsettled as I feel.

I nod.

It doesn't take us long to inspect every corner and shadow and hidden space in the king's suite. We find more dust than I'd like but no more snakes.

By the time we return to the bed, I'm shivering.

"I don't know how I'm going to do this," I admit, pulling the sheets up over my shoulder and turning toward Sara once again. "I don't know how to be a fucking queen, Sara. Lissa could have planted the snake. Hell, she could have killed the king, too, and I told Lord Hayes she should keep working! And Rowan . . . we've been friends for years. I should be thrilled to marry him—at least he's not a stranger. And he's gorgeous! But tonight—I mean, the other night—" Even in the middle of my freak-out, I remember the passages are a closely guarded secret—"I think he was thinking of kissing me, and I . . . I don't know. I've never thought of kissing Rowan before. It's like I'm a different person now. A royal who kisses *Rowan*? Sara, I don't know how to do this."

She squeezes my hands. "Okay, first of all, you may never have thought of kissing Prince Rowan, but I guarantee he's thought of kissing you."

"Sara!"

"Okay, okay." Her face turns serious. "I don't know if Lissa had anything to do with the snake. I hope not. But even if she did . . . you are not a bad person—or a bad queen—for wanting to believe the best of her. We just need to make sure she's never alone in your rooms until you find out the truth. Or you could reassign her to somewhere else in the castle. And let's not forget Theia was here too."

"Theia? Do you really think *Theia* could have done it?"

I expect her to roll her eyes, but she looks at me without a hint of amusement. "Why not? Who knows what any of us is capable of? Theia's pretty new here. I barely know her."

"But she's scared of everything," I say.

"Or maybe that's what she wants everyone to think."

Truly, Sara is diabolical.

"Okay, well, I'd rather keep an eye on both of them." What's the old saying about keeping your enemies close?

"Fair enough. Now listen, because this last bit's important." She takes a deep breath. The flickering candlelight sends golden streaks across her face. "You say you don't know how to do this. Okay, fine. But, Ruby, I believe with my entire *soul* that you will figure it out. We might not know why the king chose you yet, but he *did* choose you. You're the smartest person I know. Hell, you're the smartest person anyone in this *castle* knows. You're smart enough to be a spectacular queen for everyone, not just the nobility. You have a chance to make things better for all of us."

I raise a brow. "That's quite the speech."

She grins. "I've been practicing. I was saving it for your coronation, but you needed it now. I'm serious, Ruby. You have something no one in the monarchy has had in hundreds of years."

"And what's that?"

She squeezes my hands again, even tighter. "Perspective."

Huh. I've been so intent on finding answers about the king and myself, I haven't given much thought to what my position could offer anyone else.

I reach for her and give her a big hug. "Thank you, Sara."

She turns to blow out the candle, and then we're face-to-face again, quiet in the dark.

My eyes drift closed. "We've only talked about me and my problems. What about you? Who've you been kissing?"

For a long time, she doesn't answer. So long, in fact, I start to drift off, and I'm not sure whether her "She's the stuff of fairy tales, Ruby, truly" is a part of my dream.

As soon as Sara leaves for her duties the next morning, both of us a little groggy from our night of deep, much-needed sleep, I slither behind the tapestry by the hearth.

The king said I would be in danger—well, it's obvious I am. And I'm not going to sit here and wait to die.

I run my hands along the wall, looking for a hidden latch.

Secret passageways are handy escape routes, and given how many times I've almost died already, having an escape plan is smart. I definitely need to figure out how to lock this door, though. As glad as I am that Rowan came to my aid, I don't really want *anyone* entering my rooms uninvited.

It takes a few minutes, but I find a seam bisecting the wall. With a quiet *snick*, I disengage the latch and push the door into the darkness.

Dust motes hang in the air. It's so quiet. I step into the narrow, musty passageway and carefully examine the door to see how to open it from this side. I mess with it until I'm pretty sure I've figured out how to lock it. Though I most decidedly don't test the theory—no way do I want to be stuck in here. I already feel like a rat, scurrying in the walls. Getting trapped would be a nightmare.

Slowly I shuffle into the darkness, hands out to feel my way along.

A long hallway stretches before me, running parallel to the main corridor that serves the rooms of the royal family. It's lined with pinpricks of light that make it relatively easy to navigate. And, it turns out, to spy. The light is coming from tiny holes chiseled into the walls that peer into the rooms on the opposite side. I put my eye to each one.

The first reveals a glimpse into a well-appointed bedroom with a large four-poster bed and messy tangle of sheets. With a snort, the figure on the bed readjusts. It's Rowan . . . and he apparently sleeps nude.

I swallow back a squeak. It's not that I'm surprised. It's just . . . not something I knew about him. Once we're married, will he . . . will he sleep that way beside me?

*Of course, Ruby. What do you think marriage is?*

I move on, giving him his privacy.

The next tiny peephole shows a rose-damask sitting room, with two delicate golden chairs by the hearth and a bookcase under the window. Princess Belle is awake already, curled into one of the chairs, a thoughtful look on her face as she stares into what I assume is a fire in the fireplace. I think maybe there's a book on her lap, but she's not reading it. I hold my breath as I pass, unsure if the crackle of the fire will mask the noise.

The next three rooms are empty, two looking lived in—I assume Asher's and Cedric's chambers—the third a dusty shrine.

Prince Sorren's bedroom.

I can barely see anything; the curtains are drawn and the air heavy with disuse. The maids were forbidden to touch it. I assumed the king had the room cleared out. But Sorren's things are still here, as if waiting for him to return.

I reach another staircase, and then Queen Narissa's chambers. I knew they were a good distance away from the king's, but until this moment I'm not sure I realized quite how far.

The maids, we always knew there was no love between King Octavius and Queen Narissa. But it wasn't a scandal or anything. What king and queen ever really love each other? Royals marry for money or power; they're not given the luxury of love. Maybe it's the only luxury the lowborn have that they don't. I don't know. Even Rowan and I . . . we're marrying because we've been told we have to. At least we share a friendship. That's more than many kings and queens.

I remember feeling a little sad when Prince Asher's engagement was announced. Lady Rosaline is quite sweet; she's kind to her maids and, kitten stealing notwithstanding, she's always been perfectly poised, perfectly beautiful. The perfect noble wife for the second son of the king. But she and Asher grew up together, here in the castle. And she was never the girl he snuck into the garden with after dinner. Never the girl he chose to sit beside at the jousting tournaments held every summer. Or dance with at the endless balls. He never, well, wooed her.

And the way Lord Stone has always bragged about the match, like he should have all the credit, makes me think he does. Another arranged marriage. Another callous calculation, at the expense of his own child's happiness.

Hell, who knows. Maybe Lady Rosaline is thrilled. You'd never know one way or the other.

Beyond Narissa's chambers I find the royal library. It's empty, the fire still unlit. I wonder who's taken over my duties. I should ask Sara.

I squint, peering down the long, dark hallway. The passageway stretches far beyond these rooms. I don't have time to fully explore it now—I'm due for etiquette lessons with Governess Blake—but it doesn't matter. I've confirmed what I already suspected. What I couldn't tell Sara last night.

The truth settles deep in my chest, heavy and sickening.

All this time, I thought no one could have visited the king after Drake bid him good night and found him dead the next morning. But Narissa, Cedric, Belle, Asher, and Rowan all had access to the king's rooms. As easy as opening a door. No guards, no locks, no oversight.

That means King Octavius's wife or any of his children could have killed him in his sleep, and no one would have even known they were there.

# SIXTEEN

I'VE BARELY HAD TIME TO return to my room, figure out how to lock the secret door, and worm my way into my day dress when a loud knock scares the ever-living hell out of me.

I unlock the door to admit Lord Hayes.

He enters, his beard newly tidied but his eyes shadowed. "Good morning, Your Majesty. I trust you slept well?"

I nod and say, "You as well, I hope."

"Are you ready?" he asks, ignoring my polite response. "Princess Belle is waiting to see you."

"Princess Belle?" I repeat, surprised. "I thought I was meeting with Governess Blake."

Lord Hayes shakes his head. "Princess Belle wanted to help you today."

We pass down the corridor in silence, Reece following us. He's a lot younger than Drake, with short dark hair and big brown eyes. Some of the maids fancied him when he first began working at the castle, but we soon learned that he had a sweetheart back home. I heard they finally got married over the summer, and she lives in Ryvin now.

Lord Hayes leads me to Belle's personal sitting room, a pretty, circular chamber within the North Tower, with floral tapestries on the walls, a roaring fire in the hearth, and several chairs arranged around the room. It's odd to think I just saw her a little while ago in her own room.

Princess Belle rises to greet us, and as she moves, I notice she's not alone. Sir Henry stands in the corner by the window, his gaze caught on something outside. But his attention shifts to me quickly enough.

He bows deeply, his thick blond hair falling forward, his piercing blue eyes finding mine as he straightens.

Princess Belle takes my hand and draws me closer to the fire. I'm not sure what the royal protocol is, but her kind gesture isn't unwelcome. "Sir Henry has been telling me about what happened last night. Horrific. Are you okay?"

I nod, afraid my voice might crack if I try to talk about it. She seems to understand.

She squeezes my hand. "See? She's perfectly fine," she says, addressing the castle physician. "Now, gentlemen, you may leave." She nods to both men and watches, still holding my hand, as they bow and follow her order.

As soon as the door closes, she drops my hand.

"Well, that was disgraceful."

"Excuse me?" I look at her, shocked.

Her deference slips away, leaving the cold, impenetrable princess behind. She moves to a small desk along the wall and opens its rolltop with a key from a chain around her neck. Without looking back at me, she says, "You let me touch you. You didn't say a word when I didn't use your title. You let me speak for you, *and* you allowed me to dismiss the men."

"Okay . . ." I don't understand what she's getting at, but her disdain is giving me a prickly feeling under my skin. "Are you actually complaining about me being respectful right now?"

She grabs a pipe from the desk and lights it using a piece of kindling dipped into the fire. The process takes a few minutes, during which she studies me but doesn't answer. At last, she releases a series of smoke rings and says, "That wasn't respect. It was *deference.*"

I rock back on my heels.

She raises a finger. "No one touches the reigning monarch first." Another finger. "The reigning monarch will be addressed as Your Majesty by all. No exceptions. No one speaks of the monarch's health without permission, and no one presumes to speak for the monarch."

"Okay," I say. A blush climbs my cheeks. It's so obvious when she breaks it out like that. "You've made your point."

"There hasn't been a female monarch in Lumaria since Queen Cora," she says, her shrewd gaze inescapable. "Whether you like it or not, your position is historic. And you're acting like it's a favor, not a right."

I straighten my shoulders. "Isn't it?"

She shrugs. "You tell me. How did you earn this 'favor,' Your Majesty?"

Shit. I walked into that one. And I don't have an answer yet. If I have to tell one more person that I have no idea why the king chose me—

Wait.

"I don't have to explain myself to you," I say firmly.

The corner of her mouth quirks. "Good, yes. But even that is acknowledging the ask. Next time, ignore the question altogether. Snap an order or issue a dismissal."

Slowly, I nod. "Okay."

She takes another draw of her thin pipe. "The ball to celebrate your betrothal to my brother is in three days."

I nod. As if I could forget, after a week of dancing lessons and endless dress fittings.

"At the ball," she continues, "you'll be asked to dance by every man there, married or not, young or old. It's customary. You obviously won't have time to dance with them all, and of course you *must* dance with Rowan first, seeing as he's your betrothed. But the rest of the dances are far more important strategically. So choose wisely. The wealthiest nobles—Lords Phillip and Maddox—are good choices. The council: Lords Hayes, Stone, and Rutherford. An entourage from Tartula is coming—if Prince Trevan comes, you should dance with him. Father was working on a new trade agreement with him when Sorren . . . when Sorren died. And you must dance with Cedric and Asher, of course, to show there's no internal rebellion brewing."

"And would that sign of solidarity be for show?" I ask. "Or would it be genuine?"

She blows another smoke ring. "You think my family is planning a rebellion?"

"Prince Asher has made his position abundantly clear." This conversation feels like a chess match, each of us taking incremental steps, trying to anticipate each other's future moves.

I've never been able to get a sense of what Belle really wants or thinks. She's always been more skilled than her brothers at the games of court.

Games . . . or lies?

Cedric told me they all lie. Vipers, he called them, like the snake in my bath.

"Would Prince Asher kill me for the crown?" I ask, watching her closely.

She doesn't flinch. "He thought he would be king. He has reason to doubt you."

"So . . . yes?"

She puts out the pipe. "May I be candid with you, Your Majesty?"

Something tells me the game has suddenly changed. I nod, slowly.

With a sigh, she says, "As far as I'm concerned, neither you nor Asher is the rightful heir. Sorren should be here. He should be the one dancing at the ball, ascending the throne at the coronation. He was the one Father poured all his wisdom and knowledge—all his *love*—into. I may be Rowan's twin, but Sorren was my best friend. He was my idol, and I . . . I was his shadow. I saw what he learned, all that he was as a person and a future leader. I love Asher, and I'm sure my father chose *you* for a reason, whatever that reason may be, but neither of you has what Sorren had. Neither of you will *ever* live up to my eldest brother's memory and the king he would have been."

She clears her throat. The light of the fire shines against her damp cheeks. "It makes no difference to me if you're queen or if Asher kills you. Neither of you will ever be Sorren."

At last, as these words ring in my ears, she turns her hard gaze on me. A thin line takes root between her softly winged brows. "All I can truly say is be careful, Your Majesty. Nothing is more dangerous than a crown."

# SEVENTEEN

FOR THE NEXT TWO DAYS, I'm busy with dress fittings, dancing and etiquette lessons, training sessions with Lieutenant Gaynor and Prince Asher, and meetings with my advisors. Lord Hayes has completed his interviews with Lissa and Theia—they've been cleared, for now. He asked again if I wanted to replace them, but I think it's best to keep them close. I still don't know for sure whether the snake was a murder attempt, but I'm not taking any chances. I did add Sara as a third lady's maid. Her argument about playing favorites is less important than my safety, and she knows it.

She makes sure neither maid is ever alone in my rooms, *or* alone with me.

At night, when I can't sleep, I haunt the secret passage behind the royal bedrooms.

Nothing of interest has happened the past few nights. Belle reads a lot. Once Rowan was out; another night he was staring morosely at the fire, a tankard of ale in one hand. Cedric sleeps deeply and soundly.

Asher hasn't been in his room at all, and I wonder whether he's been spending his nights with Rosaline or off somewhere plotting my demise. A knot twists in my stomach.

I stare up into the shadowy canopy over the bed, moving like clouds in the flicker of candlelight. So indulgent of me to keep my candle lit long past dark. I blink my eyes shut, and an image of me standing beside Sara fills my mind. I'm wearing my maid's uniform. My black hair is pulled back in a braid and we're laughing and spinning, our arms entwined. That Ruby I could understand. She had friends in Sara and Lissa, a mother in Mellie, a quiet life with quiet work. That Ruby watched Prince Rowan and Prince Asher through the branches of the trees that line the formal garden. She snuck books from the library and read all night. She had a secret friendship with a prince, in which they never did more than squabble over chess. She saved kittens and yelled at another prince's dogs.

I see her so clearly in my mind, but when I open my eyes, in the dim, candlelit opulence of the king's bedchamber, I know that Ruby is gone.

This Ruby . . . she *has* to be different, and I don't understand her at all. I don't know how to be what the Queen of Lumaria needs to be.

Not yet, anyway.

I flip to the next page in King Octavius's journal.

*Garrick and I met someone today. Legs for days, hair to her waist, and a mouth that could burn stone. I've never heard such language from a woman before. Of course, she didn't appreciate us muddying her mother's sheets that she'd spent hours hanging on the line. I asked her where she'd learned her manners, and I swear if her eyes had been daggers I'd be dead. She wouldn't tell me her name, but Garrick wrangled it out of her while I collected the damn horses.*

*Esme.*

*I want to see her again.*

If I hadn't known the king held no love for his wife, his journal would have educated me. It begins shortly after he took the throne, upon his father's death. He was newly married, newly crowned . . . and apparently quite horny.

Reading each entry adds to the sense of impending doom. Nearly every moment, the king spent with Lord Garrick, his closest friend and ally. Knowing that the Great Betrayer was secretly plotting against him twists my stomach as he talks of how much he trusts Garrick, how grateful he is to have his best friend by his side.

With a sigh, I climb out of bed, wrap my chemise-clad body in a long, heavy black dressing robe that covers me neck to ankle, and slip on a pair of house shoes. Princess twists and stretches, showing off her tricolored belly fluff, but she doesn't leave her warm nest of pillows.

I take a lantern, heavily shuttered, a shawl to protect my hair from spiderwebs, and my small knife. I don't go anywhere without it these days. Happily, Lieutenant Gaynor and Asher have let me start training with it, instead of the heavier dagger. And by *let*, I mean I took Belle's lesson to heart and ordered them to.

It's later than my other wanderings, and the passageway is especially dark and musty tonight. I shuffle forward as silently as I can, with the smallest sliver of light to show my way. Even that feels like a risk, but I'm afraid I'll trip over my feet and give myself away.

Hopefully the royals are well asleep by now. Rowan's room is dark, giving me hope, but there's definitely someone moving around in Princess Belle's room. I can't see anyone, but I can hear soft sounds that suggest—

My face warms. Ah. Belle isn't alone. That's a bit different from the last couple nights. At least she won't hear me moving in the walls.

I've almost reached Cedric's room when a faint noise brings me to a halt.

I fully shutter my lantern and listen, straining my senses through the darkness.

I expect a rustling or the tiny squeak of a rat. Or perhaps the slither of a snake.

My blood runs cold.

There it is again.

Not a squeak or a slither . . . a footstep.

I'm not the only one creeping through the secret passage. Someone is ahead of me on this path, taking it to wherever it must end.

Without thinking, I slide my feet forward, sneaking along like *I'm* the rat or snake.

Rowan told me the passage was made as an escape route for the royal family, so I knew it had to go beyond their rooms, but I haven't explored this part of the passageway.

I take it slow, trying to be as silent as I can. I don't dare unshutter the lantern, even though the dark is heavy and impenetrable around me.

Excruciatingly slowly, I make my way down a narrow set of stairs, and then another and another, following the footsteps until I reach the cellars. The air is cold and damp here, and the walls have changed from the chiseled stone of the castle to curved, cavelike tunnels.

In the distance ahead of me, there's a shriek of metal.

I freeze.

Long after the sound fades, I force myself to keep moving. I come upon a heavy iron door marking the shift from cellar to tunnel. Whoever I'm following has left it open a crack—I manage to worm through without making it shriek again.

The tunnel beyond is narrow and dark as a nightmare. I can't hear or see anyone before me. I take a deep breath to fortify myself, and then I'm creeping faster, as fast I can, without knocking my lantern into the packed dirt walls, stifling a scream as spiderwebs tangle in my hood and hair. It's fear that drives me, fear of dark, buried places, but also determination.

I want to know who's out here, where they're going, and why.

The door at the end of the tunnel is closed and locked from the inside. I risk unshuttering my lantern to fiddle with the latch, and then I'm through, emerging into the fresh bite of a moonlit night. I pull the shawl closer around my head and look around.

I don't see whoever I've been following, but I can hear their footsteps crunch through the woods in an unhurried rhythm. Still too close. I need to wait a moment before I follow, or risk them discovering me.

Behind me, the castle wall rises to meet the night. This portion cuts through a small forest, and the foliage butts up to the wall in a riot of climbing ivy, fern, and bushy cedar trees. They partially hide the door from view. I examine the door more closely. Its lock requires a key that I don't have.

I'll have to ask Rowan who *does* have one.

And then add them to my list of suspects.

Leaving my lantern on the ground and the door slightly ajar so I can get back in, I follow the receding footsteps into the woods.

I stay far back, hidden, until the cloaked figure reaches the outskirts of Ryvin. There it's easier to blend in with the clumps of women taking in their laundry and sweeping their stoops, and the men heading home from their jobs at the wharf. I meander through the narrow streets, stepping around puddles of waste and the occasional beggar, keeping my head down and the knife hidden in the flow of my dressing gown. Not exactly appropriate clothing for an evening stroll, but hopefully its dark color and the dimness of the few streetlamps will hide me well enough. I worry less that someone will recognize me—my portrait is still being commissioned—and more that I will catch the eye of someone hunting the streets for a different reason than I.

Ahead of me, the figure turns the corner and ducks into a tavern called The Bloody Dog just as a sloshed patron tumbles out into the street. Shouts follow, to the tune of "keep your filthy hands off the help."

Shit. That's not a place I can enter without drawing attention. Even if I could, there would be no way to discern my quarry from all the other black-cloaked figures inside.

For a few minutes, I stand hidden across the street, watching the door and weighing my options. Doubt curls through me with each passing second. What if it's just Rowan, here to have a drink, or find a woman for the night? He made it clear the royal family often uses the secret passageway for personal reasons.

I've just decided to head back to the castle when a man steps over the threshold and into the golden light of the streetlamp. Immediately, I recognize his dark whorl of chestnut hair, the sharp edges of his jaw beneath a shadow of stubble, the savage beauty of his face.

*Prince Asher.*

# EIGHTEEN

I PRESS BACK INTO THE shadows. Asher doesn't appear drunk or on the hunt for a woman. His mouth is pressed into a grim line, and his eyes survey the road with a piercing intensity.

A tall, older man with a bulbous nose and thinning hair walks out beside him, his collar pulled high and his hat pulled low. The man is no gentleman. His coat's ill-fitting and stained; his beard and boots mark him as some kind of laborer. The man looks around before leading Prince Asher down a side street to his left—blessedly away from me.

My resolve hardens. Maybe this has nothing to do with me. But if it *does* . . .

Maids are trained to be quiet, careful, and most of all, invisible. I weave my way through the crowded streets, the tall man's hat an easy focal point. No one stops me; no one pays any attention to me at all. I follow Asher as he edges ever closer to the river, where it's darker . . . fewer streetlamps and more seedy taverns.

Suddenly, a group of men stumbles into the cobbled street, yelling and swinging fists. A cluster of harlots stands at the far corner, cheering the fighting men on, their low-cut, brightly colored gowns overflowing.

I duck out of the way, but my path is blocked, and Asher slips out of view.

*Damn it.*

Someone jostles me, a man on the outskirts of the fight. I try to sidestep him, but he's noticed me now. His hand shoots out to curl around my bicep.

"Well, well, what do we have here?" he says, slurring so much the words are barely understandable.

"Nothing." I yank my arm smartly out of his grasp.

The man puts hands on me again. "Not nothing, lass. You're in your night things. You need to be put back to bed."

My heartbeat ticks up as he pulls me closer, his eyes glassy and unfocused, his breath hot on my cheek. I try to yank free, but he's ready this time, his fingers digging into my arm.

"Let me go. You won't like what happens if you don't," I warn. My other hand tightens on my knife.

He laughs. Straight up laughs. Then he shoves his face at me. "Oh, I'll take my chances for a sweet lass like—"

My knife presses into his throat. "Take your hands off me."

The drink has kept him sloppy, but when he feels the prick of my blade, his eyes turn ugly. With an inarticulate growl he grabs for my knife hand. Quick as a snake, I nick his throat, enough to make him bleed, and slash at the arm still holding me. This cut is deeper, and he jerks back with a roar, his grip loosening. I wrench myself out of his grasp and kick at his knees.

He overbalances and goes down.

I run.

I'm not worried about following Asher anymore. I'm not worried about anything but getting away. Reaction is setting in—my arm aches, and I can still smell the man's liquored breath on my face.

That was close. Way, way too close.

Heart heaving in my throat, I aim for a gap in the crowd, just past the harlots. Behind me, there's a lot of yelling, and I can pick out the man's voice above the rest.

I should have cut him deeper.

I'm almost to the women. The noise of their siren calls, the shouts of the men fighting, it all blends together into a chaotic, discordant distraction. I glance back to make sure the man isn't following.

Hands grab me and pull me into the alley.

Panic shuts out everything but my instincts. I scream, I scratch, I hit. I try to use my knife, but whoever's got me disarms me easily. This man is bigger, stronger than the drunkard who accosted me. And he's clearly not in the cups himself. He pins my arms with almost preternatural strength and precision, drawing me deeper into the shadows and quiet, away from the crowds.

And safety.

I scream again, so hard my throat hurts.

"Stop," a voice says in my ear. My assailant tightens his grip on me, almost to the point of pain. The bear hug from hell.

I fight harder.

"Your Majesty—Ruby—*stop*."

I freeze. I twist and catch the suggestion of dark hair, a green eye.

"Asher?" I choke on his name.

His grip loosens marginally, but he's still walking me down the alley, away from the crowd.

"What are you doing?" I ask.

He slaps a gloved hand over my mouth. I bite his finger as hard as I can.

He swears as he yanks his hand away and releases me, giving me a little push until I'm flush with the crumbling stone wall of a building close to the river's edge.

"What are *you* doing?" he bites out. "Alone, at night, in the worst part of Ryvin. No guards, no protection . . . Do you know how many people want to kill you?"

"Like you?" I snap back a little wildly.

For a split second, he looks genuinely surprised. But the fury returns with a vengeance, narrowing his eyes.

He opens his mouth to say something cutting, no doubt, but his attention is caught by a movement at the mouth of the alley. Without further warning, he presses me into the wall with his body, his hands cradling my face, his lips dipping dangerously close to mine.

"What are you doing?" I hiss.

His warm breath feathers my cheek.

"Oy! That one's mine!" a voice calls. "She owes me for the blood she spilled."

An icy finger skates down my spine. It's the drunk man.

Asher leans closer, blocking my view of the alley. All I can see is the hard edge of his jaw. All I can feel is the heaviness of his body pressing against me. I can't catch my breath, not with . . . all of him . . . so close to all of me.

"Your own fault for letting her get away. She's mine, friend. Go find yourself another," Asher calls.

The footsteps get louder.

Asher's voice gets more dangerous. "Walk away."

"You gonna make me?"

The prince shifts, his arm coming up, and the man screams.

I flinch.

Asher's attention returns to my face. His finger brushes my cheek, by accident no doubt. "Don't worry. You're safe."

My breath freezes in my chest. Safe? With his shadowed green eyes staring down at me like that? With his body holding me captive?

*Safe?*

The next moment, he's pulling me down the alley and the man's shriek has twisted into a pained moan.

"What did you do to him?" I ask, entirely too out of breath for the pace we're moving.

He flicks a hand up, a tiny knife in his hand. "Throwing knife."

I stare at the knife. "*That's* what I want to learn."

He raises a brow, but the corner of his mouth quirks.

We're several blocks away before he speaks again. "How did you get out of the castle without your guard? Have they been disappearing again?"

I consider lying. But what would be the point? Maybe it's best he knows that the family secret isn't a secret from me anymore. "Your brother told me about the secret passages."

He shoots me a look. "Did he now?"

"You disapprove?" What a surprise.

"Are you telling me you didn't already know about them?"

"How *would* I know?" I ask, genuinely taken aback. "None of the servants do. Rowan said it's meant to be an escape route for the royals."

"Yes," he says, eyeing me closely, "but you and Rowan have been meeting secretly for years."

The blood freezes in my veins. The way Asher says *secretly* makes this moment feel infinitely dangerous.

"How do you know that?" I snap.

"I didn't, not for sure. But I do now." He glares at me as we slip along the slick cobbles.

"We played chess," I say, trying not to sound defensive. I don't have to defend myself to him. "We were friends. There was nothing nefarious about it, except that he's a royal and I am—was—a maid."

Asher makes a noncommittal noise as he leads us down another street, this one skimming along the riverfront. We've left the taverns behind; now it's all quiet warehouses and an occasional soldier smoking as he guards the harbor.

Boats creak and water laps against the network of docks. It'd almost be peaceful if it didn't also feel like the kind of place someone would murder you for the coins in your purse.

"Is that what you were doing tonight?" Asher asks, his voice startling me. "Escaping? Or meeting Rowan?"

"I was following you," I say. Let him know I'm paying attention.

We're nearly to the castle wall when I fix him with a stare of my own. "What were *you* doing out tonight, Prince Asher?"

He ushers me over the threshold into the tunnel and hands me the lantern I left by the door, still burning faintly. "Your Majesty?"

he asks, ignoring my question.

"Yes?" I hate how the lantern light gilds his throat and the curve of his jaw.

He runs a hand through his hair. His eyes light with a dangerous gleam. "Don't follow me again."

Then he slams the door in my face.

# NINETEEN

*Garrick has asked my blessing to marry Esme. This explains his recent mysterious comings and goings. But the news is still a blow. I had hoped—no, hope is the wrong word. I had wished for something beyond even the power of a king. And Garrick is right to embrace it. Embrace her. I will give them my blessing, even though she is a commoner. They deserve the happiness they've found.*

POOR, MAUDLIN KING OCTAVIUS. HIS whole journal is just one big, long whine about how he's in love with Esme and wishes *he* could be with her instead of Garrick. Meanwhile, it's so *obvious* Garrick is plotting something. The "mysterious comings and goings" . . . the cagey way the advisor answers the king's questions. It's clear the king was too blinded by his love for Esme to notice Garrick's increasingly suspect behavior. I don't know that any of this knowledge is helpful, but it's certainly infuriating.

It's the day before the ball, and the final dress fitting and lesson from Belle are complete. I close the journal and hide it in the king's desk. Now would be a good time to take a walk in the garden with Sara.

For the past few days, we've had little time alone, what with Beatrice and her seamstress army, Lissa and Theia underfoot constantly, and me off to one meeting or another.

"Are you sure this is appropriate?" she asks as we amble through the greenery, eyeing a gardener trimming a bush several yards away. "I'm beneath your station now."

"As Prince Asher would say, 'horseshit.' Or at least," I amend, at her look, "it should be. You're my lady's maid and my companion, Sara," I say firmly, resisting the urge to rub the weariness out of my face. Queens aren't supposed to look tired. "And who's going to talk? It's not as if you're going to get in trouble with *me*."

She nods, but she still looks troubled, which is unlike her.

I draw her to a stop at the end of a long hedge dotted with delicate rosebushes. "What is it?"

She shrugs. "Sometimes, I just wish—" she cuts herself off and starts walking again.

"Sara."

She lets out a breathy laugh. "Don't worry about it, Your Majesty. I don't know what I'm saying. Everything's fine."

"The other night . . ." I trail off. I've thought often about what she said—or might have said—as I was drifting to sleep. I'm still not sure what to make of it. "The other night, I thought you said something about a girl being a fairy tale. What did you mean? Who's a fairy tale?"

Sara freezes. The sun's starting to set, turning the sky rosy and her skin golden. I can still see the blush bloom across her cheeks. After a moment, she says, "I was talking about you, Ruby. You're living a fairy tale, right? *You're* the fairy tale."

She smiles brightly and starts walking again, trailing her hand along the top of the hedge, but I don't buy her innocent explanation for one second.

She's got a crush on someone, and she doesn't want to tell me who it is.

I want to push, cajole, *beg*. But I follow her lead. I know her well enough to know even torture won't get it out of her till she's good and ready.

"Sure," I say, matching her energy. "I'm a fairy tale."

When she realizes I won't push, her smile turns genuine.

"I heard some things about the king's last day," Sara says, clearly ready to change the subject. "You know, the questions you wanted me to ask?"

I focus instantly. "Yes. About who saw the king the day before he died. What did you find?"

I can't tell her this, but now that I know about the secret passageways, all the king's family are suspects. But the snake also showed that a threat could be delayed . . . Given the adder in my bath, I'm no longer certain that Sir Henry was right about the poison. Or venom, I should say. Which means anyone who had access to the king's chambers in the days before his death could have left the snake—or something equally dangerous—behind.

Sara taps her chin. "Prince Cedric was with the king early in the day. When he left, Bryson had an audience that lasted about an hour. Then his advisors were there, too, though rumor is he kicked them out. Lissa turned down his bed that night. The girls say she was gone for a while, but not a *long* time, if you know what I mean. She didn't seem upset and went to bed as usual. Sir Miller was ill but managed to help the king with his evening routine. Oh, and Henson brought his meals. Gareth said he tasted everything, as usual. And then, as we know, Drake came on duty, and no one else entered the room until he did the next morning."

"This is helpful," I said, laying the pieces out in my mind. The game is slowly coming into focus. But *too* slowly, I fear. "What about the rest of the royal family? Did any of them see the king that day? Did Dowager Queen Narissa visit her husband?"

One thing I will say about the king's journal—it's clear King Octavius never felt a fraction of the affection he felt for Esme toward his own wife. Was Narissa jealous? Were there indiscretions, other women through the years? Maybe she took his illness as an opportunity to get revenge. And she'd certainly love to get rid of me.

Sara pauses. We've reached the small orchard near a statue of King Octavius. Some flowers have been placed at its base in remembrance. "The only one I've heard of is Prince Cedric."

"Do you think that's odd?" I ask. "If your husband was sick, wouldn't you visit him? Or your father?"

"Well, not *my* father." Sara plucks a waxy green leaf from the bush and grinds it between her fingers, and suddenly I remember that she ran away from her abusive father to come here. I want to swallow my tongue.

"I'm sorry—"

She waves me off. "I know you didn't mean it that way. And yeah, I guess if you didn't hate your father, you'd visit him. But none of us realized he was that sick, did we? Maybe they didn't know either."

Rowan said something like that . . . that he hadn't seen his father in a couple of days. If I remember correctly, he said his father hadn't wanted visitors. Which is also what Sir Henry said. And yet, Cedric and his advisors were there that day.

I stare at the blank stone eyes of King Octavius's statue. I wish he could tell me what really happened. It feels like the closer I get to the truth, the more secrets there are to uncover.

Speaking of secrets . . . "Have you heard anything about Belle taking a lover?"

"Princess Belle?" Sara jolts in surprise. "There's never any gossip about her."

"Would you ask around, just in case? I thought I heard . . . I don't know. Something. It's got me wondering."

Sara grins, her eyes sparkling. "Sure. Now you've got *me* wondering."

But what I really want to know is more about Prince Asher and his mysterious dealings in Ryvin. "And what about where Prince Asher was the night of the king's death? With Lady Rosaline, maybe?"

Sara's step falters for a moment. She tilts her head, thinking. "Sorry, no. I don't know where he was, but I doubt it was with Lady Rosaline."

"I saw them together that morning," I say, remembering his open shirt and Rosaline's pale hand on his arm.

"Did you?" Sara shrugs. "I'll look into it. I just don't think—"

Footsteps sound nearby. I look up, surprised to find Rowan walking toward us, the setting sun turning his golden skin a fiery orange.

“Good evening, Your Majesty. Sara,” he says, bowing to each of us with a wink.

Sara curtsies. “Well, hello, Prince Rowan. How very lovely to see you. You’re looking handsome this evening.”

“Such a flatterer,” he says with a laugh. “May I have a moment alone with my betrothed?”

She gives me a quick look and I nod. With another curtsy, she heads back toward the castle.

“I’m sorry to interrupt,” Rowan says.

“It’s okay,” I say. “I’ve barely seen you these past few days.”

“A travesty, truly.” He takes my arm and draws me away from King Octavius’s statue. “Are you going to step on my feet during the ball?”

I barely contain a very unladylike snort. “It’s possible.”

“I’ll wear my strongest boots for protection,” he says, grinning down on me. “Now, tell me, am I the *only* thing you’ve been missing these past few days?”

He’s led me to a small alcove with climbing rosebushes and a small marble table and chairs. I gasp when I see what he’s gesturing to.

“Oh, can we play?” I hurry to the table with Rowan’s chess set waiting atop it. Before he even answers, I sit behind the black chessmen and grin up at him.

He sinks into the seat across from me. “It’s good to see the old Ruby.”

“She’s still here,” I say, staring at the board. “And she’s still going to kick your ass.”

He laughs, a delighted sound I haven't heard since the morning his father died.

"You go first." I watch as he places his first pawn.

"I remember the kitchen staff would set up picnics for your family at this table," I say as I make my opening move. I used to watch, well hidden in the pine tree on the other side of the hedge, as Rowan and his siblings played and wonder if that was what a real family was like.

And wish I had one too.

"Mother loves being outdoors. She finds the castle stifling." He smiles down at the chessboard, his eyes sad. "She's from Yanos, you know, a coastal kingdom . . . She grew up with sea breezes and open balustrades."

"Sounds beautiful. I've never seen the ocean, but I've always wanted to." The Talas River is large and wide, but the Hinassi Sea is boundless, powerful. Free.

Everything I've always wished I could be.

"Well, you can go now, if you want," he says. It's strange, how his smile fades as he says the words. I'm surprised the prospect of travel doesn't excite him more. It's one of the few things I'm looking forward to after the coronation. I'll be expected to visit other parts of Lumaria, as well as our nearest allies, to present myself as queen. I'll finally get to leave home, like the heroes in the books I read.

"Have you ever been?" I ask, trying to understand his response.

"When I was very small, Mother took us there for a few months. Father couldn't be away from Lumaria for so long, so he sent Lord

Hayes with us. Sorren was seasick the entire trip, but Asher and I loved it. We learned to fish for sharks." His smile appears again. "Well, we *thought* they were sharks. That's what Tareth called them. I think they were just regular fish. But big." He pulls his hands out to show me, laughing.

I relax a little. "It sounds like a wonderful trip. Were Belle and Cedric there too?"

He lowers his arms, returning his attention to the game. He makes his move. "Belle was. Cedric wasn't born yet."

"Did Belle enjoy it?" It's hard to imagine Rowan's proper twin fishing for sharks.

He shrugs. "I don't remember. Mother kept her from us most of the time. Said Belle was a lady and a princess . . . she couldn't be running around chasing sharks and falling off boats."

My heart hurts for little Belle, stuck learning the same dumb stuff she's teaching me now, instead of running wild with her brothers. But I'm not surprised.

I take his pawn. "After we're married, we can go together. I'd love to learn to fish."

"Sure," he says, but as before, his smile doesn't quite reach his eyes. I note the fine stubble gracing his jaw, the flop of his dark blond hair. He and Belle share the same nose and full mouth, but his blue eyes are brighter than hers, his hair darker. He looks so much like Sorren, it's almost eerie.

"Damn," he swears softly when I take his knight.

For a while, we play in silence.

"So," I say at last. "Did you imagine yourself marrying someone else?" His eyes flick up to my face. I laugh a little and wave my hand. "I'm not a child, Rowan. I know you've had plenty of women. Probably a few great loves, given what you've said in the past. And I'm just the lowly little maid you used to sneak out and play chess with."

"Not anymore," he says, but he doesn't sound happy about it.

"My point is, I understand. You're doing this for your family. I'm doing it for the crown. It helps that we're friends, but I'm sure that's not what you imagined or hoped for. It's okay to admit it."

He captures my rook with a flick of his hand. "Neither of us should be in this situation. You shouldn't be queen, Ruby. It's a perversion of everything the crown stands for."

Wait, what did he just say?

His words are a slap across my face. A *perversion*?

I shove to my feet, my hand knocking over half my chessmen.

"Wait, Ruby."

He follows me, pulling me to a stop under a twisted arch of ivy. All across the garden, torches are being lit by silent, unobtrusive workers, but we're standing in a little bubble of darkness. I can't read his expression in the shadows. But I don't really need to, do I?

"Ruby, you don't understand . . . I didn't mean—"

"You didn't mean that you're a snob? Slumming with the help was fine until the lowly maid became your equal? I understand perfectly, Rowan." It's a surprise, actually, how much this hurts. How I've missed the signs. But they were there, weren't they? The way he's always looking away, never speaking to me at meals or in front of his mother. Never wanting to spend time together like we used to. I've ignored Lord Stone's snide comments and Lord

Rutherford's eye rolls. I'm dealing with Prince Asher's open hostility. But *Rowan* feeling this way? My friend Rowan?

"You're not my equal, Ruby," he says, and I scoff in his face. He grabs my hands, shaking his head, something like panic coating his words. "No, I mean, you've *never* been my equal. You've always been *better.* You're smarter, harder working, more considerate of others. You're more curious, more open to new experiences, than anyone I know. You're *too good* for the monarchy."

"Rowan, that makes absolutely no sense." I want to laugh, but in truth I feel much closer to crying. What is he even saying?

He pulls me closer, into the warmth of his body, and dips his head so he can meet my gaze. "It makes absolutely no sense at all that my father got to decide your destiny, maid *or* queen. It should have been *your* choice."

The intensity of his gaze is like a physical touch. His words feel dangerous.

Delicious.

Unbidden, memories of the other night surface. Rowan holding me close, my robe falling off my shoulder.

Maybe he's thinking of the same moment, because his gaze dips lower before pausing on my lips. His hands are still clasping mine, drawing me slowly forward, closer to him.

The breath leaves my body.

Oh my God, he's going to kiss me. The butterflies are back, along with an unsteadiness, as if I've been riding in a carriage.

"Ruby, may I—"

The lamp just behind us lights, throwing us both into sharp relief. The lamplighter makes a small noise, maybe of surprise, and scurries off, but the spell has been broken. I step away from Rowan, hugging myself in the cooling evening air, confused by the relief that courses through me.

"I need to get inside," I say. "It's almost dark."

His expression shifts, not to disappointment as I expect, but to understanding. "Of course. And tomorrow is a big day."

The ball and this betrothal that's not of our choosing.

"Thank you, Rowan," I say, an ache spreading through my chest. We're both trapped. "For what it's worth, I will always be happy for our friendship."

"Me too." He chucks me gently under the chin. "We'll figure all of this out, okay? You deserve to choose your own destiny."

I lean into him a little as we head back to the castle. "So do you."

But they're empty words, aren't they? That's not the world either of us live in.

# TWENTY

*The betrayal is too great to bear. I can hardly fathom, hardly imagine . . . but it is true. I've seen the evidence myself. Garrick has fed us to the wolves. Esme, poor Esme . . . her husband a traitor. I have promised her I'll spare his life, but I can't trust myself to face him. If I do, if I see him, I don't think I'll be able to honor my vow to her. My anger is a living thing, a monster sitting on my chest. I can barely breathe for its weight. No, I cannot see him, nor speak to him. Not when I am certain I would tear him apart with my bare hands, inflict the pain on him that he has so savagely inflicted on me, on Esme, on all of Lumaria. The blood of this war is on his hands.*

"RUBY!"

I snap the journal shut and shove it under my pillow, knocking Princess off my chest in the process. She meows with annoyance.

"Hi, Sara," I say brightly.

She gives me a stern look. "What in the world are you doing?

It's time to get ready for the ball. You know, that big party they're throwing for you and Rowan?"

"Just reading. Trying to relax a little before the big night." I flash her a guilty smile, my mind full of King Octavius's rage. I never knew it was *Esme* who saved the Great Betrayer from execution. I don't think anyone does. The antiroyalists might have more fuel to fan their flames if they knew the king spared Lumaria's most hated criminal because he was in love with the man's wife.

"And you lost track of time." Sara rolls her eyes as she lays out my gown. Tonight's is an absolute embarrassment of blue velvet, gold brocade, and soft ermine. It's only slightly less extravagant than the coronation gown Beatrice is working on, and I suspect that's so I can dance, a prospect that fills me with dread.

I've got the steps down, no problem. It's the polite small talk, the strategic choosing of the men, that makes me balk. Belle has continued to give me extensive advice on the subject, but the only directive that's stuck in my brain is *dance with the council, dance with my brothers.* Maybe I'll get lucky and that will fill the evening in itself.

I know Rowan being there, the first one I dance with, will be a comfort. But his words from last night keep curling through my head. If he feels that way about me, about destiny, how does he really feel about our betrothal? And how do *I* feel about it? *Could* I have the passion of a true marriage with him? He's gorgeous, his blue eyes bright gems, but I've never seen him as more than a friend before. I've never pined for him, dreamt of him, not like—

I cut the thought off. That doesn't matter. The question now is: Could there be heat between Rowan and me? Could we make this forced arrangement something more?

I try to imagine dancing with him. Kissing him—

A sudden image of dancing with Prince Asher fills my mind, hard as I try to keep it at bay. Asher's body pressed to mine, his hands trapping my waist and hand. His breath warm against my ear, close as we were in the alley. He whispers my name in that low growl of his. And he's wearing his armored leathers for some reason.

I shake my head, dislodging that picture.

That's enough of *that. Get it together, Ruby.*

There's a knock on the door, and Sara runs to admit Lissa, who's brought a whole case of additional makeup.

"Perfect," Sara says, and they go to work on me with a vengeance.

By the time my hair is twisted up with pearls and strands of gold, my makeup shimmering with golden powder and my lips dyed a dark red, my fingers adorned with rings, including the simple gold band the king left for me, by the time my gown has all its many parts fastened and pinned and sewn and buttoned, my heart is tripping over itself.

Theia enters, her arms full of flowers. She hands the bouquet to me. "Drake says they're ready for you, Your Majesty."

I take a deep breath, raise my chin, and put Belle's lessons into practice, gliding across the floor. Drake opens the door for me and I swirl out, my huge skirts just making it.

The castle is a hive of activity, servants rushing from the kitchens to the Great Hall to the ballroom. Guests are filing in through the main doors, so Drake takes me along the terrace from the opposite direction. I have to make a grand entrance, of course.

We've almost reached the ballroom when Rowan steps in front of me. "Your Majesty," he says, bowing deeply. "I have a message for you from Lord Hayes."

He looks painfully handsome in a light blue velvet coat that brings out his eyes and sharp black breeches that hug his thighs. I resist the urge to check his feet for sturdy boots.

"Yes?" I ask.

He glances at my guard. "It's of a personal nature, Your Majesty."

That's . . . interesting. I hope everything's okay. I'm already a tightly knotted ball of nerves; I don't need any new drama to add to my plate.

"Give us a moment, Drake," I say calmly. "You can go ahead and make sure the way is clear. I'll be right there."

"Of course, Your Majesty." Drake bows and continues to the doors leading to the ballroom.

I step to the edge of the terrace, as far from the guards lining the walkway as possible. Rowan follows.

"Ruby, you . . . you look . . ." He swallows visibly as he takes in my gown, until at last his eyes linger on my face.

Under his gaze, I feel like a silly little girl playing dress-up. "I know. This getup is ridiculous."

His eyes glint. "That's not what I was going to say."

"What's happened?" I ask. "What's Lord Hayes's message?"

His blond hair falls into his eyes. "That was just a line. Everything is progressing as planned. I just . . . I wanted to see you before we run the gauntlet. After last night . . . I just wanted to make sure you're okay."

"Are *you* okay?" I search his face. "All your talk of me choosing my own destiny, but this betrothal is as little a choice for you as it is for me. Are you sure *you* want to do this?"

He starts to reach for my hands, then realizes I'm holding flowers. For a long moment, he doesn't say anything, his face drawn into thoughtful lines. The sounds of clinking glasses and laughter filters through the night.

At last, he seems to come to some decision. "Ruby, we don't have to do this by their rules. We don't have to let anyone else decide for us. *We* can decide. We could leave, right now. Tonight. We could make our own destiny."

His words aren't registering. Leave? Make our own destiny? I don't understand. "What are you saying, Rowan?"

"We'll walk into the gardens, right now, and we won't come back. We'll disappear." He steps closer and cradles my cheeks in his warm hands. The intensity of his gaze is unlike anything I've seen on his face. His eyes practically burn me. "Ruby, we don't have to play this game. It's too much. It killed my brother. And now it's killed my father. I don't want it to kill you too."

My mind goes muddy and quiet. This is Rowan, carefree rake and rebellious chess partner, prince and brother, saying he wants to run away with me. Rowan, who, when he caught me spying on him, decided he should make me his friend instead of turning me in. I've never, never, heard him speak like this.

"Oh, Ruby," he murmurs. He takes my face in his hands and

dips toward me until our lips touch. He's gentle and sweet, and the kiss is as comforting as a mug of warm tea.

For a moment, I let myself imagine it—us sprinting into the garden maze, running away from the ridiculous notion of me being queen. Running away from the king's murderer and all the other people who want me dead. Maybe we'll find a small cottage somewhere far away. I'll be a maid for a minor lord, and he'll be a merchant, and maybe we'll even get married for real and have children and live a quiet life. With comfort, and safety, and respect.

Maybe, with time, the passion would come.

A month ago, running away with Rowan would have felt like an adventure, the promise of something new.

But now, it feels like the coward's way out.

King Octavius trusted me. He handed me a whole kingdom and asked me to keep it safe. I can't leave my duties behind. That's not a choice I'm willing to make.

There are tears in my eyes when I break our kiss. "I'm so sorry, Rowan. I can't run away with you."

The glint in his eyes dies, even as he says urgently, "Please, Ruby. Please come away."

Reluctantly, I shake my head. "I can't. But I understand if you need to go. We can break the engagement. I'll find another way to keep you and your family supported."

Almost angrily, he says, "This isn't about that. This is—"

Abruptly he stops. Sucks in a deep breath. Smooths his hands down his coat.

When he continues, his voice is almost light. "We'd better get to the ball. They'll be waiting on us to make our big entrance."

For a moment longer, I stare at him, wondering at this abrupt shift. But he just gives me a sad smile and threads his arm through mine.

Together, we walk toward the giant set of glass doors leading to the ballroom.

"Are you sure you're okay?" I murmur under my breath just as Drake reaches us.

Rowan pulls me gently into his side. "It was never me I was worried about."

As Drake opens the doors of the ballroom, my hands clutch at my bouquet of flowers, at the not-so-ceremonial dagger strapped at my waist, encased in a jewel-encrusted sheath.

Rowan and I step toward our future, and I can't help but wonder which destiny I've just slammed the door on.

# TWENTY-ONE

A DEEP BLUE CARPET STRETCHES from the doorway to the center of the room, and a crowd of finely dressed nobles glitters in the light of a thousand candles. At the other end of the carpet, the rest of the royal family waits. Even from this distance, I can see the twist of Queen Narissa's mouth. She's standing at the head of the receiving line, but it's clear this honor—which I insisted upon when Lord Stone gave me the options for welcoming the ball's noble guests—is not sufficient.

I keep my chin up, my face as blankly regal as I can make it. Like Princess Belle, whose entire demeanor is impressively neutral. Asher's expression is a storm cloud made of green eyes, dark hair, and hate. Cedric keeps shifting from foot to foot, looking deeply uncomfortable.

The string musicians wrap up their song, and the trumpets take over, bright and loud. After the flourish, a great, deep voice announces, "Queen Ruby Zara Giovani Alyssa Veracruz and her betrothed, Prince Rowan Victor Finneas Maxwell."

Oh, such ridiculous names. All of mine but the Ruby are made up—Lord Hayes said I had to be called something more than just Ruby the housemaid. I picked them from various books I've read over the years, a combination of fictions for the ultimate fiction of my royal name.

I step forward, releasing Rowan's arm for a moment, as we practiced. As one, the crowd folds into bows and curtsies. The effect is overwhelming.

Intimidating.

Dizzying.

*Breathe, Ruby.*

Slowly, in just the way I practiced with Princess Belle, I reclaim Rowan's arm and walk down the carpet to join his family. When we reach them, the music resumes.

Narissa can't hide her disdain. Her curtsy is so shallow and half-assed, even I can tell it's an insult.

"Good evening, Dowager Queen," I say, emphasizing the *dowager*.

She tries to impale me with her glare.

Prince Asher barely looks at me, bowing over my hand like it costs him something. To his brother, he says, "I hope this is what you want."

Next comes Princess Belle, who curtsies deeply and breaks her neutrality enough to give me a small, encouraging nod.

Prince Cedric kisses my hand after a subtle prodding from his sister. His eyes keep darting to the side, but he offers me a smile. "I'm not a very good dancer," he says. "Sorry in advance."

I smile and wish I could whisper, "Don't worry. I'm not either." But that seems like the kind of thing the nobles watching us closely would gossip about.

Once the royal family has greeted me, we all stand in a line to receive the rest of the ball guests. No one touches me, but I have to say hello and repeat their names back to them. A lot of *welcome, thank you for coming,* and not a lot of time to calm my racing heart.

One older noble, white-haired and resplendent in a black fur cape and embroidered jacket, stands before me without bowing and says nothing. I look him in the eye, refusing to lower my gaze, but a prickle of sweat touches the back of my neck. I don't need Princess Belle's lessons to tell me this is a power move. A refusal to acknowledge me as queen.

"Your name, sir?" I ask lightly, though I've already heard Asher greet him as Lord Maston.

He takes a moment to look affronted that I don't know who he is, so *I* take the moment and move on to the next noble. This he dislikes even more. But he thinks better of whatever he might have said when Drake personally escorts him to another part of the ballroom.

"Your Majesty," Lady Rosaline says with her sweet voice, when it's her turn. She curtsies deeply. She looks beautiful and poised in a deep purple gown with puffed sleeves. Unlike her father, she has chosen understated jewelry: a single golden ring, two thin strands of pearls around her neck. She's almost past me when she murmurs, so only I can hear, "I'm very sorry about the kitten thing."

My eyes widen. I didn't expect her to ever acknowledge that moment . . . or even remember that the impertinent maid was me. I nod, but she's already gone.

At long, long last, the receiving line is complete, and a footman brings me a goblet of wine. My bouquet of flowers has disappeared. I think Theia said they'd be given as favors to the young eligible women of the nobility.

"May I have this dance, Your Majesty?" Prince Rowan holds his hand out to me with a bow. As I set my goblet down and take his arm, I catch Prince Asher's scowl.

Does that man ever smile?

Rowan draws me onto the dance floor and into the first steps of the waltz. The precision of the dance soothes me. Like chess, dancing has a very precise and predictable set of rules.

Every eye is on us. There are a few smiles, but more frowns and whispers behind hands. The gossips are enjoying the show, the maid who mysteriously has been named queen.

I fix my gaze on the white rose in Rowan's lapel and try to smile like I mean it.

"This is terrifying," I admit in a whisper as he leads me across the dance floor. "How long do we have to do this?"

"Well, balls usually last until dawn . . ." He laughs at my horror. It's nice to see this lightness in him again. "But it doesn't mean you have to stay. You're the queen. Your word is unto God's. Isn't that what Tareth said?"

I roll my eyes. "Do I really look like a god to you?"

The amusement in his face shifts, deepens. He gives me a long, slow look, from my feet to the crown on my head. "No, not a god . . ." he says softly, pressing into me as we move through the dance. "But perhaps a goddess."

My cheeks warm.

"Seriously, though, you should leave before dawn," he says more seriously. "Don't wear yourself out. The people here aren't worth it."

"Rowan, I'm sorry . . . about earlier. I just—" I don't know what I want to say, exactly, but I don't want him to keep doing this, talking to me and dancing with me like everything is okay, like he didn't just admit that he wants to run away with me.

Before I can finish—or he can respond—the song ends. Rowan spins me dramatically to the edge of the dancing area and dips me. Then he twirls me out and his sister in, winging Belle across the floor. Lord Something or Other is waiting for my attention, practically quivering in eagerness for his turn. Behind him, Asher is glaring at me. Again. Shouldn't he be dancing with Lady Rosaline?

When he sees me looking, he turns and stalks right out of the room.

I let the nobleman bask in my attention for a moment before excusing myself.

I should be dancing, but Belle insisted I had to dance with all her brothers first. That means Asher and I are supposed to dance. If he just walks away . . . I can't imagine that will look good for me, or for Rowan. We can't let the gossips think there's a rift between them.

I'm following Asher away from the party, into the dark and echoing hallway beyond, when a hand shoots out and pulls me into an alcove beneath the spiraling stone of a staircase.

*Not again.*

"I told you not to follow me," Asher growls.

A single candle burns in his other hand, throwing tongues of light across his shadowed face. He's so tall, so large he fills the space, bending over me to avoid hitting his head.

"Then stop sneaking away," I snap back. "And stop yanking me into dark corners. Not appreciated."

"I hate balls. They're—"

"Horseshit?"

His lip quirks, despite himself. "Yes."

"Seems to me you were having a different issue," I say. There's something wrong with my voice; it's too breathless, too low to be mine.

"And what is that, Queen?" He places the candle on a ledge beside him.

"You didn't want to dance with me." For some reason, my heart is racing, my skin shivering under my dress.

He laughs in a way I think he means to sound cutting. But it doesn't, not really. "Is that a problem?"

"It's protocol." I try to hold on to my annoyance. "I'm supposed to dance with you and Cedric, and you're not cooperating."

"Oh? And you want me to cooperate, do you?" The candlelight flickers across his mouth. The way he says *cooperate* sounds indecent. "Rowan can fulfill the family duties. He's your betrothed, after all. I'm not interested."

His words sink in, bracing as a dip in a frozen lake.

What am I doing here?

Asher is engaged to Lady Rosaline, and he hates me. Of course he doesn't want to dance. And I, the queen, just embarrassed myself chasing after him. *That's* what the gossips will talk about.

"I'm sorry," I say, heat suffusing my cheeks. I don't know what's wrong with me. Something. Something to do with who Asher used to be, maybe, and the way I used to watch him from a distance. "I know you hate me. I shouldn't have tried to make you dance with me. It was unfair."

I know I'm breaking one of Belle's rules—probably a lot of them, actually—but I don't care. This moment has me too unbalanced. I need to get back to the ball. *I* need to do my duty.

I step out into the hall.

"Ruby. Wait."

I pause, shocked to hear my given name on Asher's lips.

"Come back here. Please."

I turn around, my gown swishing. He's stretching out a hand; in a daze I let him draw me back into the small alcove. I stare into his eyes, greenish gold in the candlelight. His fingers slowly, carefully twine with mine.

His other hand slides around my waist.

He leans forward to murmur into the delicate curl of my ear, "Hate has never been our problem."

A delicious shiver skates along my skin. We begin to sway, our bodies pressed together, but this is no waltz. His cheek brushes mine, sending tiny electric shocks through me. Our mouths are so close. We're so close. All those moments over the years, when I watched him in secret. And recently, when he saw me, *stared* at me, like he couldn't help himself.

Oh God, he's right. This isn't hate.

And it is *definitely* a problem.

Suddenly, a flash of light breaks across Asher's face. A gigantic rumble follows, strong enough to shake the floor.

My eyes widen. "A storm?"

Asher cocks his head, a strange expression stealing across his face. He shakes his head. "I don't think—"

That's when the screaming starts.

# TWENTY-TWO

WITHOUT HESITATION, ASHER DARTS OUT of the alcove and sprints toward the ballroom. I run after him, cursing under my breath as my unwieldy gown tangles around my legs.

By the time I reach the room, knife in hand, smoke is billowing in suffocating clouds, bringing with it an acrid stench. Everywhere, people are running for cover. Swords clang and a woman screams loudly near the doorway, her bare shoulder smeared with blood. Glass litters the floor. I can't see Asher—or any of the royal family—in the chaos.

Suddenly, Drake appears through the smoke. His face and sword are streaked with blood. The expression in his eyes is the closest to panic I've ever seen from him.

"Your Majesty!" He rushes over to me. "I've been looking for you. Come on, I need to get you to safety."

"What's happening?" I ask, straining against his grip, trying to see around him to make sense of what's happening. "Are we needed here? Should we help?"

"You are the queen," he says sternly. "You must go."

Reluctantly, I let him lead me down the hall, away from the noise and crowd. Away from Asher and Rowan. My chest tightens.

"Are the others safe? What's happening?" I ask again, out of breath already from the weight of the dress.

"An attack," Drake says. "An explosion, and an attack. Princess Belle was injured. As for the others . . . We can only hope they are okay."

It takes me a moment to understand where Drake is taking me—the secret passage in the walls of the royal wing isn't the only tunnel beneath the castle. There are also the crypts. Nowadays, the royal dead are buried or burned beyond the castle walls, but once, the bodies of nobility were interred beneath the castle. Deep beneath, beyond the reach of the living.

He's opening the heavy iron door, releasing a musty puff of air from the narrow, dark passageway. There's no way my dress will fit through the doorway.

With a silent apology to Beatrice and her hardworking helpers, I pull my knife from its sheath and start ripping at the precise stitches holding the skirt in place. Despite my shaking hands, it only takes moments to release the huge skirt from the rest of my gown.

In the distance, shouts break the silence. "Quickly, Your Majesty," Drake says, panic in his eyes as he shoves the fabric down the stairs, then leads me into the dark.

A series of caverns lies beneath the castle. Torches burn in the far cave, where the mausoleums of the first kings and queens rest, but the long galleries in between are filled on either side with bones and darkness. I've been down here only once, when Rowan dared me to sneak in with him. It still has the same stifling air, the same deathly quiet. The hairs on the back of my neck stand on end.

For a moment, Drake and I pause at the base of the stairs,

panting. The lack of light wraps us in a suffocating blanket. The rest of the world feels a universe away.

Drake is a heavy presence beside me, his breath overloud in the silence.

And suddenly, I remember his absence at my door when I found the snake in my bathroom.

His assertion that he was the last person to see the king alive, and the first to find him dead.

A chill washes through me. Why didn't we go to my chambers, where the door locks? Where a secret exit provides safe passage out of the castle?

Why are we trapped down here instead, with no means of escape should anyone gain entrance?

What if someone is down here waiting for me already?

My breath quickens, the dark pressing in on me.

Did Drake bring me down here . . . to get rid of me himself?

"We should find another exit," I say, my voice cutting through the silence. "We can't stay down here."

"We can't risk that much time in the open," he replies. The urgency in his voice sounds real. But it doesn't ease my frantic heart. "Antiroyalists have stormed the castle. They'll be looking for you. You're the one they want." Drake's hand finds my arm and urges me to move away from the base of the stairs, deeper into the cavern.

I balk.

"I don't think this is the safest place." I hate the way my voice shakes.

"Please, Your Majesty. We need to move farther from the door."

Drake uses a flint to light a torch at the base of the stairs. Its glow flickers sickly across the skulls that line the walls. "Is that better?"

I turn to face him—

And see another face looming in the darkness just over his shoulder.

I don't have time to scream before the man plunges a dagger into my guard's back.

# TWENTY-THREE

DRAKE GROANS, HIS BODY LURCHING from the blow. Even still, he staggers forward a step, blocking the narrow passage. Putting himself between me and his attacker.

There's a squelching sound as the man removes his dagger. Slowly, Drake sinks to the ground, the torch wobbling in his hand. His gaze meets mine. As blood stains his lips, he yells one word.

"Run!"

Then he lifts his shaking arms and uses the torch to light the man's clothes on fire.

Shadows and flame jump. The man yells. Drake groans again, and I see the moment life leaves his body.

With a shuddering sob, I turn and run.

Behind me, the man utters a string of curses, and I hear the sound of frantic hands patting fabric, the scuff of a body rolling on the floor.

I pray that it will be enough, that the flames will finish him. There's a moment of silence. But before relief can flood my body, the haunting echo of footsteps fills the air.

*Shit.*

I weave through the long galleries of bones, trying to find the darkest corner, the quietest hiding place. I gutter torches as I go, plunging the room into ever more darkness, knowing its cloak will be my only cover. I keep sprinting, praying for another way, for the hall to continue, but soon, too soon, I reach a dead end.

The path forward is blocked by a wall of bones.

I swallow down another sob, then double back, ducking into an alcove containing three sarcophagi.

I crouch behind one, my small, paltry blade in my hand, and try to quiet my shaking breath.

Silent tears chill my cheeks.

I listen desperately for his footsteps, strain my eyes for the faintest glimmer of light.

It feels like forever and no time at all before he finds me. I cower behind the sarcophagus for as long as I can, hoping the glint of torchlight won't reach me.

But soon he's upon me.

He makes a sound of triumph, but in his enthusiasm he moves quickly, and the torchlight flashes sickeningly against the walls of bones around me. This saves me from his first, hurried thrust. But there's no chance of escape. He's enormous, a shadowed giant blocking my way.

A giant who doesn't know I'm armed.

I surge forward, channeling all my terror into the one move Asher drilled into me over and over. The smaller knife helps. The strength of abject terror helps more. The knife sinks deep into the man's stomach. He staggers backward, roaring, and I'm so shaky and shocked, I can't keep my grip on the dagger. He goes down, taking my knife with him.

Shit, shit, shit.

I've got nothing to defend myself with now.

I back up until I run into the wall of bones, panic pulsing in my temples, as he regains his feet and advances on me again.

This is it. I'm gasping, scrabbling along the wall, tearing at the stone and the bones, looking for any crack, any crevice that could indicate a hidden door, a final hope. My fingers are bloody, rubbed raw, and I know it, deep in my heart.

There is no way out of this. I'm going to die.

The man knows it too.

He raises his dagger in one hand, the torch in the other.

The light illuminates his face, the cruel smile on it.

I gasp.

Oh God, I recognize him.

The man in the top hat from Ryvin. The one Asher met with.

He grips his weapon, about to plunge, when suddenly his jaw slackens. The dagger falls from his hand and clatters to the stone floor, the torch along with it.

In the flickering light I see it: the bloody point of a sword thrusting out of his chest. And just behind him, temple bleeding and jacket torn, is Asher.

# TWENTY-FOUR

I STARE, DISBELIEVING, AS ASHER pulls his sword free and climbs over the dying man, crunching bone, kicking aside the torch to reach me.

"Are you injured?" he asks, his voice full of a dark and unexpected protectiveness. My body responds, urging me to throw my arms around him, sink into him, breathe in his safety.

But I hold myself rigid, my spine coated in ice.

"Asher," I say hoarsely. "I saw you—I saw you with this man, in Ryvin."

The memory flashes before me, Asher leaving the tavern with him, walking down the dark street deep in conversation. For all the flickering darkness that night, I know who my would-be assassin is. Who he was with that night in Ryvin.

"What did you do?" I ask, as the shadowy bones of the kingdom's dead press close around us. "Why was he trying to kill me?"

Asher doesn't answer. Instead, he grabs the torch off the ground.

"I don't know why Colin targeted you," he says, his voice rough and low. "My meeting with him had nothing to do with this. Now, come on. We need to get out of here." He strides back down the gallery without waiting for me to follow.

I don't know if I believe him. But I definitely don't want to stay here, in the darkness, with a fresh corpse. I scramble, stepping gingerly over the body.

"Asher, wait," I call in a near whisper. My voice isn't working properly.

Neither are my legs. They're weak as water and wobbly as all hell.

The hardest part is stepping over Drake's body.

Guilt and grief wash over me in waves. The way I doubted him. The way he protected me, at the cost of his own life. It's unbearable leaving him here, among the dead in the crypts. I vow to return as soon as humanly possible, to make sure his sacrifice is known and rewarded. To make sure he is given an honorable burial.

"Faster, Ruby," Asher urges, pausing on the last step of the narrow staircase, waiting until I join on still-trembling legs. We emerge into the hallway, which is warm and smoky compared to the cool damp of the crypts. Asher walks quickly down the corridor.

"Where are we going?" I ask, the words sticking in my dry throat.

"To your room," he says. "Lord Rutherford will be calling a council meeting shortly. Lord Hayes is setting up a makeshift infirmary in the Great Hall. Lord Stone is . . . well, hopefully not still hiding in the corner squealing like a pig."

"Shouldn't we go straight to the council meeting?"

He turns around to look at me and raises a brow. "In that?"

My gaze flies down to my body. Oh. Right. The thin white underskirt of my butchered gown flutters around my bare thighs.

The bodice is in tatters, most of the beads shorn off in the fight, the remaining boning barely containing my chest.

My cheeks flare with heat.

"Fine. Proper clothes first, and then we'll deal with everything else."

We walk in silence to the king's rooms. The castle echoes with shouts and commotion, but it's a more controlled chaos than before. Calls for aid, rather than the booms of explosions. The sound of sobbing echoes from somewhere nearby, and my heart clenches at the thought of everything that happened this evening, everything I still don't know about the invasion.

Asher keeps glancing back at me, his eyes raking my body. To disapprove? Or reassure himself I'm in one piece?

With him, it's impossible to tell.

We make it to the king's door without encountering a single soul, which, given my state of undress, is probably a blessing.

"I'll meet you in the Great Hall," I say, making to shut the door in Asher's face.

"I'll be out here." Something about his grim expression makes me pause.

"Do you think . . . ?"

"Do I think there could still be rebels in the castle?" His eyes are hard. "I'm not taking any chances."

It's strange seeing him standing there, in Drake's place, and a sick feeling settles in my stomach. I close the door and lean against it for a moment, trying to breathe.

I bow my head under the heaviness of this day. Of Drake's death.

Of the unrest in Lumaria. Of the man—the man Asher knew—nearly killing me. Of Asher himself, inexplicably saving me.

I thought Asher wanted me dead, and here was the perfect opportunity—he wouldn't have even needed to get his hands dirty. If he'd just waited a second, if he'd paused . . . I would be gone, and he'd have had what he wanted.

There are moves in chess where you sacrifice short-term gains in service of a longer strategy, but the goal is always, ultimately, to win.

I'm not sure, now, that I know what Prince Asher wants to win.

Without a maid to help me, I choose the simplest of my gowns, with laces that tie up the front. I wash my hands and face, scrubbing off the gold and kohl that's already streaky from my tears. When I rejoin Asher in the hall, I look more like Ruby the maid than I have in weeks.

Asher stares at me for a long moment before heading down the hall.

Before we even reach the Great Hall, I can hear the chaos within. Crying, groans, shouts for more assistance. We walk into the smell of blood and ash. Along one wall, bodies lie wrapped in white. The number is staggering. There are servants carrying bodies even now.

On the other side of the room, pallets have been set up for the injured. Sir Henry is busy, moving from one to the next, several maids assisting him, or gathering supplies at his direction.

Narissa is sitting off to the side with Belle and Cedric. All three of them have bandages on their faces and blood on their clothes.

Belle's staring at her own shaking hands, and for once her expression conveys how shaken she actually feels. Cedric is bent forward, face buried in his hands.

Where's Rowan?

When Narissa sees Asher, her face crumples. He rushes to her side and lets her curl her arms around his neck and weep.

Behind me, lines of soldiers patrol. I'm sure they've spread throughout the castle, looking for rebels.

Lord Hayes notices me, his whole body jerking with surprise. He strides to where I stand in the middle of the room.

"Your Majesty, why aren't you in hiding? Are you injured? Sir Henry should examine you." He gestures to a pallet beside Cedric.

"I'm fine," I say. "Where's Rowan? I don't see him."

Lord Hayes's face changes. "Come on, the council is waiting for you."

I don't like that. No, I don't like that answer at all. My stomach drops, and I glance wildly around the room again. Rowan has to be here. Lord Hayes is *not* going to give me bad news. He's not.

My gaze finds Asher's. His brow is furrowed, his own expression betraying his concern. With a last squeeze of his mother's shoulder, he follows me to the throne room with Lord Hayes.

Lord Stone and Lord Rutherford are already there, along with several senior officers, including Lieutenant Gaynor. No sign of Rowan.

*Oh shit, oh shit.*

I should have run away with him. If I had, he'd be safe right now.

"Tell me what happened to Rowan," I demand, my voice ringing out across the quiet murmurs of the advisors.

Lord Hayes clears his throat and nods toward the two thrones set at the end of the room.

Every delay in answering my question makes my heart beat faster. I make my way to the king's throne and perch on it, as told, feeling like an absolute imposter. Of all the events and activities we've done to celebrate my coronation, nothing has felt more real—and wrong—than me sitting in this chair.

"Now," I say, gritting my teeth, bracing myself, knowing what they're going to say. "Tell me *now*. Where is Rowan?"

Lieutenant Gaynor steps forward, addressing me in a way that includes Asher, as the commander of Ryvin's military. "A group of well-organized, armed antiroyalists stormed the ballroom, breaking the windows with bottles filled with alcohol and lit on fire. They attacked the guests, shouting antiroyalist propaganda and slogans."

"Prince Rowan was attacked," I say for him. "Is he . . . is he one of the bodies in the Great Hall?" Bile rises in the back of my throat.

The words *Rowan is dead* pound in my skull so loudly I can barely hear what Lieutenant Gaynor says next. "Your Majesty, Prince Rowan . . . he was seen coordinating with the attackers. He led them away from his siblings and took up arms with them. My men arrested him. He has been detained."

It takes me a moment to process what he said.

"Rowan did . . . Rowan did *what*?" I must have misheard.

Lieutenant Gaynor bows his head. Asher swears, slamming his fist into his thigh.

Lord Stone startles at the outburst. His finery is drooping and smoke-stained. "That boy's always smirked too much. You could just tell he was up to no good."

Before I can react, Asher is in his face. "That's my brother. Watch what you say."

Rowan was working with the antiroyalists. I can't wrap my head around it. He's a royal himself. It makes no sense.

Is that why he wanted to leave? Was he trying to keep *me* safe?

And then the worst question of all: Did he know about the assassin?

My stomach churns. I really think I might be sick.

"During the chaos," I say, my voice hoarse, "an assassin followed me down to the crypts. He killed Drake, and he nearly killed me."

Lord Stone's face goes ashen. My gaze shifts to Prince Asher. Do I mention he saved me? Or that he knew the assassin? Oh God. A terrible thought unfurls in my mind. What if Rowan and Asher were working together? What if this whole attack was cover for them having me assassinated?

But then why did Asher stop the man? If he was part of the plan, surely he would have just let the assassin—Colin, he called him—kill me.

Lord Stone clears his throat. "Your Majesty, it's clear that you are in danger. Given the attempts on your life, and the fact that your betrothed is currently imprisoned, you must declare a successor. If you do not, the country will fall to chaos when you are killed. Name Prince Asher, so there will be a plan in place."

His words ricochet through me like a bolt of lightning. Did he say, When *you are killed*?

Lord Hayes steps in with an apologetic look. "Your Majesty, please forgive Lord Stone. He's never the coolest head in a crisis. King Octavius mostly relied on him for financial matters."

Lord Stone huffs but doesn't deny this.

Lord Hayes continues, "Lieutenant Gaynor, send some men to the crypts to recover the bodies." With a quick bow, Lieutenant Gaynor hurries from the room.

"What has Rowan said?" I ask, trying to keep my voice even.

But Prince Asher's question comes at the same time, all business even as I'm breaking apart. "What was their point of access?"

"The windows. As the lieutenant said, bottles were thrown through the glass," Lord Hayes reports.

"What has Rowan said?" I ask, more loudly, too loudly. "Did he actually say he was working with them?"

Lord Hayes swallows, looking pained. "He hasn't said anything yet. But he'll be questioned. If there's a mistake, we will release him."

"How many rebels do you estimate?" Prince Asher asks, continuing his interrogation. I think I see his eyes dart to me for a split second. I don't think he's nearly as calm about this as he seems. He *can't* be.

"Perhaps twenty-five? We'll get a clearer count in the morning, after all the bodies have been recovered," Lord Hayes says.

"And how many casualties among the ball guests?" Prince Asher is asking all the questions I should be asking. But I'm still caught, gasping, on the knowledge that Rowan may have participated in an attack designed to hurt the family he claimed to love. To hurt *me*.

Lord Hayes replies, "Last report was ten deaths. Two nobles, three servants, and five soldiers. But that number will likely rise."

"We need a successor, Your Majesty," Lord Stone says again.

I round on him. "Lord Stone, your opinion has been noted. And, since you've nothing additional to contribute, you're dismissed."

He starts to sputter. But I'm not done. One murder attempt is too many, and I've had, what? Three? I don't trust these men to keep me safe.

Cedric was right. I can't trust *anyone*.

"Lord Rutherford, see to it that Drake and all the other soldiers who died have a ceremony to honor their sacrifice. Send out a statement, too, showing we're in control of the situation. Make sure it's clear I'm fine, and that we're looking for all perpetrators behind the attack. I want approval of all statements and plans beforehand. Prince Asher, do what you can to fortify the castle. More soldiers, more guards, whatever it takes." I turn next to Lord Hayes. "I want to know the identity of the man who tried to kill me, and whether he was doing so at the direction of the antiroyalists. Was I their primary target?"

"Of course, Your Majesty," Lord Hayes replies.

Lord Rutherford snuffles into his mustache and says, "That's all well and good, but we must show decisive action toward the traitors. At least four rebels have been caught and imprisoned. A hanging can be arranged as early as tomorrow at dusk. It would show the swift justice of the queen."

A cold sweat chills the back of my neck. An execution, as early as tomorrow . . .

"No!" The word might as well have been wrenched from my chest, but it's actually Lord Hayes who speaks it.

Lord Stone raises a brow at him. "This betrayal of the kingdom and danger to the queen's life cannot be left unanswered. You know that, Tareth. There *must* be consequences."

Lord Hayes turns to me, looking genuinely distraught. "I'm sorry, Your Majesty. I spoke out of turn. It's just . . . King Octavius entrusted me with the care of his children on more than one occasion. Rowan's betrayal is a devastating blow. I haven't fully wrapped my head around it."

I think of Rowan's story about their trip to Yanos, when Tareth taught the boys to catch "sharks." The way he got Asher to back off when he attacked me.

"I understand," I say. "We're all in shock. I'll make no decisions on punishment until I speak with Rowan. We all deserve to know the truth."

Lord Hayes nods, but he still looks shattered. Just as I feel shattered.

*Oh, Rowan, what have you done? And what will* I *have to do?*

# TWENTY-FIVE

AS SOON AS THE DOOR to my room is closed, I sink onto the floor. Princess climbs into my lap, chirping to get my attention. I bend over her, my hands curled into her soft fur, and let her lick the tip of my nose.

In the other room, water runs in the bath. When I straighten, Sara is sitting on the floor facing me, her expression a mirror of my grief.

"They're saying the rebels will be hanged," she says, her voice a cracked whisper.

My shoulders sag. "I don't know what I'm going to do, Sara. What was Rowan thinking?"

She shakes her head. "I don't understand it. He's a royal himself! And he was going to marry you!"

*We don't have to let anyone else decide for us.*

All his talk about destiny . . . was he being coerced? Was he trapped in some plot? He obviously wanted to run. If I had gone with him . . .

Would the assassin have found me anyway?

"Penn and Rushman were part of the attack too," Sara said, shaking her head. "Penn was killed, but I heard Rushman ran."

Penn and Rushman. A valet and a footman . . . we all knew to stay away from Penn when he'd been stealing spirits from the kitchen. But Hessa could never catch him in the act, and he worked for the truly odious Lord Locklan, who was even worse and did nothing about his errant servant. I make a mental note to follow up on Lord Locklan's whereabouts tonight, as well as his loyalties. There have always been theories that nobles must be secretly funding the antiroyalists. I refuse to believe Rowan was . . . or was the only one.

"So many people were injured. I was so scared. If something had happened to—" Sara's voice cracks, leaving the *you* unsaid.

I know it's not queenly or royal, but I lean forward and hug her. We stay that way, crying into each other's shoulders, until Lissa returns from the bathroom.

"Your bath is ready, Your Majesty," Lissa says, looking uncomfortable. Slowly, I disengage from Sara's embrace and tip Princess out of my lap.

My bath is hurried and not at all restful, as I keep my eyes open and trained on the spigot the entire time. Right now, the whole world feels full of vipers.

It's well past midnight when Sara banks the fire, inspects my bed for nasties, and wishes me a good night. I sit on the bed with the king's journal in my lap, but I don't open it. My brain is too tired for more of the king's agony over Garrick's betrayal, but my body is too tense to sleep. For a while, I watch Princess prowl the room, happy there's another living creature here with me.

But the night presses on me. Drake dead. Prince Asher secretly meeting with an assassin, then killing him before he could finish the job.

Rowan in a cell, a suspected antiroyalist.

Could he have killed his own father, in service to the antiroyalist cause? Is that why he knew I was in danger? The king thought the threat was coming from his inner circle, but maybe it was part of the wider antiroyalist movement too.

With Rowan at the center of it all.

My stomach roils. I spring up from the bed and throw my dressing robe over my night shift. With the king's journal tucked under my arm, I sneak into the darkness of the secret passageway. I give a cursory peek into each room as I pass—Rowan's empty room is lit by a flickering fire in the hearth, probably kept burning by his valet since before the attack. I swallow back a sob. Belle is sitting beside Cedric on his bed, the two of them speaking in low tones. Asher's and the dowager queen's rooms are dark. I pause for a moment and listen, wishing to hear something, anything, that will answer the questions swirling in my head.

There's nothing, of course.

I follow the corridor down a small flight of stairs, running my fingers along the rough stone of the walls until I reach the library. My hands are still tender from my fight with the assassin, and it's difficult to unlatch the hidden door to the library. Finally, I get the door open and trip into the room, only to stop short.

Asher is sitting next to the chess table, a pawn in his hand, staring at me.

I jump, clutching my robe to my chest and dropping the book in the process.

"Asher," I sputter. "What are you doing here?"

Memories flash through my mind—his face bent close to my

assassin's as they walked through the streets of Ryvin together, their faces close again when Asher stabbed the man in the back. Asher's eyes, glittering and feral as he nearly pushed me off the battlements. Does this man want to kill me or save me? What is his game?

Slowly, he stands up, the pawn still in his hand. He offers a small bow. He has bathed and changed as well. His fresh white shirt gapes at the neck, and his breeches cling to his hips. Oh God, his feet are bare.

Another memory flashes, of a narrow alcove and the words *hate has never been our problem* pressing against my ear.

He's giving me a similar assessment, his gaze lingering on my loose, damp hair and the drape of my robe. The thin fabric of my nightgown burns against my skin. I should leave. Everything about this moment is so wrong.

Then my gaze catches on the chess game, and suddenly I'm not worried about what I'm wearing.

"Was it you?" I move closer so I can study the state of play. "Rowan would never say, but he swore it wasn't him."

At the sound of his brother's name, a shadow of pain washes across Asher's face. He passes the pawn from hand to hand. After a slight hesitation, he places it on the board.

He's opened up his bishop to an attack. I play out the possibilities in my head. Is he sacrificing the piece for some greater gain? If so, I can't see it.

I take the bishop.

He curses softly.

My lip quirks.

He moves another pawn. "When I was young, my father taught me to play. He taught all of us . . . we would have little tournaments. There are six different boards stored in this room. There used to be a board in his living quarters as well, but he put it away when Sorren died."

I move my knight. As he stares at the board, I move the chair by the fire closer, so I can sit down.

"Who taught you? Rowan?" he asks, assessing my move.

"Your tutor. I knew long before Rowan and I started playing."

"Ah." His lip tips up in a half smile. "Sorren was the best of us. Father played with him nearly every night."

He makes another unforced error, and I take his other bishop.

"But he never let us touch this board." He looks up, suddenly, his green eyes burning in the firelight like emeralds. "And I never did, not until the day after he died."

A strange feeling settles over me.

His attention refocuses on the game. "Apart from Sorren, none of us could keep up with Father's intellect. We could never make the game a challenge for him. But someone did. *This* board with *this* game was reserved for an opponent he found worthy. He never told us who it was."

But Rowan knew.

All those early mornings spent dusting the books, stoking the fire, sweeping the floor. Glancing at the chess pieces, strategizing my next move . . .

My pulse pounds in my throat. "Are you telling me that all

this time, I was playing chess with the king?" And Rowan never breathed a word.

Asher holds my gaze.

"Your Majesty," the prince says, with an edge that sends a chill down my spine, "I think it's time you tell me how you knew my father."

# TWENTY-SIX

I STARE AT THE CHESSBOARD, my brain whirling. I *didn't* know the king. He never spoke to me about chess . . . or anything of consequence at all. I'm still trying to understand how he could have possibly been the person I've been competing with all these years.

*Why did Rowan never tell me?*

It also bothers me that Asher's the one demanding answers when he's certainly not the only one with questions.

"I would, if there was anything to tell." I move my rook to threaten his knight. He's right about one thing: He's not nearly as good as his father. "Personally, I'm more concerned with how you knew the man who tried to murder me tonight."

His hand bumps a pawn. He straightens the piece before moving his knight to safety. Well, it's not safe, but he clearly thinks it is. "His name was Colin. He worked the docks of Ryvin, and—"

"And he was an antiroyalist," I supply.

He studies the board, refusing to meet my eyes. It takes him forever to make his move, but it's more astute than I was expecting. "Check," he says. And then, when I'm about to upend the whole fucking table because he's still not saying anything useful, he adds, "Yes."

"So, how did you know him? And why were you speaking to him that night in the city? You said it wasn't related, but you must see how it looks. Were you . . . were you working with Rowan?"

King Octavius suspected that one of his family members or, at the very least, someone in his inner circle, would kill him. Asher had the most to gain—he'd become king himself. Were he and Rowan using the antiroyalists to further this end?

Just the thought makes me want to scream. It butts up against everything I know of Rowan. Maybe Asher was the one coercing him?

Except he killed the assassin.

It's the piece that, however outlandish everything else sounds, just does not fit.

Asher runs a hand through his wavy chestnut hair. I hate that my eyes catch the gesture, that I can't look away. "You have a lot of questions, and yet you barely answered mine. Here's another. Do you really expect me to believe you yourself have nothing to do with the antiroyalists?"

Caught utterly aback, I laugh in his face. "Excuse me?"

He narrows his eyes. "You and Rowan have been meeting secretly for years. You conveniently left the ballroom before the danger began—"

"So did you!" I practically shout. "And my friendship with Rowan—it had nothing to do with the antiroyalists. I had no idea, I had—" My voice breaks. I still don't believe it.

He shakes his head angrily and focuses on our game again. "Just tell me how you knew my father. Were you his lover? A spy? A saboteur? Whose whispers have had the queen's ear?"

“No one’s tried to whisper in my ear,” I snap.

“No one? Not even my brother?” His curls fall forward over his forehead as he tips his chin down to meet my eyes.

For a moment, we stare at each other. Behind me, the fire blazes. That has to be the reason for the warmth in my cheeks, the heat sliding like fingers across my chest and down to my stomach.

I clear my throat.

His eyes dip to the neckline of my robe before he looks back at the chessboard.

We’re not going to get anywhere if we keep asking questions without answers. Maybe, if I give a little, sacrifice a pawn, he’ll open up a little too. “Rowan and I are friends. Only friends. And I wasn’t King Octavius’s lover, nor a spy, nor a saboteur. I swear it. I have no idea why he chose me as his heir. Why he played chess with me all these years. I don’t even know why or how I started . . .”

A memory surfaces, one of my first days working in the castle. I was so excited, ready to finally have something to do, a way to pay back the royal family for letting me grow up here, a war orphan with nothing but a necklace to my name. It was Bryson himself who walked me to the library and showed me where the broom was, who walked me by the table with the chessboard. He’d said something, very casually, what was it?

“It was Bryson, I think.” I try to remember. “He said something about the board. Something about it being a practice board, that anyone was permitted to move a piece if they wished. It had felt like permission. So, after I was finished sweeping up and building the fire, I made my first play."

Asher studies my face, like he's trying to peel away the layers to reveal the lie. But this is the truth, and eventually the tension in his shoulders eases. He shifts his attention to the board. I watch him make his move, and I see it. My win. Right there, plain as day.

Three turns, and I'll have him.

"Why did you leave the ball tonight? Where would you have gone if I hadn't followed you?" I move my queen.

He shrugs a little, but he's softened enough to say, "I told you, I don't like dancing. I knew everyone expected me to dance with Rosaline, and I was trying to delay the moment."

"You were hiding?" I ask skeptically. He's never seemed the hiding type to me.

He shrugs, but the tips of his ears are slowly turning pink.

"You still haven't explained why you were speaking to Colin two days before the ball," I say, focusing with an effort.

His expression shifts to something like wariness, but this time, he finally answers. "I knew Rowan was connected to a faction of antiroyalists in Ryvin. He was seen at a protest a few months ago. I wanted to know if you were involved too. I was there to ask Colin about you."

"I've never seen that man before in my—"

But Asher is suddenly on his feet, the movement scattering our chess pieces. He stares toward the fire, his hand on the hilt of the dagger at his hip.

"Come with me, Your Majesty."

He puts a hand on my lower back and urges me to the door. I try not to notice the heat of his fingers through my dressing gown.

"What's going on?" I whisper.

He throws a dark glance back toward the fire—toward the secret door just beside it. "We have an audience."

# TWENTY-SEVEN

ASHER STEERS ME INTO THE hallway and suddenly we're rushing, nearly running down the corridor. His bare feet slap against the cold stone while my flimsy slippers threaten to fall off.

Someone was in the secret passage watching us. But who?

And why didn't Asher just confront them, instead of running away? It had to be a member of his family. Narissa or Belle or Cedric. Maybe he doesn't want them to know about Rowan and his history with the antiroyalists.

So here we are, rushing down the hallway as if chased by ghosts.

We reach the Old Tower, and when I stumble, he grabs my hand. The spiraling stairs go on for an age, and my world is reduced to the heat and firmness of Asher's hand, and the vision of his strong, muscular thighs climbing the stairs before me. Torches are lit at intervals, but we're in the shadow more than the light. Each time I falter, he urges me on with a squeeze of my hand.

Finally, as before, we burst onto the parapet, only this time the night stretches before us, cool and sparkling with stars.

The wind whips my hair into my face, obscuring my view. Dizziness overcomes me and I falter, flashing back to our last encounter on the battlements, when he shoved me up close to the edge, his body pressing against mine, his voice low and threatening. But this time, Asher draws me to a protected corner, well away from the edge of the battlement. Here the wind is blocked by the angle of the stone tower behind us.

"Why did you bring me up here again?" I ask, now that we're truly alone. And indeed, it feels as if we're the only ones in the whole world, cocooned as we are by night and stone and wind.

"The garden is crawling with soldiers, and everywhere else in the castle has ears. Surely you know that. Inside, someone is always listening."

"Do you come up here a lot?" I ask, because there's something about the way he leans into the wind, breathes deeply for what feels like the first time, that has me wondering.

I feel him shrug. "I have been . . . more often . . . since Sorren died. And I wonder why . . ."

His voice trails off.

The sudden, overwhelming desire to squeeze his hand, to hug him, makes me do the opposite. I step back.

I can't forget that just days ago, Asher had his hand around my neck, that he threatened to push me from these very battlements.

That he met with Colin two days before the man tried to kill me.

That I'm engaged to his brother. At least, for the moment.

"Why did you ask that man about me, Asher?"

The darkness makes him a ghost. There isn't enough light to read his expression, or even really see his face. The rough timbre of his voice rumbles under my skin as he says, at last, "I thought you killed my father. I wanted to know why. If you were an antiroyalist, it would make sense. I was hoping . . . I was hoping it was you, not Rowan."

My breath hitches. "You thought *I* killed him? When *you've* got the most to gain?"

"You don't deny he was murdered, then?" he asks sharply.

So he knows too. And suddenly I cast the past few weeks through a different lens. Asher's threats, his violence. Were they actions of a killer—or of a grief-stricken son on the hunt for his father's murderer?

I take a deep breath. Other than Sara, I don't trust a soul in this castle, but I need Asher to trust *me* . . . so I give him the truth. "The king left me a hidden message. He didn't tell me why he chose me to be his heir, but he did say he thought someone close to him was trying to kill him. He tasked me with discovering the truth."

For a long time, the only sound is the scream of the wind.

"How do you know the note was meant for you?" Asher asks at last.

I reach for my necklace and I raise the stone off my skin. "It was in a box, and my necklace was the key."

Asher exhales sharply.

"I have as many questions as you do. But I swear, I had no knowledge of the king's plan. I had no idea he even knew who I was."

He shifts, and then his warm, calloused hands are on my face, cupping my cheeks. His eyes search mine, as if he could find some truth written there. "Who *are* you, Ruby?" he asks gruffly.

Some part of me wishes I could lean into his hands and tell him everything. Satisfy his every curiosity, give him the resolution he wants. But I can't, because his search is also mine.

"I don't know who I am," I say, the wind nearly stealing my words.

"No one else seems to either," he says after a moment, letting his hands drop from my face to my shoulders. "Colin had never heard of you. No connections to the antiroyalists, and also no information about who you are or where you came from. Even the story the other servants know—of you being an orphan of war—I couldn't corroborate it."

His words lodge in my chest, cold and hard.

What does he mean he couldn't corroborate it?

A cold breeze whistles around the corner and unconsciously I lean closer to him, drawn by his heat. "Thank you," I murmur. "For stopping Colin."

"I swear, I had no idea what he planned to do."

"If you didn't hire him," I say, my voice barely more than a whisper, "then who did? Or was he part of the attack? Perhaps the whole point of it was to get to me."

"I don't know." His voice hums in the darkness, warm against my face. "What I fear most—" He chokes on the words.

"What?" I ask, cheeks flayed by the screaming wind.

With a rough growl, Asher says, "Is that it's Rowan behind all of this . . . that he killed our father and tried to kill you too."

"We don't know that it was him," I say, even though that very fear has crossed my mind. "It could have been any number of people."

"But Colin's no mastermind himself. He's a mercenary. So *someone* hired him. And you're in danger until we figure out who."

I nod, but the pronouncement doesn't strike fear the way it

would have even four weeks ago. I've been in danger from the moment Lord Hayes read the king's will. I'll likely be in danger until the day I die.

Asher steps closer. "You're shivering." He presses the warmth of his hand into my back, and I fight the urge to arch into the touch. My robe snaps against my legs as the cool night air whips against my cheeks. And still, the air is too thick between us. We're so close, I can see the glint of moonlight in his eyes.

His gaze flits to my lips. And gently, so gently, he brushes a strand of hair off my forehead.

It takes me a moment to realize I've stopped breathing. My body sways closer, seeking his warmth, seeking him—

But, as if remembering himself, a shadow passes over Asher's face, and he takes a step back.

"Come on," he says gruffly. "Let's get you back inside."

# TWENTY-EIGHT

BELLE LOOKS TERRIBLE. SHE HAS a deep scratch on her cheek from a flying piece of glass and a sprained ankle from tripping over a chair while trying to flee. Dark shadows circle her eyes, which are currently wide with disbelief.

"You want me to be an advisor?" she asks.

We're in the sitting area of my room, and I'm sure I don't look much better. I slept terribly last night, haunted by nightmares of men trying to kill me and memories of Rowan asking me to run away with him. I've spent the morning caught in the same painful rumination the king once suffered over his own best friend and subsequent betrayer.

I woke up knowing I couldn't be like the king, refusing to see his friend. I have the strength, at least, to face Rowan.

I think.

But first, I need to talk to Belle.

"I need someone whose judgment I can trust," I say. Lord Stone assumes I'll be dead within days, Lord Rutherford ignores me in my own council meetings, and Lord Hayes, the most respectful of the three, still treats me as a daughter to be shielded rather than a monarch to be obeyed.

"You know the castle and the kingdom inside and out," I say to Belle. "You've already been advising me; you know how to deal with men who don't respect you, and you've been trained in all the royal etiquette. There's really no other choice."

"What about Tareth and Liam and Simon?"

I shrug. "I'll replace them all in time. There's no rule about how many advisors a queen must have. I just . . . those men don't make me feel safe."

Belle gives me a knowing look, and already the weight on my shoulders feels lighter. She understands. Good.

"I would be honored to become your advisor. I think my father's men have . . . well, let's say they have gaps in their knowledge, vast as it is. I hope I can become a trusted resource."

"You already have," I say, with a sincere, if tired, smile. "I really value your understanding of my . . . situation."

"My situation" being the fact that I'm a woman, worse a maid, who has to grip any power I manage to gain with an iron fist.

"What can I do for you now?" Belle asks. Her spine, usually poised to the point of rigidity, has an exhausted slump to it.

I wave her off. "You should rest. Maybe go see Sir Henry. That cut on your face looks painful. I need to . . ." I pause, searching for the right word, at last landing on, "Speak to your brother."

Her mouth twists, a tiny, agonized break in her marble armor.

"Rowan told me once that you could read each other's minds," I say quietly.

She smiles at the floor, a tear escaping down her cheek. "I wish. I'd ask him what the hell he's playing at."

I touch her arm. "I'll ask him for you. I—I think there must be more to this story. I just can't believe . . ."

She nods and pulls herself together, straightening her spine.

With a shaky breath, she says firmly, "It'll undermine your authority and status as queen if you show him leniency. But strength doesn't have to mean brutality."

The tightness in my chest eases slightly. I nod.

"Please rest. I'll let you know what I learn." I walk her to the door and watch as she limps down the hall.

Both Reece and Garon are on duty. Prince Asher has doubled the guards all over the castle. With a last glance at Princess, curled tightly in a chair by the fire, I close the door and stride into the hall myself.

When I reach the Old Tower, Reece takes the lead while Garon follows behind me. We climb several loops of the circular staircase before we reach the floor that functions as a prison. We walk down a long row of cells with heavy wooden doors and iron-barred windows. There are several other guards spread along the hall; they bow smartly as I pass.

We arrive at Rowan's cell a few short moments later. Reece and Garon retreat to the end of the hall at my nod.

Rowan doesn't notice me at first. He's sitting on the one small stool in his cell, shoulders slumped, picking at a scab on his finger.

"Rowan?" I say quietly.

He looks up, and then stands up quickly, but he doesn't approach the door.

"They said you wanted to speak with me," I say, searching his face.

According to Lieutenant Gaynor, Rowan said he would only speak to me. No one else.

Not even his own mother.

I have so many questions, so many feelings churning in my stomach.

"I'm so sorry, Ruby," Rowan says, his face crumpling. "It all went too far. I wanted to tell you—I tried to get you out of there. When I saw Belle and Mother with blood on their faces . . . God, I am the world's biggest fool."

The agony in his eyes breaks something inside of me. But he's also not denying anything. "You're an antiroyalist. How is that possible, Rowan?"

He shrugs a little, and begins to pace the small, empty tower room. "It always bothered me how vastly different people's lives are, and for what? Because you happened to be born to a poor laborer instead of a prince? Because your mother was a maid rather than a noble? I watched Sorren learn so much about the kingdom, and yet all Father's teachings, all the books I read after Sorren, talked about 'leveraging' the lower classes. Never about how to support them or lift them out of their circumstances. And then I met you, a whirling dervish of falling leaves and exposed ankles." He smiles a little, as if remembering. "I'd been told the common people weren't intelligent, that they needed us to manage their lives . . . and yet you kept beating me at fucking chess. It made me look harder at the other maids, at my valet, at Bryson, who keeps an entire castle running smoothly. I couldn't understand how my father had gotten it all wrong."

"So you killed him?" I ask, as gently as I can.

He looks at me blankly, pausing his rhythmic pacing. "Who?"

"Your father," I say.

He laughs a little and then sobers at the look on my face. "Wait, are you serious?"

I nod.

The blood drains from his face. "Of course I didn't kill him! I may have given a little coin to a couple of the protests, and I kept a close eye on their demands and the progress they made, but I would never hurt anyone. I thought I could convince him to do more to help. I persuaded him to raise wages last year, remember?"

"The attack last night was more than a protest," I remind him, not so gently. But for the first time since I walked down this hall, I feel like I can breathe. If I can ease Asher's worst fears about his brother, all the better.

"I left the group when you were named queen, you have to believe me. But the attack on the ball was in motion so quickly . . . I didn't help them, but I didn't share what I knew with you or Asher either." He runs a hand down his face. "I should have. I'm responsible. I tried to get the rebels to leave my family alone, and that's when the guards saw me."

"Rowan," I say, knowing everything hinges on my next question, praying I don't see him scratch his ear, which has been his tell since he was a kid, "did you ask me to run away with you because it was your job to draw me away from the party? Were there . . . was there anyone waiting for me out in the garden?"

His eyes widen. "Ruby, I would never do that. *Never.* I told you . . . I wasn't helping them. I was just trying to keep you safe. The only reason I—" He swallows whatever he was about to say. I study his face, the wild certainty in his eyes. I note his hands, tight around the bars of the window in his cell door. No scratching his ear. No deflection or denial.

Just Rowan.

"What?" I ask. "The only reason you what?"

With a sigh, he presses his forehead against the bars of the small window. "*You're* the only reason. The reason I joined the antiroyalists. The reason I wanted to run away. I've . . . I've been in love with you since we met. It killed me that there was no chance we could ever be together, that the most I could offer you was a secret affair. All those romances you thought I was having . . . most of them were excuses to sneak out for antiroyalist meetings. When Father chose you . . . everything went sideways. Suddenly, we were betrothed. What I've wanted since we met, it was finally possible, and it wasn't even your choice."

My heart is running like someone's chasing it. I'm wide eyed. Speechless.

Rowan *loves* me?

"You never said," I murmur, my voice hoarse. "I didn't know."

"Of course not," he says. "I didn't want to put pressure on you, or make you think I was trying to take advantage."

This revelation is more than I can handle.

Because Rowan is in a cell. And because I know my love for him is different from his love for me. I think . . . I think he's right. If I'd *had* a choice . . . I might have made a different one.

I suck in a breath. I can't tell him that. His handsome face is already twisted in agony and shame. So I stick to what I'm here for. Getting answers. "There was an assassin—his goal was to kill me. He very nearly succeeded. Was the larger attack a diversion so he could get to me?"

Rowan backs away from the door, horror suffusing his face. "No, no. They were just supposed to sow chaos. Make their voices heard. No one was supposed to be *killed*. I swear, if the goal had been to hurt you, I would have told you. I would have gotten you out of there, no matter what. You know I would have."

"So I wasn't a target?" I flash back to the crypts and the darkness and the man who tried to kill me. "But surely the antiroyalists want me dead. Down with the monarchy, all that."

Rowan shakes his head. "The point was to get your attention, that's all. I swear it. Though the whole endeavor did get out of hand."

His words swirl through my head. I'll have to confirm with the other prisoners, but if what Rowan is saying is true, that means the assassin was working under someone else's orders. The attack was a diversion. The people carrying it out just didn't know it.

"Do you know someone named Colin?" I ask, studying him. "Big guy, scary looking."

Slowly, he nods. "Yeah, Colin's one of the leaders of the movement. I didn't see him last night, but he would have been involved in the planning. Did they catch him?"

A flash of memory leaves me breathless. "Something like that."

Rowan bows his head, the shadows under his eyes making him look haggard. His fine blue velvet jacket is singed, one cuff black with dried blood. "Please tell my mother I'm sorry," he says, his voice a raspy memory of itself. "I'm so sorry, Ruby. I hope . . . what you said about taking care of my family . . ."

"I'll find a way," I say.

"I would have spent my whole life trying to make you happy," he says, almost wistfully. "I would have tried to earn a true, loving marriage with you. You're the best of us, Ruby. You'll help all of Lumaria. I'm sorry I won't live to see it."

The ache in my chest threatens to split me apart. I put my hand through the bars of the window. He takes my fingers gently, rubbing their chill away between his two palms.

"You think I'll have you put to death?"

"You won't have a choice." He squeezes my hands. "Think of the Great Betrayer. It's been twenty years, and a whole rebellion has grown on the back of the king's weakness. I know these people, Ruby. Don't embolden them."

"Did you kill anyone last night?"

The look on his face is almost comical. "Of course not."

"Then your death wouldn't be justice. It's not weakness to do the right thing." I lean my forehead on the bars for a moment, wishing I could hug him. Wishing we could have one moment together, wishing I had time to process Rowan's feelings for me. Was I always destined to break his heart?

Well, fuck destiny.

Rowan starts to release my hand, but I hold on for one moment longer. I take him in, his familiar blue eyes, his artfully messy blond hair, memorize all of it, knowing nothing will ever be the same between us again.

Reece, Garon, and I return to my chambers, only to find someone unexpected waiting for me.

"Your Majesty," Queen Narissa says. Her head is still bandaged, but her eyes are clear and canny. She dips into the tiniest curtsy. "I seek an audience with you."

"Of course, Dowager Queen." I gesture her into my room, realizing after the fact that I should have met her on more neutral ground. What if she was the one who planted the snake? What does she have hidden in her skirts, in her hands, that could be of danger to me?

I watch her closely. Even Princess gives her a wide berth.

She moves to stand by the fire, her gaze cast into the flames. "Belle said you saw Rowan this morning."

My heart is still stuttering. "I did."

"I find it impossible to believe that my son is an antiroyalist. There's been a mistake." She twists to stare at me accusingly, like *I'm* the one to blame for this error. It's her usual glare, but she can't fully hide the pain behind it.

Almost gently, I say, "I'm sorry. He has confessed. He didn't actively help plan the attack, but he knew in advance that it would happen and he gave no warning."

The damning words break something within her. With a shudder, her usual mask of disdain cracks fully. She hides her face behind her hands as she cries.

Narissa has shown me nothing but dismissal, judgment, even hatred. Maybe she killed her husband. Maybe she tried to kill *me.* But I can't help feeling for her now. Whatever else she is, she's a mother who loves her children.

"He told me to tell you he's sorry," I say. "For what it's worth, I think he was trying to help Lumaria."

She takes a deep, shuddering breath and straightens, her face smooth and cold once more. "Please do not put my son to death, Your Majesty. I realize his crimes are great, but"—she pauses to gather herself—"but his role was minor compared to others'."

For a moment, I stare at her. She's here to beg for her son's life. It's clear the act is humiliating to her. She, the dowager queen, asking *anything* of a maid. But she's here. She's doing it anyway.

I let the silence grow until she's visibly uncomfortable.

Then I tilt up my chin. "Rowan did not warn of the attack, though he knew full well it would occur. He must be punished for his crime and to send a message to others who would plan harm. But"—I raise a hand to halt her before she interjects—"he didn't kill anyone or actively take part in the attack. I am certain he will cooperate and provide what information he knows about the rebels. Therefore, a punishment of death would be unjust. He'll be sent to the Reaches to serve a term of . . ." I scramble to come up with a reasonable time frame. "Five years."

There was no chance I was going to sentence Rowan to death. *I* wouldn't survive it. But he's right that there have to be serious consequences.

If the Reaches has held the Great Betrayer all these years, it will hold Rowan.

Narissa bows her head, and in a voice that could cut stone, she says, "Thank you, Your Majesty, for your mercy," before sweeping out the door.

# TWENTY-NINE

I SIT IN FRONT OF the fire in my room, Princess purring on my lap. I don't know if she can sense my distress or if she's just feeling affectionate today, but she's turning circles, rubbing her face against mine, and kneading her sharp little claws on my thighs. I run my hands along her soft fur, trying to concentrate on breathing.

Rowan will go to the Reaches, just as Garrick did twenty years ago. He wasn't the one behind my assassination attempt, I'm certain of *that*, but he also helped antiroyalists protest, even threaten, the monarchy. Of which I'm now a part. I think back to all the time we spent together, sneaking around, playing chess, talking about the various petty injustices of our lives.

And all that time, he was in love with me.

It was his love for *me* that radicalized him.

I can't seem to wrap my head around it. I thought I was an amusing diversion for him. Somehow, I missed the obvious . . . the fact that he chose to befriend me to begin with.

But there's more weighing on my mind.

The betrothal, broken.

I'll have to find another answer before my coronation, yes, but that's not what claws at me and tastes a lot like guilt. I'm . . . not sorry that Rowan and I won't be marrying. As much as I care for him, as handsome as he is, every time we got close, every time we almost kissed, when we *did* kiss, I could feel my body, my heart, resisting. He would have been a good companion, a friend. But we would never have had passion.

As queen, probably passion isn't something I should expect or hope for. But that doesn't mean I'm not a tiny bit relieved.

I dip my head, shame curling through me. Relieved? That Rowan will be imprisoned for five years? I don't know what I'm thinking. And it's not as if the next prospect will be any better.

Princess bites my finger gently, sparking tears.

"No, baby, that hurts," I say, but I'm grateful for the distraction.

Suddenly, a knock sets us both on edge.

"Come in!" I call.

Lord Hayes hurries into the room. With the slightest bow, he immediately says, "Your Majesty, I heard that Rowan spoke to you. What did he say?"

"Are you well?" I ask, a little alarmed. The advisor is usually so stoic and unmoved. Today his beard is untidy, his eyes glassy, and the knot on his cravat is askew. Is he so worried about Rowan?

"Yes, yes, I'm fine," he says, waving a hand. Then amends that to, "I haven't slept, no surprise. But I'm fine. I'd like to know about Prince Rowan, please."

With a sigh, I recount our conversation.

"So he won't be executed?" The man looks like it's his own neck in the rope.

"Of course not. He wasn't a full member of the attack, and he knew nothing about the assassin. I'm having him sent to the Reaches for five years. I suppose that's something you can arrange?"

He nods. "Of course, Your Majesty. It will take a few days."

"As for the other rebels, their punishment should be on balance with their crimes. If there's proof they killed, they should suffer the same fate. Otherwise, time in the Reaches seems fair."

He bows, more successfully this time. He runs a hand through his hair, and I notice the weariness in his face, the age that's settled into the grooves around his eyes. The king's death, this attack . . . it's wearing him down.

He's been a fixture in this castle since before I came here as a baby. Given his age, his time as an advisor may be ending in the not-too-distant future. Even though that's what I told Belle I wanted, I still find a small ache in my chest at the thought.

No one likes change.

Or unanswered questions.

My conversation with Asher runs through my mind.

*Ruby, who are you?*

"Lord Hayes, do you know anything about where I came from or the person who brought me to the castle? When I was a baby, I mean."

To his credit, he takes the change of subject in stride. But he shakes his head. "Nothing official, if that's what you mean. If I recall, it was the cook who took you in. I always thought the story she told about a stranger was just that . . . a story. I have always assumed you were her illegitimate child."

His words break my world apart.

He thinks—has always thought—that *Mellie* is my real mother?

"Where's Miriam?" I ask Hessa, poking my head into the kitchen.

Hessa jumps, splashing soup onto the fire. "Good Lord, love, don't scare a woman like that! Oh, I mean, Your Majesty. I'm sorry. I didn't realize it was, uh, you."

What she really means is that she forgot I, Ruby, am no longer someone to scream and snipe at.

"It's fine," I say, waving a hand. Regally, probably. "Where's Miriam? I need to speak with her. Urgently."

Hessa shrugs. "Last I saw her, she was in the yard. Weeding she said, but with her old eyes, I expect she's pulling up all my thyme."

I turn. She shouts another belated "Your Majesty!" to my back.

The long servants' hall lined with tables is mostly empty this time of day, but one of the footmen, Lucas, leans against the wall, a mug of something hot and fragrant in his hands.

He bows as I pass him on my way to the kitchen yard.

As I step into the sunlight, I suffer a sickening moment of déjà vu. My gaze rushes to the spot by the chicken coop where the coyote ravaged Princess's family, expecting blood and snarls and sorrow.

But the yard is quiet, the coop tidy with a fresh bed of straw and a new mouser curled up asleep in the sun. Automatically, I glance at the gate, prepared to shut it. Asher's fool dog probably—

But the gate is secure. In fact, it's not just closed—it has a new latch, silver and shining in the sunlight. I hurry over.

There's a full-on lock now, no shoddy lever a dog can muscle its way through.

I look questioningly back at the castle, but that's when I spot Miriam in the garden, elbow-deep in the basil.

"Miriam, I need to ask you a question," I say. Well, shout, really. Even so, it takes a couple tries to get her attention.

"Do you know where Mellie settled when she retired?" I ask, once she's gotten over the shock of me in a proper gown.

Miriam thinks for a moment, her wrinkled face screwed up like a withered peach. She's been old my whole life; she's even older than Mellie. But she doesn't have a family outside the castle, so she'll remain here until she passes.

"I think she lives in Spyrian with her children." She putters around in the dirt, picking a few more bunches of herbs. "Bryson can probably tell you more."

Spyrian. That's only a couple hours from here.

After I thank her, I hurry back inside, followed by my guard-shaped shadows, and track down Bryson. He's able to give me more precise directions, and I study him closely, watching to see if he gives me a pitying look that signals that he, too, assumes that Mellie is my mother and I'm just too naive to have realized.

He doesn't tip his hand, but I have to wonder: Does *everyone* assume she's my mother? Or was that just Lord Hayes's idea?

It's true that Mellie was always a mother figure to me; my stomach is sick with wonder at the thought that she could actually *be* my mother.

But if so, why wouldn't she have told me?

Or taken me with her when she retired?

I hurry past the Great Hall and down the stairs to the armory.

"Asher?" I call, stepping into the cavernous room. According to Garon, he's normally addressing the castle guards this time of day, but when we got to the training yard, Lieutenant Gaynor said he was taking inventory.

The room is dim, just two torches lit. Golden light gleams against the swords mounted on the walls. Reece and Garon stay close behind me.

"Asher?" I call again.

"Your Majesty." He steps out of the shadows at the back of the room, his voice pitched into a dangerous growl. His armored leathers creak ominously. "Do you need something?"

For an instant, I think about turning around and forgetting the whole thing. It's clear Asher wants to be alone, that I'm the last person he wants to see.

But I can't stop thinking about what Lord Hayes said. And I can't stop thinking about Asher's fears.

"I saw your brother," I say. I glance back at my guards, asking them with a look to give us a little space. They wait outside as I step farther into the room.

"And?" Asher stands in the center of the training ring, half of his face still in the dark. His hair falls across his forehead, its own kind of shadow.

"He says he had nothing to do with your father's death, actually laughed at me when I suggested it. He also admitted to knowing Colin but had no idea he tried to kill me." I wish I had more definitive proof for him. But all I can offer him are Rowan's words and my own belief that he was telling the truth.

For a long moment, Asher stares at me. At last, he lets out a long breath.

"Thank you for telling me," he says, with a little less hostility.

It's not a very big opening, but I'll take it anyway. "Also, I've been thinking about the question you asked me, about who I am. Would you . . . would you be willing to go with me to maybe find out?"

He raises a brow in question.

I suck in a deep breath. "Lord Hayes thinks Mellie, the old cook, might actually be my mother. I want to go to Spyrian and talk to her."

"What kind of protection are you planning?" He shifts a little closer. I'm aware of every inhale of his breath, the lethal beauty of his face.

I shrug a little. I hadn't even thought about that. "Reece and Garon? I could add another guard, if you think it necessary?"

"If I think . . . If I—" He breaks into a short, humorless laugh. "Yes, I do think it's necessary. You're going to need a whole detail. I'll get it organized. We can leave tomorrow morning, if that's acceptable to you."

"We? Are you sure—"

"You asked me to accompany you. I will not refuse my queen."

Asher calling me *his* queen does something to my insides, something I absolutely refuse to examine. "Thank you," I say, flustered. "Tomorrow is fine."

I turn to leave, but his gaze lingers on me, heavy and unspoken, as if he knows exactly what his words have done to me—and all at once I can't shake the nervous anticipation of what tomorrow will bring.

# THIRTY

"CAN YOU TAKE PRINCESS DOWN to the kitchen yard?" I ask Sara. It's almost time for my trip to Spyrian with Asher. I tell myself the strange flip-flop in my stomach is definitely nerves over seeing Mellie, nothing else. "She gets restless all by herself up here."

"Of course," Sara says. Predictably, it takes her another five minutes to catch the little terror, who's already shredded a wrap I left draped over a chair and kicked the sand in her box everywhere.

"I noticed the gate in the kitchen yard was fixed. *Finally.*" I stare at myself in the mirror in the bathroom. My hair demurely twisted back from my face. My dress a relatively understated pale green gown with a mink collar. There's a chill this morning, with low, gray clouds crowding the sky.

Will this be the dress I'm wearing when I discover I've known my real mother all along?

The dress I'll be wearing when I ask her *why*? Why did she lie?

"It was actually Prince Asher himself," Sara says, kissing Princess's nose. "Not long after King Octavius died, the prince came down with that ridiculous dog and watched him open it. He engineered the new latch himself."

My reflection's eyes widen. *Asher* fixed the problem?

"Well, that's good. It's about time."

Sara gives me a weird look as I emerge, and suddenly I don't know what to do with my face. Am I giving her a weird look too? Why would I look weird? Why do I feel weird?

Oh, hell.

"I'll be back by nightfall." I lean down to kiss Princess's nose and catch a noseful of fur. She's already squirming.

"Tell Mellie I send my love," Sara says. "I hope she has answers for you."

"Me too."

Sara heads out before Princess can wriggle free. I touch my necklace, the stone warm against my skin. I don't want to get ahead of myself.

It's weird to hope someone's lied to you your whole life. But if it means I'm about to learn the truth, there we are.

There's a knock on the door, and I am surprised to see Lissa slip inside the room. This isn't her usual time to be here. Sara brings my breakfast and lights the fire in the hearth—when I haven't gotten up and done it myself already—Lissa and Theia don't come until the afternoon, sometimes evening, when it's time to bathe and dress for dinner.

Sara and I've planned it that way, so I'm never alone with Lissa.

She closes the door behind her, and my heart skitters in my chest, just a little faster than usual.

"Lissa, is there a problem?" I ask.

She twists her hands into her apron. Her lovely round face has two pink washes of color along her cheeks. Her eyes glitter.

"Your Majesty, there's something I need to say." Her voice

wobbles, and she clears her throat. "I know . . . I know most people would have arrested me and Theia. And I just want to say, well, thank you. You owe us nothing. But you didn't throw us to the wolves."

There's something in her voice, in her face that makes me ask, "Did I make the right call? Or is this the beginning of a confession?"

Her cheeks go even redder. "I—I just want you to know you're safe with me. No matter what."

"Well, thank you. I should hope so," I say, a little awkwardly. But given what I've heard her say about the king in the past, this feels meaningful.

"Come on," I say, gesturing to her. "I need to leave, and there's nothing for you to do in here while I'm gone."

She might be feeling grateful, but that still doesn't mean I trust her.

Asher is waiting when I step outside the castle.

He's wearing a black velvet jacket, this one embroidered with silver thread. No armor this time. The white of his shirt accentuates the sharp edge of his jaw, which tenses further when he sees me. As he helps me into the carriage, I can't help noticing how his breeches cling to his thighs.

Calen joins the coachman, while Reece leaps up on the back. Several other soldiers accompany us on horseback. Asher wanted to allocate even more guards, but I drew the line at a half dozen. I don't want to draw unwelcome attention to Mellie.

One of the carriage horses neighs, shaking its head against the bit as we start moving forward. Asher sits beside me, his velvet sleeve brushing against the thin silk of my gown. The wide cushioned bench seat and polished wood of the king's carriage, large and ridiculously opulent by nearly any measure, still feels small with Asher's tall, muscled body so close. Every breath I take smells like his spicy orange soap.

Part of me wants to move away, to put more space between us. But he doesn't seem at all bothered, and I don't want to admit that I might be, so I stay where I am. Acutely aware that our arms are touching, that only an inch or two separates our thighs. I stare out the window, fixedly.

The city grows around us, stone by stone. The carriage takes a route similar to that of the parade, down the wider main street that leads to the riverwalk. We turn off before we reach the river and continue through narrow streets lined with small taverns, street markets, and women hanging wash.

"I trust you slept well?" Asher says.

"Actually, I did not. Princess—my, uh, cat—decided my feet needed to be hunted."

He lets out a surprised chuckle.

"You?" I ask, since apparently we're doing the small-talk thing.

He doesn't answer.

I sneak a glance at him; he's staring at his hands, quiet and still on his knees. There's a callus on his thumb and jagged scab on the back of one knuckle. Scars, too, and a crooked pinkie that looks like it was broken and badly set. His hands don't match the boy I watched from my perch in the garden trees. The boy who'd stretch on the grass for hours, reading and sketching caricatures of his parents and tutors, his fingers calm and graceful.

"Thank you for fixing the kitchen yard gate," I say.

His hands close into fists, and his gaze shifts to my face. "I didn't realize Rocky was causing harm. I'm glad you brought it to my attention."

We sit in silence for a few minutes, our arms bumping as the road shifts from cobbles to dirt and we leave Ryvin behind. The run-down cottages at the edge of the city transform into green pastures dotted with wide-canopied trees—the kind that make for good climbing.

I've never been outside of Ryvin before. At least, not that I can remember.

"Have you ever been to Spyrian?" I ask as casually as I can manage.

"A few times," he replies. "It's along the route to Ploughton, where we keep a standing company of infantry troops."

"Oh," I say, a little embarrassed. It didn't occur to me we'd have companies of troops beyond the city walls, but of course we do. And it *should* have occurred to me. Or my advisors should have told me.

"Have you ever traveled, Your Majesty?" Asher seems to be making the same realizations I am.

I shake my head. "A maid has no occasion or reason to. But a queen . . . I should be traveling all over, shouldn't I?"

With a pang, I remember talking to Rowan about Yanos, about

him taking me there and teaching me to fish for sharks. I wonder whether Asher has visited his brother in the Old Tower, or whether Rowan is still refusing to speak to anyone else. I find I can't bring myself to ask.

"Once it's safe, you should." Asher glances at me and for once doesn't look like he's trying to decide how to kill me. "We have a few things to sort out first, don't we?"

The vagueness of his words reminds me that we're not alone—there's the carriage driver and Calen in front of us, the soldiers riding to each side, and Reece on the bench just behind.

After a moment, Asher says, "Spyrian is much smaller than Ryvin. It's really no more than a village. But it's a wealthy place, with the military to support the farmers and laborers in the area. It's a good place to live."

"I hope Mellie's happy," I say. Thinking of the hard-working, red-cheeked cook who raised me, I can't hold on to whatever royal veneer I've managed to create over the past few weeks. I settle back a little bit, let my shoulders fall. "Why wouldn't she have told me?"

"Maybe it would have endangered her, or her job," Asher says. He's staring out the window, his hair curling softly against his temple. I'm tempted to push it back a little, so I can better see his face—

No, I'm not. I cast the word *tempted* right out of my mind.

I glance up at Calen. Dipping my voice to near a whisper, I murmur, "The king—your father—seemed to think history was important, that it would explain things. I was hoping he meant *my* history. But if I'm just the secret daughter of a cook in the castle, I don't see how that would help make sense of anything."

"But you'll know," Asher says quietly. "That's just as important as some cryptic note my father left you."

I don't know about *just* as important.

"I need to figure out who has been, uh, threatening me. I can't just sit around waiting for them to succeed." I'm careful not to mention our suspicions about the king being murdered. The threat on my life isn't much of a secret, after the snake and ball.

"We won't let them succeed," Asher says firmly.

Which is a nice thought and all, especially after spending the last few weeks thinking *he* wanted to kill me. But I'm not entirely comforted.

I turn to him, and he brings the full force of his brilliant green eyes to meet mine. "Asher," I say, "surely you have spies and other sources of information, given that you're head of Lumaria's military. Now that you've crossed Rowan off the list, is there really no one you suspect?"

To my shock, his cheeks redden. But he holds my gaze like it costs him something. "Unfortunately, I, uh, put most of my energies toward uncovering whether *you* were the threat, Your Majesty. You can be sure I'll be casting a wider net now."

"What about your family?" I ask quickly, still so quietly my voice won't carry over the rumble of the carriage. "Your father thought someone close to him was the danger. I don't think it was Rowan. What about . . . well, it's hard to imagine that Belle or Cedric would have done anything to him. Right? What about your, um, your mother?"

What an incredibly awkward, insensitive question to ask someone. But Narissa . . . she's been so antagonistic, so determined that I marry *her* son, that *her* family still have claim to the throne. And the king's journal has thrown into even greater relief the cold relationship between him and his queen.

Asher's sharp jaw tightens. "We've all been mourning Sorren. It's hard to imagine anyone seeking out *more* death."

For an instant, a shadow crosses his features. He clears his throat.

"I'm sorry," I say quietly. "Everything that's happened . . . it's not what any of us wanted."

He raises a brow. "Even you?"

He probably won't believe me, but I give him the truth. "I was a maid. Of course I dreamt of an easier life, one where I didn't have to be alone and invisible. But becoming queen didn't give me a family or love or friendship. It certainly didn't make my life easier. And what's the difference between people only seeing an apron, or only seeing a crown?"

Asher looks at me for a long time, so long I can feel heat travel up my cheeks. The air leaves the carriage, and the space between us thickens. I can't read his expression, but I can read the frantic beat of my own heart clearly enough.

His lips part, to speak or maybe to breathe, but the flick of his tongue along his lips draws my every nerve ending to the surface.

"I do appreciate all the pillows," I say.

He blinks.

It's at this precise moment that the carriage wheel hits a rock and jerks to the side, spilling me into Asher's lap.

We arrive at Mellie's early in the afternoon. She lives in a little cottage at the edge of the village, with several other houses grouped around a communal vegetable garden.

Prince Asher helps me down from the carriage, his hand warm and firm on mine. I hope he can't feel the dampness of my palm. I haven't been able to look at him since I rolled into his lap and we spent several minutes trying to untangle arms, legs, and gown. He was a perfect gentleman, because of course he was—he's betrothed, for God's sake—but for some completely unfathomable reason (I was also just recently engaged, for God's sake) it took everything in me not to stay right there in his lap. If I don't look at him, I won't know if he knows. I'll just continue not knowing. That seems best.

Right now, I have other much more important things to think about. Asher's steel arms and soft jacket get locked away in my mind, well away from any other body parts.

This is Mellie's house.

The ivy that climbs the walls has been carefully trained to frame the bright red door. The stoop is brushed clean, and a neat stone walkway leads from it to my feet, encased in soft leather traveling boots.

Everything is precise and well tended. Of course.

I haven't seen Mellie in almost two years. But before that, she was there every day, nearly every hour. Guiding me, teaching me, standing back and letting me teach myself. She was a warm hand on my forehead, a hot cup of milk when I couldn't sleep.

In all but name, she was my mother.

My hands are shaking by the time Calen pounds on the bright front door.

An age passes before the painted wood slowly creaks open. An old woman stands on the threshold. She squints at me, her face folding into its familiar, well-worn grooves. "Ruby, honey, is that you?"

It doesn't matter than I haven't seen her in two years, or that she might have lied to me my whole life, or that I'm queen. I hurry up the walk and right into Mellie's arms.

# THIRTY-ONE

MELLIE INVITES ME IN LIKE I'm the girl she taught to fillet fish and wash her own hair, not the Queen of Lumaria. And I love her for it. For the first time since King Octavius died, I feel like I'm still myself.

"Come sit, my dear. Come sit," she says, leading me to a long wooden table and bench in the kitchen. Asher follows a little awkwardly and declines to sit down. Instead, he stands in the doorway like he's guarding me.

"Mellie, how are you?" I ask, suddenly feeling horribly guilty for not visiting her sooner.

She putters around her small cave of a kitchen, and then there's a plate of apple tarts in front of me and she's waiting, hands on her hips.

I know my job.

I take a bite and melt at the buttery crispness, the spiced warmth of the filling. She smiles and hands one to Prince Asher before finally sitting down before me.

"Hips give me a bit of trouble, but otherwise I'm grand. My children live next door, and I'm overrun with their little ones. Busier than I was in the castle, I expect. Everyone wants a treat from Granny Mel." Her eyes twinkle as she winks.

"I'm so glad," I say. My heart aches as I imagine her caring for her children and grandchildren as she cared for me. Was I illegitimate, as Lord Hayes thinks? Are her children my half siblings? "Truly. We miss you in the kitchens. Hessa's . . . well, it's an adjustment."

Mellie laughs with a sound like a squeaky door. "It's a gift and a curse being indispensable."

"I'm sure your family knows you're a gift, just like I do." I study her face, looking for similarities. The curve of her cheek, the angle of her nose.

I look for myself in her.

There's nothing glaringly obvious, but oh, I've missed her shrewd eyes and soft smile. Her unique combination of kindness and no-nonsense honesty.

And yes, the apple tarts too. I take another, and she smiles approvingly.

"Now, Ruby, my girl. I saw that royal carriage out front. I couldn't believe when I heard, but I suppose it's true. You're really our new queen?"

I nod, the tart sticking in my throat. In this room, I don't want to be.

She crosses her arms over her chest. "Well then, you didn't come to talk to me about Hessa or to reminisce. What do you need?"

I wonder if she knows what I'm going to ask. Her clear blue eyes reveal nothing. A good secret keeper. She has to have been, to keep this from me all these years.

With a quick glance at Asher, whose face also reveals nothing, I shift my focus back to Mellie.

"I need to know . . . are you my mother?" As soon as the words leave my mouth, a heaviness settles in my stomach.

Mellie looks at me for a long moment, her expression unreadable. I can't even tell whether she's surprised. Then, abruptly, she stands up and bustles to the hearth. "I'll bet you want some warm milk with those tarts."

"Mellie."

"You've always had questions." Her friendly tone has turned tense, and she's brushing me off, just like she used to.

Frustrated, I reply a little too loudly, "Of course I have! You told me I was a war orphan. That I was dropped off by a stranger. Were those all lies? *Who am I*, Mellie?"

The clay pitcher of milk slips out of her hands, shattering on the edge of the stone hearth. Her voice shaking, she says, "I've told you what I can."

I rush to her side. She's crying, rough sobs that shudder through her.

I kneel at her feet in my stupid, fancy gown, and clean up the mess. As I've always done. As she could trust I would always do. More gently, I say, "Please, Mellie. I need to know."

She lets out a long, shaky sigh. "The truth is not at all what you think."

"So . . ." The words stick in my throat. "You're *not* my mother?"

We move back to the table, and I help her sit down. She twists her hands together on the table, staring at her fingers as if they hold the answer. Softly, she says, "No, I'm not your mother, honey. There is no indiscretion in the world that would have kept me from claiming you, if you were mine."

I can't stop the tears from streaking down my cheeks.

Ever since Lord Hayes suggested Mellie was my mother, the thought has been tearing me apart. Her words, the look of love on her face, are a balm.

"But it wasn't my secret to tell. In fact, I was told to keep it or forfeit my very life."

My stomach seizes. All the air leaves the room. The fire in the hearth is too hot, and my heart is beating too fast. "So there *is* more to the story. Mellie, you must tell me. I'm queen. I will *not* let your life be forfeited for revealing this secret."

The king made it sound like history, maybe even my history, was important to Lumaria. He may have meant the Seven Weeks War or some other ridiculous, arcane piece of Lumarian lore. Right now I don't give a shit about any of that. *My* history is important to *me*. The parents I've never known, the questions I've never had answers for. Do I have my mother's eyes? My father's hair? I've focused on my gratitude for my life, my survival for so long. But that doesn't mean there isn't a deep and lasting wound, an empty hole where all I've been missing should be. The truth of where—who—I came from.

Mellie grips my hands in hers. "The one I made my promise to is dead now. But I don't want to give you the burden of this truth. Are you sure you must have it?"

A deep shiver runs down my spine as I nod. I've come too far now.

I glance at Asher. He's still in the doorway, facing away from us, but as I watch, his hands slowly clench into fists.

Mellie leans back a little and steeples her arthritic fingers.

Staring hard at the faded cloth covering her table, she begins.

"I remember everything about that night. I even remember exactly how it started. I was tired. I had two little ones at home already, and it was late. I knew I'd get home after they went to bed, and I was sad over it. Queen Narissa had asked for speckled trout pastry for breakfast, and the dough had to be set the night before. I'd sent everyone else home or to bed.

"I was elbow-deep in dough when the door flew open. Practically gave me a heart attack, it did." She puts a hand to her heart, like she's feeling the shock all over again. "And then, the bigger surprise: It was King Octavius himself standing in the doorway, soaking wet with rain, his eyes wild."

"King Octavius?" My mouth drops open.

She nods. "Yes, the king himself. Wet to the skin and carrying a wailing mess of blankets. He handed me the child and told me to dry her off and get her warm. So I did. I stoked the fire, found some clean kitchen rags, and got you all dried off and warmed up. You kept crying, with your angry little face, until I found some goats' milk for you. Then you settled right down."

My heart is doing something weird, and I can't help looking at Asher's back.

"Are you telling me . . . are you telling me I am King Octavius's child?"

Mellie shakes her head. "The king wasn't your father. Though I understand why you ask. It was my first thought too. But King Octavius needed warming up as well, so I made him some hot tea and a bit of bread, and he confessed the full story. He was grieving, I think. Else I doubt he would have told me so much."

I nod, urging her to keep going. I'm squeezing my hands together so hard, the nails are biting into my palms.

She reaches out and takes my hands in hers, gently prying my fingers out of the clawlike shapes they've twisted into. "Your mother was a woman named Esme, and the king was in love with her."

My breath stops.

*Esme?*

"But she married his best friend. Because he was king and married already. Because she loved him but loved Garrick more. They got married, a union the king blessed even as it broke his heart. Then not two years later, Castella attacked our border, and the king discovered Garrick had sold information to help them. He had to punish him, of course, but even in his anger, he couldn't bear to execute his best friend. So he sent him to the prison camp in the Reaches. Your mother had just given birth to you a few months before. She was, of course, devastated. She always maintained Garrick's innocence. The king . . . he went to visit her, to see if she could tell him anything about why Garrick had betrayed him and all of Lumaria, but he found her dead and her house ransacked, with her child hidden in another room, weak and hungry. He didn't know what to do, except that he had to save Esme's baby. He couldn't leave the child."

"So he brought me to you?" My voice is so faint, the question is barely audible. Her words are still playing in my head, over and over, the shock of them sending out echoes, like the ripples of a stone dropped into a pond. Or waves flooding the shore.

King Octavius wrote of Garrick's betrayal, even of his love for Esme. But he never mentioned a baby, never even spoke of Esme's death. It was as if Garrick being sent to the Reaches ended his story once and for all.

Why didn't he write about me? Because it was too painful? Or to protect me?

My father . . . my father is the most hated man in Lumaria.

The Great Betrayer himself.

"Well." Mellie gives a sad chuckle and squeezes my hand. "In truth, I don't believe he was thinking that clearly. He saw the kitchen lit and knew he couldn't bring you to Narissa. He knew what it would look like if he showed up with an infant. He felt so protective of you . . . he didn't want you to grow up in the shadow of your father's betrayal. When he saw me that night, he chose to entrust me with your story. He swore me to secrecy on pain of death. He knew I had a family of my own and couldn't claim you as my child—my husband wouldn't have taken kindly to that—so we created the tale of the stranger and the family torn apart by the war. I cared for you after that, along with the rest of the servants in the castle. And King Octavius himself, dear. He made sure you were taught by the royal tutors, and given every opportunity he could provide without revealing your secret. And now . . . well, look at you. He truly gave you everything he could."

She brushes her hands across my wet cheeks. The tears are streaming so fast, I can't see her. "Oh, my dear. My dear Ruby."

"The . . . name? The necklace?" I croak.

"The necklace was the king's gift to Esme on her wedding day. A bit inappropriate to my mind, if I'm being honest."

I choke out a laugh.

"Your name," she continues. "Ruby, your name was given to

you by your mama. We had to pretend you were a stranger's child and say that I named you. But it was a story. Esme named you. Your mama gave you your name."

"Oh, Mellie." I'm too overcome to say more.

She gets up and moves to sit beside me. She hugs me, her warm, cinnamon-scented body so comforting and familiar, I start crying all over again.

"So . . . Garrick. The Great Betrayer."

"I told you this truth would be a burden. But remember, you're not *his* legacy. You're the king's. You will be good for this country."

I try to hear her words. I try to believe them.

"Your mother . . . her grave is in the cemetery just a short walk from here. King Octavius arranged for me to live here when I retired . . . he asked me to care for her grave. I was the only one who'd understand, wasn't I?"

"Yes," I say hoarsely. "Yes."

I hug Mellie tightly. I owe her everything. For the care she gave me as a child. For the truth she's giving me now.

I take a small, heavy purse from my reticule. She shakes her head, but I leave it on the table. "For the apple tarts, Mellie, and for breaking your silence. It will help you care for your grandchildren. And . . . and for Esme's—for my mother's—grave."

When she says goodbye to me at the door, pointing to the gates of the cemetery in the distance, there are tears in her eyes. "There's a monument," she says, her voice uncharacteristically gruff. "You'll find it easily. The angel—the angel has your mother's face. Take care of yourself, Your Majesty. You are always welcome here. I'm . . . I'm proud of you, Ruby."

Her voice cracks. She turns away and closes the door before I can answer. Before I can hug her one last time.

I stand before her house, and I can't find Queen Ruby. I can't find the maid called Ruby either. There's a new person in me now, a new Ruby, daughter of Esme and Garrick. Daughter of the Great Betrayer of Lumaria. I don't know how to live with this Ruby inside me yet, and so I'm frozen. I'm stuck. I'm completely, utterly, and fully overwhelmed.

Asher leaves for a moment to speak to Calen, Reece, and the coachman. When he returns, he takes my arm. "Let's go to the cemetery."

My legs move, ushering me down off the stoop and along the stone walk, out to the pitted dirt road. They turn me toward the cemetery, and we're walking. The sun is hanging lower in the sky now, gilding the edges of the storm clouds building in the distance. We'll need to leave soon if we want to make it back to the castle before dark.

"It makes more sense now," Asher says softly, almost to himself.

My heeled boots wobble on the uneven ground. He tightens his grip on my arm. "What makes more sense?"

"Why Father would choose you. You're the daughter of his best friend and the woman he loved."

"I'm the daughter of a traitor." Garrick's been the Great Betrayer of Lumaria my whole life. He's been written about in countless history books, his name analogous to treason. Treachery. Disloyalty.

The king wrote in his own journal about how hurt he was, how mystified that his closest friend would turn on him. But he never, ever wrote about me. Nothing about Garrick's child.

Why?

Is this the history I was meant to learn? How does it help me discover the king's killer? And what does it mean for my position in Lumaria that my father is the most infamous and reviled traitor in the entire kingdom?

I glance over at Asher, my stomach twisting. Will he use this to delegitimize me? It would give him a stronger claim to the throne.

I can't bear to ask the question aloud.

"I don't understand," I say instead, as I pick my way along the grass-and-stone path to the cemetery. Whatever Prince Asher said to the guards, they're giving us space, waiting back at Mellie's house. I appreciate this more than I can put into words. My tear-streaked face isn't fit for being seen, let alone issuing orders. "In the note he left me, your father said the key to this whole mystery was in history. Is this what he meant? I don't see how. Garrick's still imprisoned, and my parentage isn't some royal revelation, is it? If I was *his* child, it would make sense. But this . . . this just makes me even *less* worthy of the crown."

Asher studies the ground, mulling over my words. "Maybe he wasn't sure about your father's guilt?"

That gives me pause.

*I still struggle to believe he conspired against me. There was never a sign, never a hint that I shouldn't trust him. And Esme, oh, her faith in him . . . she hasn't spoken to me since he was taken to the Reaches.*

King Octavius *wasn't* sure about Garrick's guilt. But he was so angry, so hurt, he never confronted him. He sent him to the Reaches without once speaking to him. So he wouldn't rip him apart with his own hands.

Asher opens the cemetery gate for me, and almost immediately, I understand Mellie's final words. The monument—an angel with its wings outspread—dominates an entire corner of the graveyard. I pick my way over to it, my boots soaking through in the damp grass. There, carved stark into the marble, is Esme's name, her birth date, and her date of death, just months after my own birth. An inscription underneath reads, "Beloved for all time."

And above . . . the angel stares blank-eyed down at me, with my mother's face.

With *my* face.

The sky dims. In the distance, thunder rumbles ominously. The wind rises, biting at my skirts. Ignoring all of it, I kneel before the grave of my mother and weep.

# THIRTY-TWO

I DON'T KNOW HOW LONG it is before I wipe my face and say a final inner goodbye. My skirts are damp and stained at the knees. I feel weak and shaky; there's so much going on in my mind, it's like I'm playing five different chess games with five different opponents at the same time.

I get to my feet just as a crack of lightning flashes across the sky.

"Your Majesty," Asher says, "we have to hurry."

The sky opens up before we make it to the gate. The world becomes a wash of slick grass and darkness, pricked with blinding flashes of lightning. Asher starts to reach for my arm, but it's too late. I slip and fall, twisting my ankle and scraping my arm against a headstone. *Damn.*

I brush off my arm and stagger to my feet. Asher helps me to the rutted dirt road, which isn't any easier on my ankles. I tip my head up to the sky, letting the cold rain wash away my tears. In seconds, I'm shivering.

"We need to get out of this storm," Asher says. "Come on."

He leads us back toward Mellie's house, but we don't get far, because Calen and Reece are bringing the carriage to us. The horses are stamping and shaking their heads, as uncomfortable in the driving rain and frequent lightning as I am. Just as we reach them, one of the horses tries to bolt, and the carriage jerks widely, nearly colliding with Asher.

He stumbles backward into me and for a moment we do a strange sort of off-balance dance, ending with us standing at the edge of the road, arms wrapped tightly around one another. He smells like rain and spiced oranges and Mellie's apple tarts.

I breathe into his neck for a moment, until we're both steady.

"The horses don't like this," Calen yells. "We need to get them under shelter until the storm passes!" Our entourage of soldiers has already dismounted. No one wants to be thrown by their horse at the next crack of thunder.

Asher turns to me. A flash of lightning illuminates his face, wet hair plastered to his forehead, his eyes bright, his skin pale. "We can't make it back to Lumaria tonight, Your Majesty. I'd like to send the men to the barracks to dry off and care for the horses. There's an inn near here . . . I've stayed there before. You can rest there, and we'll return in the morning. Is that acceptable to you?"

"Will I be safe there?" I ask. My teeth are starting to chatter. Whatever we're doing, we need to do it soon. I glance back toward Mellie's house, but the storm has hidden it. I don't want to bother her anyway. She's already given me so much today.

"I'll make sure of it," he says.

I nod, and he snaps into action, giving Calen and the rest of the soldiers their marching orders. Reece comes with us.

Asher leads me back onto the road, in the opposite direction of the carriage. We turn into a twisting neighborhood, with slick stone pathways and the occasional candle in the window. The sun hasn't set yet, but it might as well have; the storm has reduced the world to a shadowy swirl of rain. Each time lightning flashes, a different detail stands out, frozen in an afterimage behind my eyes: the sharp corner of a building, the bulge of an ornamental tree, the regal slope of Asher's nose.

Reece stays well behind us, so unobtrusive I nearly forget he's there.

"How far is the inn?" I ask, pulling my soaking, heavy dress forward and trying not to wince when I put weight on my twisted ankle.

Asher points to a golden glow at the end of the street. "There."

Another wave of rain tries to wash us away. He grabs my arm and suddenly we're running, dashing toward the welcome beacon of that warmly lit window.

We pound on the door together, and the innkeeper answers quickly, looking disgruntled. "We're full," he barks, and starts to shut the door.

Asher shoulders it back open, using the hand that bears his royal signet.

The innkeeper pauses, studying Asher—and his ring—more closely. Suddenly, his eyes widen. "Your Highness, I apologize. I didn't get a good look at you."

Asher gives him a small, damp smile. "Well then. Now you have. And I'm sorry to put you out, Finch, but I do need a room."

"Of course, Your Highness. I'm afraid . . . ah, I've only got the one. I don't rent it normally on account of its size. It's probably quite musty."

"Has it got a hearth?" Asher asks.

Finch nods.

"A fire's all we need." He slides his arm through mine and draws me across the threshold and tight into his side. The sudden physical contact sends a shock through me. I freeze. My cheeks heat at the innkeeper's knowing smile.

I twist to ask Asher what game he's playing, but he tightens his grip further and shoots me a look that says, *trust me.*

Reluctantly, I let him continue touching me and try not to like it.

The room beyond the entranceway is low-ceilinged, smoky, and loud. A few of the men crowded near the bar glance our way; others are distracted by several women in low-slung velvet gowns, their makeup exaggerated.

Is that what Asher is making me out to be? A harlot?

Behind us, I hear footsteps—Reece has arrived.

"Now," Asher says, "can we see the room?"

The innkeeper straightens and says, "Of course, Your Highness. Follow me."

He leads us, dripping and limping, up two flights of stairs and down a hallway to a small door that opens to a tiny closet tucked up under the eaves. There's one narrow bed, a cold grate, and a rickety chair that looks like a stiff breeze would turn it into kindling.

"I'll send a maid up for the fire," the innkeeper says, but I shake my head.

"No, thank you." As a grudging nod to Asher's deception, I add, "We don't want to be disturbed."

He shrugs. "Suit yourself. What about the soldier?" He jerks a thumb at Reece, who followed us up the stairs. "There's room in the stables—"

"I'll stay here," Reece says, standing in position as if this tiny door were the massive gilded entry to the king's chambers.

With a bow, the innkeeper retreats down the hallway, his face red despite the chill in this neglected corner. As soon as he's out of sight—and presumably earshot—Asher says to Reece, "Go get yourself some dinner. See if you can do a little reconnaissance, listen for any rumors flying around. I want to know if anyone's talking about the queen, especially now that the wider public knows the castle was breached. I doubt anyone recognized her tonight, but check for that too."

Reece nods.

Asher ushers me into the room and closes the door behind us. It's cold and musty, as promised, but more than that, the space is small.

Very small.

Asher's tall, muscular body seems to fill the entire room.

He looks at me in an appraising way. His hair is black and slick, the curls flat against his forehead. His shirt is so wet it's nearly translucent. If he took off his jacket, I'd be able to see his chest clearly.

I'm staring.

And it takes effort to tear my eyes away.

"I'm sorry for taking liberties," Asher says, and for some reason he sounds like he's been running. "But you'll be safer if no one recognizes you."

"I understand," I say, and I sound a little breathless too. Maybe it's because I'm so damnably cold. "Though, for Lady Rosaline's sake, I wish the lie hadn't been necessary."

He laughs without humor. "Believe me, Lady Rosaline doesn't care about any of my transgressions, real or imagined."

I narrow my eyes, surprised. But, I remind myself, Asher's love life is none of my business. My business, right now, is the damp clamminess of my skin, the chatter of my teeth.

I shift my attention to the fireplace. It only takes me a few moments to build a small, hungry fire. As I stand up, I realize my dress is streaked with mud . . . and the weight of it has pulled the bodice considerably lower than intended.

Asher clears his throat. "We need to get out of these wet clothes."

But then he just stands there, staring at me.

The small room warms quickly, the space between us humming with heat. There's no hope for privacy. Glancing around for something to cover ourselves, I pull the blankets from the bed and toss one into his arms. "Here."

"You go in that corner," I say, pointing to a clear spot by the fire. "I'll go over by the bed."

I turn my back to him, wrap myself in the blanket, and work on removing my sopping dress from underneath. As quickly as I can, I strip down to my chemise, which, while damp, isn't as soaking wet as my gown. Then I wrap myself tightly in the blanket.

"You're bleeding."

I whirl to face Asher. He's removed his jacket but not the rest of his clothes. The blanket in his hands is wet, like he rubbed himself dry with it.

Thunder crashes, shaking the inn.

Asher points at my arm. There's a scrape from when I fell in the cemetery. It's not deep, but it burns. He approaches me slowly, like I'm a skittish horse. I stare at him. Prince Asher, terrifyingly handsome prince, commander, and erstwhile heir to the throne of Lumaria, wants to tend my wound?

He bends over the broken skin, blowing cool air against the scrape.

"The rain's washed it pretty clean," he says softly. He removes his cravat, exposing his throat. He's so close, I can smell the spicy scent of his soap and the fresh rain on his hair. He wraps the damp linen around my arm, squeezing gently as he ties it in place. "This will keep the blood contained, at least. We can get proper care back at the castle."

I'm still shivering. My ankle aches. My arm burns. My heart . . . I don't know what my heart is doing. Part of it is happy, so happy, to finally have answers about my parents. But another part is cracked open and exposed.

"Asher," I say. And because I'm obviously dying of cold or at least severely addled, the words "*I* would care. If it were me, I'd want you all to myself" come out of my mouth.

His hands are still on my arm. He raises his chin to look at me.

His green eyes are washed clean, fresh as grass after a storm. I can feel the heat of his hands on my arm. On my skin.

Without my conscious will, my hands reach for his face, curl along his jaw, to his rain-slicked hair.

I don't have any more room in my mind for regrets or revelations. Only the words *hate has never been our problem*.

Only his voice, breathless from running through my thoughts, day and night.

"Ruby," he murmurs, drifting closer, as if there's a string pulling tight between us. His forehead presses against mine, still damp. "This is a terrible idea."

But his hands are in my hair, pulling gently to tilt my head back. The butterflies that plagued me when Rowan and I stood this close don't trouble me now. Thunder splits the sky and the fire leaps in the hearth, and I hold my breath and hope I won't regret what I'm about to do. My eyes drift closed. My lips part. His breath flutters against my mouth—

A loud knock shatters the breathless quiet.

Our hands drop, and we step away from each other as if burned.

"Come in," Asher barks.

Reece opens the door, bearing a tray with steaming bowls of stew and a couple crusty rolls. Asher hands me my dinner and steps into the hall with his, joining Reece.

My skin flares with heat. I sink into the spindly chair by the fire, wrapped in the blanket from the bed, and try to convince myself the interruption was good. Try to convince my heart to slow, my cheeks to cool.

Try to convince myself that I should absolutely *not* be kissing Asher. No matter how much I might want to.

# THIRTY-THREE

I STARE AT THE CHESSBOARD in the library. The pieces are all precisely set, ready for a new game to begin.

But I'm not here to play.

It's been two days since we returned from Mellie's. I haven't seen Asher. He's busy helping Lord Hayes plan the transfer of Rowan and the other rebels to the Reaches. And I'm busy . . . not thinking about Asher.

*We almost kissed.*

This time, I know it for sure. There've been moments before when I wondered, when I admitted only to myself that I'd been thinking about his lips, about their heat and how I'd like to know what he tastes like.

But this time, this time his hands were in my hair, his forehead was pressed to mine. This time was real.

Not that it changes the reality that kissing Asher would be an absolute calamity. I was recently betrothed to his brother. He's *currently* betrothed to Lady Rosaline.

Until a week ago, he thought I had murdered his father, and I was sure he wanted to murder me.

After his talk with Reece that night, Asher returned to the room and told me that my identity was safe, and therefore *I* was safe, for the moment anyway. There'd been no rumors about the attack on the castle, beyond a few murmurings that the antiroyalists were getting stronger, which we already knew.

And then he curled up on the floor by the fire like a cat, wrapped the blanket around himself, and fell asleep, leaving the bed—and the agonizing silence of *what if*—to me.

The memory of that *almost* has its teeth in my throat, worrying at me like an animal trying to rip me apart. Of all that happened that day, of all I learned, it's what I *almost* learned about Asher's mouth that I can't escape from.

With an effort, I force the memory away, ashamed at the thoughts running through my head. I have bigger problems to turn my attention to.

Namely, my father. The Great Betrayer.

I pick up a pawn and turn the piece over in my hand. I still can't figure out how he might be connected to everything going on now—the king's murder, the attempts on my life—but he's certainly part of Lumaria's history, and now I know he's part of mine. So I *have* to believe he's key to this in some way. *He's* the history the king was talking about. He must be.

And then there's the secret passageway. If what Drake said was true, no one came into the king's chambers from the main hall before he died. But his wife or one of his children could have used the secret passage to visit him. Asher has the clearest motive, as the presumptive heir. But he seems less and less likely as a suspect. First, he doesn't seem all that interested in becoming king. And second, he thought *I* murdered his father.

Then there's Rowan. As an antiroyalist, he certainly had reason to kill his father. Except, with four living children, it wasn't as if the monarchy would die with King Octavius. And I saw Rowan's face when I asked him. He seemed genuinely shocked, like the idea had never crossed his mind. I also have the years of our friendship as evidence. Rowan loved his father. He spoke of him often, and always fondly. If anything, he was sad he didn't get to spend *more* time with him.

I place the pawn down and pick up the knight, turning the piece in my hand, my gaze unfocused as I continue with my list of suspects.

Belle. She had access through the passage, but I can't think of a single reason she'd have to harm her father. She was never going to be named heir, so ambition wouldn't have driven her, and as far as I know she's not been pushed into any unwelcome marriage contracts or other repugnant responsibilities. By all accounts among the maids, Belle got along just fine with her father. She's certainly knowledgeable of the court and the duties of a queen, as she's helped me assume this new and *very* unfamiliar role. I suppose I could think of reasons she might want *me* dead? Revenge for taking the crown from her brother being the chief one. But it's hard to imagine her sneaking a snake into my bathroom or hiring an assassin. And as for the king, I doubt she'd have had the strength to smother him.

Last of the siblings is Cedric, of course. He's also the only one who knew the king named me as his heir. Maybe Cedric was upset about it? Maybe he snuck back in that night and tried to change the king's mind, and killed him in a rage when he was unsuccessful? The knight's helmet digs into my palm. Cedric always seems a bit vacant and disengaged. But he *did* tell me everyone in his family lies. Could he have meant himself too? Is he struggling with guilt or shame? He wouldn't have killed his father for his own ambitions, but he's a loving brother. Maybe he'd do it for Asher?

I set the knight back on the board, an uneasy feeling coiling tightly in my stomach. Could *Cedric* be the viper he himself spoke of?

I have no proof. I can't just go and accuse him of killing his own father and trying to kill me. And the history piece doesn't connect, unless the king told him of my true parentage. I would have to make a lot of leaps on that one.

Lastly, there's Dowager Queen Narissa. Trapped in a loveless marriage, bitter at the death of her eldest son—might she have wanted King Octavius dead? She would have assumed Asher would be heir. And she's certainly been hostile to me. I pick up the queen and roll the chess piece between my fingers. But she also wanted me to marry Rowan. She's stayed out of my way for the most part, aside from a nasty look now and then. Would she really risk her position and that of her children to kill the king?

And, of course, there's the possibility someone else knows about the passageway. One of the advisors or a lover of any of the siblings. Lady Rosaline perhaps? Or maybe someone was bribed to give up the secret to the antiroyalists. With the protests gaining traction and the antiroyalists growing bolder, they could have staged something like this. Or contrived to poison the king in some way, with a snake or a toxin in his food. Sir Henry didn't think it was poison, but I saw the purple cast to the king's skin when I visited his body. I saw the grit of his teeth. Maybe it's not *probable* that it's poison, but it's still *possible.*

Which basically leaves me with . . . no true leads, other than maybe Cedric and Narissa.

But certainly no clear evidence or connection to "history" . . . or to my new knowledge of my father.

King, queen, rook, bishop, knight, pawn . . . all the players are moving across the board, but I can't see the pattern yet. I don't know who's who.

Mostly importantly, I don't know who *I* am.

The king, who must be protected at all costs? The queen, powerful but constantly under threat?

Or am I just a pawn?

Princess, who's been quietly hunting in the corners of the library and playing in the sunbeams under the window suddenly trots to the door, a little meow catching my attention. A moment later, Lord Hayes bustles in. "Your Majesty, there you are."

"Yes, Tareth?" I say, rising to my feet.

"Prince Asher asked me to inform you that preparations are complete for the journey to the Reaches. He will accompany the, ah, prisoners. They plan to leave within the hour. If . . . you know. You wanted to say goodbye."

I freeze, an ache spreading across my chest. No, I don't want to say goodbye to Rowan. I thought he was going to be here, my friend, forever. I thought we were going to get married and make every attempt to deepen our friendship into love and passion. I thought we had a *future* together.

The past interrupts my thoughts.

The Reaches.

My father.

"Tareth, is Lord Garrick Donahue still being held in the Reaches?" I ask abruptly.

He looks truly taken aback at the change of subject and stutters for a moment. "Why on earth would you ask?" he says finally, then snaps his mouth shut at my expression. *A queen never needs to explain herself*, Belle's voice intones in my mind. He continues, as if he hears her too. "Apologies, Your Majesty. The answer is yes. I believe so."

"Thank you," I say. I stoop to collect Princess and head for the door.

"Your Majesty? Is there something I can help you with?" he asks, looking flustered as he rushes to my side.

"Yes," I say. "Send Sara to my room along with a trunk. And send word to Asher to hold the transport."

"For what? For how long?" he asks, confusion carving deep grooves in his forehead.

"Just long enough for me to pack. Please inform Prince Asher I'll be joining him."

"You're—you're what?" Lord Hayes shudders to a stop.

I flick a look over my shoulder at him and say in a tone that brooks no argument, "You heard me. I'm going to the Reaches."

I'm not ready to say goodbye to Rowan quite yet.

But I *am* more than ready to meet my father.

# THIRTY-FOUR

"ABSOLUTELY NOT," ASHER SAYS, IGNORING the fact that he should *absolutely not* be speaking to his queen that way.

"It's not up to you," I remind him. This is the first time we've spoken since our charged moment at the inn. And it's going so very well.

He paces near the fireplace. I wave at Sara and Theia to keep packing.

"It's too dangerous. There's already a good chance the caravan will be targeted by antiroyalists, and your presence will just make it more attractive to those who hate the monarchy. I won't be able to assure your safety." He looks almost agonized at the thought, which I admit is a lot more pleasant than when he glared at me with violence in his eyes.

I'm tempted to put a hand on his arm, but I don't dare with Sara and Theia in the room.

"No one will know the queen is traveling with the caravan," I say. "I'll be dressed as a maid. Sara is coming with me. We'll just be two servants there to care for the soldiers along the way."

It's almost funny how scandalized he looks.

I step into his path, forcing him to stop.

He knows about my father. He knows about my friendship with his brother. Surely he can understand why doing this is so important.

“I’m going,” I say softly, capturing his gaze with mine. Willing him to understand. “I need to.”

I don’t need his permission. But it’ll be an easier journey if he isn’t mad at me the whole time.

He stills, silent as a statue, his eyes searching. At last, he huffs a sigh.

“Yes, Your Majesty.” He bows. “I’ll see about getting us some extra security.”

“You have your dagger?” Asher asks me, worry drawing his brows together. But his voice snaps with all the businesslike precision he shows his soldiers.

I nod, patting my apron pocket to confirm.

Putting on my old maid’s uniform was strange but also sort of wonderful. For one thing, I’m so much more comfortable. I’m not crimped into a corset, and my skirts fit into the carriage bench without any effort at all. Even better, I’m free of the heavy jewelry Theia’s always hanging around my neck. The only piece of gold I wear is the ring the king left for me. Even if I had my royal signet—which is being made in time for the coronation next week—I couldn’t wear it on this trip. But it feels good to have the thin golden band on my finger, a secret reminder that I’m still trying to fulfill the task King Octavius set for me.

Beside me, Sara is practically bouncing. “I can’t believe we’re leaving Ryvin,” she murmurs, completely unperturbed by the narrow look Asher gives her.

Seeing that we’re settled—and resolute—he wheels his horse around and moves to the head of the caravan.

Our party is composed of twenty-five mounted soldiers, a large, enclosed carriage with bars on the window for the five rebels we're transporting, including Rowan, who I haven't been able to catch a glimpse of yet, and several additional carriages and carts full of supplies. Sara and I occupy one of these carriages, as maids employed to help care for the soldiers, but our carriage also contains Reece, Calen, and Garon, who have the singular job of keeping me safe.

Sara is here as my lady's maid and chaperone . . . and to help sell the deception. She found someone—one of the maids, I think—to keep Princess while we're gone, but I can't help wishing I could have brought her with us. Her antics have a way of calming me down.

"Are you nervous?" Sara asks.

The carriage creaks beneath us. It's not one of the royal carriages with thick, plush cushions and better suspension. As we pass into the outskirts of Ryvin, wide fields stretch from the horizon to the river. Many are being harvested now, though a few have already been prepared for winter. The breeze that bites at my cheeks hints at the cold to come, even as the sun shines brightly from a cloudless sky.

I'm glad I brought a thick woolen shawl with me. For once, I almost miss the multitude of fur stoles at my disposal as queen. How soft I've gotten.

"I'm not nervous about the journey," I reply. "This part is exciting."

Her mouth curves into a smile, though she's too busy watching the farmland rumble past to turn my way. "But the destination is a different story?"

"Yes" is all I say. And, like Asher and *no one* else, she knows why.

"What if he's exactly what the world thinks he is?" she asks quietly, her voice barely audible over the *click-clack thud-thud* of many hooves.

Of course he will be. The king might not have been fully convinced of Lord Garrick's guilt, but he also never found evidence to exonerate him. He never spoke to him, as far as I know. The most likely outcome of this meeting is that I'll confirm everything I've been taught about Lumaria's Great Betrayer. But at least I'll know. At least I'll see my father with my own eyes.

My whole life, there's been a ghostly kingdom within me, full of the family I imagined was mine. Parents who lived in a little cottage in a small village near the border with Castella. A mother who loved me enough to hide me when war came. I've imagined conversations with them, imagined what they looked like, what parts of myself were gifts from them.

Ever since I spoke to Mellie, those ghosts have been changing, reforming. Now, my mother has the face of a marble angel, a face I can see myself in. And my father . . . well, my father is, for good or ill, a living, breathing man. He's someone I can face.

That's a chance I can't pass up, no matter how much it may hurt.

The journey to the Reaches will take us two days, which means Sara and I will sleep in a well-guarded tent tonight. A first for both of us.

By the time we stop and set up camp, my back is screaming for the king's soft featherbed. Alas, it will have to make do with the thin bedrolls Sara packed for us.

I catch a glimpse of Rowan as the prisoners are led out to relieve themselves and get a bit of food, but Asher thunders between us on his horse and shoots me a warning look before I have a chance to approach him.

I suppose Asher has a point—why would a maid be granted a private conversation with a prisoner?—but it still makes my heart ache not to speak to him.

Rowan's artfully messy blond hair is just plain messy now, and the simple pants and shirt he's wearing are streaked with grime. Knowing how much time he used to spend on his appearance, I'm sure the lack of cleanliness is bothering him.

I wish I'd been able to spare him this. But he confessed to working with the antiroyalists. People were killed in the attack that night. Whether he was an active participant or not, he gave money to antiroyalist efforts. He tried to help some of the rebels evade capture.

If I spared him, a royal, the punishment for his crime, it would just fan thc flames furthei.

But that doesn't make any of this easy.

I can tell by the tension running along Asher's body, the way he barks orders, that it isn't easy for him either.

It's strange to think of the two of them, side by side. I wonder what might have happened if Rowan and I *had* gotten married. Would we have come to find the passion of a marriage for love instead of duty? We had such a good foundation. And there's no denying that

Rowan is brutally hot. With him, I felt . . . possibility . . . if not open attraction.

But that future promise, that possibility, is dead now.

And I'm left with a mess of tangled, heated feelings for his brother that I absolutely cannot act on.

Asher draws the line at Sara and me actually serving the soldiers, so he makes us our own little fire and has Reece bring us food. I watch him flit through the shadows, ensuring each of his soldiers has what they need. Just before the prisoners are led back to their carriage, Asher speaks to Rowan.

"Are you not hungry, Ruby?" Sara asks, nodding to the tin plate in my hands, still heaped with bread and dried meat.

At her reminder, I eat a few bites. "It's strange to think about sleeping outside."

Sara shrugs. "My father used to lock me outside to punish me. I slept curled against the chimney. Sometimes it was warm. One night, wolves howled from just over the ridge for hours. He never let me in."

I nudge her with my shoulder. I remember the nightmares she'd wake from screaming when she first came to the castle. We'd sneak into each other's rooms and sit together, holding hands in the dark, until we could keep the dreams at bay.

"There will be no wolves tonight," I reassure her. "But with all these men and their clanking tack and stomping boots, I can't promise you quiet."

As it turns out, neither of us sleeps well. But at least we have each other.

By the next afternoon, we've left the farmland and forest

behind and have started climbing into the foothills of the Fortuna Mountains. I stare out of the carriage at the barren, rocky hillside. The land here is covered with scrubby trees and exposed rock, very different from the verdant farmland along the Talas River.

"Sara," I say, my thoughts circling aimlessly, my body sore from the long day bouncing along uneven roads after a night sleeping on uneven ground, "Is there much gossip about Prince Asher and Lady Rosaline in the kitchens? You always seem to know what they're up to."

Sara stiffens beside me. "Oh? I don't know that I know anything special. It's just as it's always been, no? The two of them don't seem particularly interested in each other."

*Asher's breath against my mouth, his forehead pressed to mine . . .*

"Do you think Lady Rosaline is sad she's not in line to be queen anymore?" I muse. Asher acts like he doesn't care, but for the past six months, everyone assumed it'd be Asher and Lady Rosaline when the king died. Maybe she cares a lot. Should I more seriously consider her as a suspect?

"Definitely not," Sara answers quickly. Confidently. "She's relieved—I mean, I imagine she's relieved, given what everyone says."

I glance at Sara—is she blushing? Wait . . .

"Sara, are you—"

A loud whistle cuts through my question. The carriage slows. At the head of the line of horses and carriages, I catch a glimpse of a giant iron gate emerging from the rock itself.

The Reaches. We've arrived.

Slowly, the gates scream open, and then our entourage files into an open field embraced by walls of natural cliff. The Reaches is more than a prison—it's a mine, reaching deep within the Fortuna Mountains. Here, prisoners are put to work, mining for the iron ore that will become the steel swords of the Lumarian army.

A small lake serves as a boundary to our left. A veritable village of stone houses climbs into the cliffside to our right. And, straight ahead, a dark hole—the entrance to the mine. Soldiers stand guard throughout the compound, while a constant line of prisoners flows into and out of the mine.

As soon as our carriage stops, I climb down, Sara just behind me. Asher rides up and dismounts, his armor clanking.

"Your Majesty, they're preparing a private room for you. It'll be just a moment." He looks harried, his hair stuck to his temples with sweat and his helmet in his hand. His eyes dart around, taking in our surroundings and any potential hazards.

"I want to see Rowan," I say. "I need . . . I want to say goodbye." Now that the moment is nearly here, my stomach turns over. I don't actually know that I can do this.

Asher nods. "Of course. And . . . the other meeting you were hoping for?"

"Yes, please arrange that as well," I say firmly.

He pauses, his gaze finding mine. For a moment, he gives me his full attention, ignoring the controlled chaos around us. "You are sure you want to face him."

It's not exactly a question, but he searches my face as if for an answer.

I draw in a breath. I appreciate him giving me a final chance to change my mind, but it's not going to happen. Lord Garrick Donahue, the Great Betrayer, can fly into a rage and try to kill me, and it will still be better than the unanswered questions that have haunted me all my life.

My hand goes to my throat, and the red stone nestled there. I nod, decisively. This is a gambit I've got to play.

Something in me breaks when Rowan ducks his head to step into the small stone hut they've appropriated for my use. His hands are bound before him, and the heavy workpants and shirt of his new life are a far cry from the velvet coats he loves. Asher holds him by the arm, but I think it's an excuse to stand close to his brother one last time. Reece, Calen, and several of the prison's guards fill the small room. Sara stands just behind me, her warm presence a bolster.

When Rowan sees me, his dirt-streaked face breaks into a smile. "I've missed Ruby the maid."

I glance down and remember I'm still dressed in my uniform. It's impossible to hide the tears that fill my eyes when I raise my gaze back to his. "She will really miss *you*."

His brave smile wobbles. "Thanks for being my friend, Ruby. Whether you believe it or not, you'll *always* have a friend in me."

"And a worthy chess partner," I whisper, my tears flowing freely.

"Oh, I was never that," he says, and his smile cracks. He reaches for me, and without thinking I step into the circle of his arms. One last embrace, one last—

Asher jerks Rowan away and shoves himself between us. "No touching."

They share a look, and for the first time I wonder if Asher trusts what Rowan told me. Does he think Rowan knew more about Colin's activities than he admitted to?

Either way, the tension between them is clear.

Over Asher's shoulder, Rowan manages a cheeky grin. "Don't worry, Your Majesty. It's only a few years. You'll see me again."

I nod, my heart squeezing. "Take care of yourself, Rowan. Don't do anything stupid."

"Who, me?" He tries to smile, but it doesn't land. His eyes are too serious. Too . . . scared. A prison work camp is the antithesis of the life he's accustomed to.

I take a deep breath, my throat clogged with tears. This is it. This is our goodbye. This is the end of any future we might have had . . . as friends or as husband and wife.

Rowan's eyes flick to his brother, and just before he's escorted out, he says, "Ruby, don't trust anyone. *You* take care of *yourself*."

I nod. "Goodbye, Rowan."

And then he's gone.

It takes longer for Asher to organize my meeting with Garrick. The prison guards won't allow him to come to me, and I'll have to wait until his shift in the mine is over before I can go to him.

We're trying to keep my true identity confined to as few people as possible, but the man who runs the prison does come to see me and bend the knee. He eyes my clothes askance, but Asher's presence provides the necessary legitimacy.

Sara and I try to rest on the hard wooden cots in the little hut while we wait, but my mind is whirling and my stomach won't settle. I go back and forth on whether I should change—do I want him to see me as a maid or as the queen?

As a maid, I can show him the life I lived without him.

As queen, I can show him what I've become.

Ultimately, I choose to stay as I am. I'm incognito, after all.

"This way," a grizzled old warden says, leading me across the yard. The sun has dipped beneath the rim of the mountain, plunging us into darkness. Lit torches are carried by guards stationed throughout the work camp. Even in the dark, prisoners stream into and out of the mine.

Sara stayed behind, but Asher is with me. He keeps glancing over, like he's trying to gauge how I'm taking everything.

I don't know what my face is telling him.

We reach a long stone building, and when we enter, it's immediately obvious that we've cleared everyone out. A narrow walkway leads between cells on either side, but they're all empty right now.

Empty save one.

A door clanks. And then the hallway is filling with a large figure, shadowed in the dim light.

I notice the man's hair first, black and thick. His frame, tall and lean. And his face, haggard but handsome, with striking gray eyes. His hands and feet are shackled.

My breath seizes in my chest. I watch, as if in a dream, as his gaze latches onto the necklace at my throat. As the blood drains from his face. As his mouth opens in shock.

There's no longer even the smallest doubt.

This is Lord Garrick Donahue. The Great Betrayer.

My father.

# THIRTY-FIVE

I LOCK MY KNEES SO I won't fall down.

"Lord Donahue," I say, amazed my voice sounds remotely normal.

Nothing about this moment is normal.

"It's just Garrick now," he replies. His eyes explore my face with both hunger and despair, the way a drowning man might gaze at a shoreline that remains just out of reach.

My whole life I've heard stories about this man, and in every one of them he was so fearsome, so villainous, that I pictured him as beyond human. Ten feet tall, eyes glowing red, a soulless sneer twisting his lips.

But standing before me is just a man. No sneer, no anger. No flickering, cunning intelligence. No indication that he intends to play this conversation like a chess match.

Still, I brace myself.

"Everyone out!" I shout, before anyone says more. "Asher, you may stay."

The guard who led us into the building hesitates, but Asher murmurs something to him and he files out after Reece and Calen. Asher takes the place of the guard, watching Garrick closely with his hand on his sword.

Garrick observes this exchange with raised brows. It must be strange, seeing a maid ordering grown men around. Or maybe he's plotting an escape attempt.

Once the three of us are alone, I ask, "Do you know who I am?"

Garrick studies me, his expression caught somewhere between agony and hope. "I would say you are Ruby Donahue. But twenty years ago, I was told my wife and daughter died."

My heart gives a giant thud. *He thought his daughter was dead, just as I thought my father was dead.*

"My mother Esme was killed," I say, the words rough against my throat. "But first, she hid me. I survived. I was raised as a maid in the castle, ignorant of my history and my parentage. I only discovered the truth recently."

Before I even finish, his face crumples. He raises his bound hands to cover his mouth, but he doesn't let his eyes leave my face. Tears spill over his hands.

He doesn't look like the villain of Lumaria, but I try to harden myself. To remember that two things can be true—this man can be happy I'm alive *and* be a treasonous snake.

"Ruby? It's really you?"

I nod, my own eyes filling despite my best efforts.

"You look just like your mother. *Just* like her. I thought—I thought I was seeing a ghost." His voice rasps, and it's clear he's holding himself together with effort. I find myself wishing I could offer him a chair, a moment to collect himself, but I can hear voices outside. Someone is clearly unhappy about this unconventional meeting.

Still, I can't help the hand that reaches toward him.

His gaze catches on my finger. "That ring . . ."

I tilt my hand so the thin gold band catches the torchlight.

He takes a breath like it'll be his last one and says, "It looks like your mother's wedding ring."

I see the truth so suddenly. The king visiting Esme, her body lying on the ground, bludgeoned to death. The ring on her finger, a symbol of the love she could never give him. The love that spared her husband.

"It belonged to Esme," I murmur. "The king left it for me."

Hidden in a box with my name on it. A piece of my past, and a mystery to solve for my future.

"I need to ask you something," I say, when I want to ask him *all* the things. When I want to run away. "The king made me his heir before he died. Do you know why he would do that? He said the answer could be found in history. I think he meant *your* history. Or, well, mine."

He glances at my simple dress and apron, wrinkled now from our long days of travel. I wonder if he thinks I'm lying. "So the king *has* died. There've been rumors, but the guards like to keep us uninformed."

I nod.

"And he named *you* his heir?" His brow furrows.

"Even though he has four living children," I clarify. He doesn't seem to recognize Asher, and it sounds as if news is hard to come by here, so I don't know if they've heard of Sorren's death.

"Does he now?" Garrick says, and for the first time his face darkens with the anger, the murderous intent, I expected from the Great Betrayer. I take a step back, even as Asher steps forward, half drawing his sword.

With an effort, Garrick gets his emotions under control. "You're telling me King Octavius made you queen upon his death, despite having more obvious choices?"

"Yes," I say. "Do you know why?"

All at once, his face clears. "I can only hope it means Octavius figured out the truth before he died."

"And what truth is that?" I ask, impatience creeping into my voice. Why couldn't the king have just *explained* things? Every scrap of knowledge, every small revelation seems to lead to more mysteries, more questions.

"For one thing, I never sold anything to Castella."

I know every criminal in history starts by denying their crimes, but that doesn't mean I don't want to believe him.

"The king had evidence. You were his best friend. It wasn't some kind of witch hunt. It would have had to be irrefutable."

He gives an angry shrug. "I was framed for a crime I didn't commit, I was afforded no trial or recourse, and Octavius never spoke to me or asked me what happened. You say he was my best friend, and yet he never even gave me a chance to defend myself."

"You betrayed him. He was angry."

*No, I cannot see him, nor speak to him. Not when I am certain I would tear him apart with my bare hands, inflict the pain on him that he has so savagely inflicted on me, on Esme, on all of Lumaria.*

The king's words come back to me, his anger a palpable thing. He thought not speaking to Garrick was a mercy, in service to his vow to Esme. And yet, I can see how it might have looked from Garrick's perspective, if he was never given a chance to defend himself.

"He may have felt betrayed," Garrick says, echoing my thoughts, "but he wasn't the only one. He had snakes in his ears, whispering their evil nonsense. If he'd only *spoken* to me, I would have told him what really happened, and why."

"So tell *me* why," I say, clearing my throat. I want to believe him, but that's why I don't trust his words. They too easily absolve him. "Why would someone frame you?"

He straightens his powerful shoulders, and again, Asher steps between us, his hand on his sword. Garrick ignores him. "I discovered something so dangerous that I had to be silenced. I lost everything. My wife, my daughter, my life. I've lived in this hell for twenty years knowing the king let himself be deceived. That I could have given him the truth if he'd only asked."

A hum of certainty fills me. This is it. This is the reason for all of it. I can feel the pull of the truth in my bones. "Tell me," I say. "Tell me what you discovered. *I'm* asking."

He gives me a long look, flicks a glance at Asher, then, almost reluctantly, shakes his head. "It's too dangerous."

I want to throw up my hands and scream. Why are these men so *difficult*? No one can just *say things plainly*. "It's *already* dangerous! Someone is trying to kill me. Maybe this is why." My heart pounds, and I resist the urge to wipe my damp palms on my apron. "You said you've wanted to tell the truth for twenty years. This is your chance."

Painful regret crosses his features. "I'm sorry, truly, but the not knowing is not nearly as dangerous as knowing. Trust me, if I tell you, you will not survive to wear the crown. I can't live with that, Ruby. Come back and see me after your coronation. Then, perhaps, it will be safe enough to tell you."

I want to kick him in the shins like an angry child. But that's not the way to win this game. So instead I say calmly, "If what you say is true, if I can find proof you were framed, I can release you. No more wasted time. You can enjoy the rest of your life as a free man, fully vindicated. But I have to know where to look."

He takes a deep breath, drinking me in with his eyes, a small smile playing at the corner of his mouth. "Just like your mother," he murmurs. "Be careful, Ruby, my girl. Don't trust anyone in that castle. *No one.*"

Then, before I can say another word, he yells, "Guards!" and steps back into a cell and away from me.

# THIRTY-SIX

THE NIGHT PASSES IN A blur of back pain and burning questions. Sara and I never get a chance to talk, as the warden stations two guards just inside the door of our little hut. I barely sleep, Rowan's goodbye and Garrick's words spinning through my mind.

Asher wakes Sara and me before dawn for the journey home.

I turn every word Garrick said to me over and over, searching for some clue I can connect to what I know. I wish I'd thought to ask *how* he was informed his family had been killed. Was my death an honest mistake, a lie the king himself spread to protect me? Or did someone actively deceive Garrick? Did the king truly never speak to him again? How damning *was* the evidence against him?

And of course I have to consider: What if everything my father said was a lie to protect himself? What if there *was* no dangerous secret he discovered, no plot to frame him? All I have are his words, the look on his face. The shattering sorrow as he turned away from me.

I give Sara the update under my breath as the carriage bumps over the rough road. By the time we stop for the night, my voice is hoarse and my joints are creaking.

Without the prisoners to protect, the camp is more relaxed, the sounds of laughter and clink of tin dishes providing a backdrop to the snap of our little campfire. Asher eats with us; more than once, I catch him staring at me across the flames.

It doesn't take long for Sara to notice.

"That man tracks your every move," she whispers as we try to get comfortable on the hard ground in our tent. "I can't quite tell if he sees you as a conquest or as prey."

I bump her arm. "I think he sees me as a duty . . . and maybe a pain in the ass."

I haven't told her about the night in Spyrian, the moment of heat between us. I'm not entirely sure why. Maybe because I should have known better, and I'm afraid she'll tell me so.

"Well, he *sees* you, that's for sure." A small furrow appears between her brows, highlighted in the light of our small lantern. "Do you think he'll tell anyone the Great Betrayer is your father? He could make a play for the crown. We're a week away from your coronation. It's not much time, but it could be enough to overthrow your claim."

Sara's thoughts echo my own. Ever since Mellie's revelation, I've wondered whether I could trust him . . . or if he was biding his time. I want to believe he wouldn't do that, but then again . . . *everyone* is telling me not to trust anyone. Honestly, it's exhausting.

Long after Sara falls asleep, I sit in the darkness, stewing in my thoughts. In the questions I should have asked, in my sorrow for Rowan and Garrick. In my tangle of feelings for Asher.

The boy I watched from the trees long ago, the one I tried to comfort after Sorren's death . . . that Asher I would have trusted.

The hard-edged man who thought I killed his father? The commander of Lumaria's army?

I don't know.

I can't stop thinking about the way Garrick's eyes flicked to Asher when he told me not to trust anyone.

I roll over again, my brain refusing to quiet, my back aching as a rock digs into an already sore spot. With a huff, I extricate myself from my blankets and sneak out of the tent.

The night air hovers between brisk and cold, the black sky holding the glittering stars like a bowl of diamonds. The small fire outside our tent is still burning, so I head for it, hoping to warm my hands.

It isn't until I've reached my cold fingers toward the flames that I realize I'm not alone.

"Asher!" I say, startled.

"Couldn't sleep?" he asks, his voice gruff in the inky quiet.

After a moment's hesitation, I sink to the ground beside him. "I can't stop thinking about, well, everything."

"Did you believe him?" he asks.

I stare into the jumping flames. "I want to. But also . . . twenty years in a mine for a crime you didn't commit? The whole kingdom believing you're the worst of men? How do you survive that?"

He makes a small noise. "I think it's easy to say there's a dangerous secret without sharing what it is."

I hug my knees to my chest, the knife in my apron pocket bumping against my chin. "You know all my secrets. Does that make them dangerous?"

I don't know why I'm asking now. I don't know if he'll even understand. But I can't breathe with this tangle in my chest anymore. I can't keep myself from pressing the bruise.

For a moment, he doesn't answer. When his voice rumbles up from the darkness, I glance at him, golden in the firelight. "Your parentage doesn't change my father's edict. He knew who you were. He made his decision."

"You could use this knowledge to build a claim to the throne. You could delegitimize me." Why am I pushing?

"As far as I'm concerned," he says, his voice low, "when Sorren died, so did the only legitimate heir. I'm no more qualified or worthy of the throne than you."

For a while, we sit in silence, watching the undulations of the fire.

"Will Rowan be all right?" I ask.

He sighs. "I think so. He understands how lucky he was not to be made an example of."

I shake my head. "Even if he'd hired Colin himself, I don't know if I could have done it. We were friends for a long time."

"Surely you were more than that?" His question drops into the quiet night like an anvil.

My gaze flies to his face.

He raises a brow, his lip quirked. "You were going to be married. And I've never seen Rowan as eager for a royal duty in his life."

Heat swarms to my cheeks. I turn my attention back to the fire. "I . . . I do think Rowan—" I break off. This is so awkward. But I forge ahead. "For me, it was friendship. I think, for him, maybe it was more."

"Hmm." He doesn't say more. I don't say more. We just . . . sit. In the dark. With the fire warming our faces.

"Try to get some sleep," Asher says at last, standing up. "It'll be another early start."

We arrive home early in the afternoon, and it's clear that runners were sent ahead, because a whole host of people await us as the carriages roll to a stop before the castle's great doors.

When we reached Ryvin, Asher stopped to water the horses and so I could change into a more appropriate gown.

As soon as I step out of the carriage, Lord Hayes approaches. "Your Majesty, welcome home. We have been eagerly awaiting your return."

"Thank you," I say, a little taken aback by his enthusiasm.

"If you're not too tired from your journey, we'd like you to call a council meeting. There's an . . . item of some delicacy . . . we need to discuss."

Ah. It's not eagerness. It's anxiety. I can see it in the tension at the corner of his eyes, the way his beard seems to quiver as he speaks.

"What's happened?" I ask, a little too sharply. "Has there been another attack?"

Lord Hayes shakes his head. "No, no. Nothing of that nature. Please, Your Majesty. Just a moment of your time before you rest from your journey."

"Of course." I lead the way into the castle, Belle and the lords falling into formation behind me. Somewhere behind us, Sara will be returning to her own room and hopefully getting some time to relax before her evening duties. And Asher . . . I wonder if he's here or if he has soldiering things to attend to. I don't risk a look back to find out.

Lord Hayes exudes an energy that puts me on edge. He's nearly hopping, he's so tense. What's wrong with him?

Narissa is waiting in the throne room, her face drawn into severe lines. Which tells me nothing, really, as she always looks at me that way.

As soon as I'm settled on the throne, Lord Stone jumps in. "Your Highness, your coronation is days away. And, once again, you have no prince consort."

Without warning, my gaze flicks to Asher, who has indeed joined this little gathering.

But it's Lord Hayes who speaks up. "It must be Prince Cedric."

I stare at him, wondering if he's gone mad. "Prince Cedric? Prince *Cedric*?"

"Yes, it is all arranged."

I look around for the youngest of the king's children, but he's not even in the room. That doesn't bode well.

"Where is he?" I demand. "Is he even aware of this plan? Did he consent?"

Belle takes a small step forward, drawing my attention. Surely she can't be okay with this. She's so protective of Cedric. Always so concerned. "Cedric wished to be here, but he was feeling unwell. He has, of course, given his consent for this union and looks forward to his future with you, Your Highness."

Like hell. I *remember* Cedric saying he had no interest in being king.

Unless that was a lie?

Unless he's the viper in our midst. But then why isn't here, welcoming this development?

I turn my attention to Narissa. What does she think of this union? Of one son being substituted for another? She certainly doesn't look *happy*. I'm about to ask what she thinks when Lord Hayes clears his throat.

"Prince Cedric is your age, Your Majesty. He's unattached. And most importantly, he's a member of the king's own family, ensuring unity and stability at a time when it's desperately needed. There's no difference between Prince Cedric and Prince Rowan, as far as the good of the kingdom goes."

My chest feels as if it's filling with sand. Because he's not wrong on *every* point. Strategically, the benefits are still there. Especially considering what I've just discovered about my parentage.

If it ever gets out that Garrick is my father, the threats on my life would double. The hatred for Garrick is as common as air. So many died because of his alleged treason. It wouldn't just be the antiroyalists out for my blood. Being married to one of the king's sons—any of them—would help limit the fallout. But . . .

*Cedric.*

Then again, what is the alternative?

I hate that I find myself looking at Asher. That *his* is the reaction I'm really waiting for. What would happen if he stepped forward and said he wanted to break his engagement? That *he* should be the one marrying me?

I meet his eyes, and I don't think I'm breathing. But he says nothing, only turns on his heel and leaves the room.

Air rushes into my lungs. "I will not marry Cedric unless I hear, from *him*, that he consents to this marriage. For all Lord Hayes's logic, these brothers are *not* interchangeable. They are their own people, and they deserve to choose their own destinies." My heart aches. I can almost hear Rowan's voice, speaking of destiny.

I meet Narissa's eyes, my expression hard as shattered glass. To my surprise, she gives me a small nod.

Lord Hayes claps his hands. "We will take care of it. You'll see that Prince Cedric is not only willing but eager for this union."

Why is he pushing this so hard?

Lord Rutherford says, "I'll finish drawing up the decree."

I spin and head for the door, my whole body aching. Four days in a carriage has taken its toll. And now my heart is aching too. I don't have the energy—or the will—to wait for someone to fetch Cedric now.

"Tomorrow morning," I say. "I'll speak with Prince Cedric tomorrow morning. Then I will decide." I leave them with my orders as the last word.

But if chess has taught me anything, it's that queens are always the means to an end.

They never win for themselves.

# THIRTY-SEVEN

A BATH WARMS MY BODY and eases my tired muscles, but it does nothing to relieve the roiling mess in my mind. *Cedric.*

I don't want to marry Cedric.

Rowan and I were friends. At least we had some connection, some affection, to build from. But I know very little of his younger brother. Cedric seems young for his age, and somehow even less prepared than I am for the life of a monarch. According to Belle, he often needs Sir Henry's tinctures to help him sleep, and he rarely attends council meetings. When he does, it's anyone's guess whether he's actually paying attention. I know it's important to show unity, but I can't help but think there *has* to be a better option. Both for me *and* the country.

*Hate has never been our problem.*

I pull myself up out of the bath and dry off, rubbing my skin savagely.

They announced my marriage to another of his brothers, and Asher just walked out. No arguments, no opinion at all. Why *did* he almost kiss me, if I'm so easily dismissed?

I throw on my chemise and dressing gown, half-heartedly run a brush through my wet hair. I need to go to bed. All the travel has exhausted me. The revelations about my father, this new betrothal . . . I need to *rest.*

But, instead, I pace before the fire, replaying every moment with Asher over the past couple of weeks. My pulse races, sending the tingling thrum of my heartbeat into my throat. There are no answers in this room, no release.

I hurry to my armoire and flip through a few dresses, but the tension is winding tighter in my chest, the restlessness crawling through my legs. I don't want to take the time. I don't want to wait. At the last second, I strap my knife belt around my waist—because I also don't want to meet any would-be assassins unprepared.

Fully aware that I'm probably making a massive mistake, even as heat coils insistently low in my belly, I head for the secret doorway.

If nothing else, Asher and I need to have a conversation. We need to clear the air.

When I reach his room, he's standing before his hearth, gilded by firelight, a tankard in his hand. He's still wearing his armored leathers. For just a moment, I watch him. I want to know what he's thinking. But he's just staring blankly at the fire.

A pressure builds in my chest, an itch crawling under my skin. I'm going to call it anger. I look at him, and it's all-consuming. I try the latch for his hidden door without knocking.

It swings open, and suddenly we're face-to-face.

Somehow, he manages not to look surprised.

"Your Majesty."

His leather armor clings to his chest and shoulders, his loose white shirt flowing around his arms. Tight leather breeches protect his legs. His whorl of chestnut hair falls over his forehead, doing little to hide his brilliant green eyes. Dark circles crowd beneath them, and I'm thrown back to that moment in the library, just before everything changed . . . when he was up this early because he hadn't gone to bed yet. He smelled of smoke and ale, and he had Lady Rosaline giggling at his side.

I haven't seen him look that unmoored since. But he doesn't look at peace now either.

"Why are you here?" he asks, his gaze raking my body. Despite my lavender velvet dressing gown, I still feel naked.

I can't tell him why I'm here, about the anger and the restlessness and the heat in my belly. I don't know why I'm here.

My own stare catches on the knife strapped to his thigh.

I unsheathe my blade. "We haven't trained in days."

"Of course not—" he starts.

I lunge, my "ceremonial" dagger aimed at his throat.

He dodges backward and unsheathes his own dagger.

"So you thought now would be a good time?" He knocks my blade away. "In my room?"

I've grown in strength, if not in skill. I keep my grip on the knife and use the momentum to spin and lunge again, this time for his heart.

"Why not?" I ask, shoving against his block. "It's important for me to know what to do when I'm under threat, even if that threat is hidden behind closed doors. A woman is *never* safe."

He slides out of range before attacking me again. This time I'm the one blocking, breathing in his breath and heat as he pushes against me, trying to get past my guard.

"Who has threatened you, Ruby?" he asks, the words rough and low.

I want to scream, *You! You have threatened me, you have made me question everything.*

"I don't know, Asher, I'm on my second arranged marriage and I'm not officially queen yet. That feels awfully threatening." His surprise gives me an advantage; as his arms slacken, I twist, breaking his grip.

Asher growls and flicks his hand out, a second blade appearing in his other hand. Like an avenging angel, he advances on me. "You know you can say no."

Fury bubbles up inside.

I slam his first blade away and shove my chest against his, a move so surprising he forgets to block. My knife caresses his throat. "And risk *your* family's future? Everyone wants something from me, *needs* something from me. You really think I can just say no?"

A storm breaks across his face. "What do you want *me* to do?"

"What do you think?" I'm so angry tears are sliding down my hot cheeks. "Say something! Protect your brother from this ridiculous marriage. Tell them you don't want to marry Rosaline! Stop pretending you don't give a shit, and—"

"I am doing my fucking duty," he snarls, pressing into my knife like he *wants* me to cut him. We're so close his breath feathers my hair. He's got his hands on me, but he isn't pushing me away. He's not fighting back. He's . . . holding me, clenching me against him, my knife the only thing between us. My chest heaves.

"Yeah, and how does that fucking duty feel now?" My brain directs my body to pull away, but somehow as my shoulders are making space, my hips are rolling forward into his. My fury has lit me on fire.

My whole body is going up in flames.

"Like . . ." he says, and his voice drops. His gaze drops to my mouth. "Like agony."

With a groan, he pushes into the knife, like he'd risk *death* to kiss me.

I yield, letting the blade drop from my tingling fingers. His knives fall to the ground with a clatter and then he's fisting his hands in my dressing gown, pulling me closer. I meet him with my mouth and my hands and my hunger.

We kiss like it'll kill us if we don't.

"Ruby," he murmurs against my lips.

He's so big, so much taller than I am. His arms around me feel like iron. I kiss him harder and he matches me, capturing my lower lip between his teeth.

But the moment I soften, the moment I pause for breath, he loosens his hold. He gives me space. Still, I kiss him again, drawing his very breath into my lungs.

His hands drift lower and suddenly he's lifting me, my dressing gown tangling around his legs. He presses my back against the cool stone wall. I hook my ankles around him and invite him closer.

"I don't want to be a duty," I murmur on a gasp, as he kisses the sensitive spot at the base of my throat.

He grinds into me, his breath hot against my skin. "I've never envied my brothers before. I tried . . . I tried to hate you . . ."

His mouth burns a line of fire along my collarbone. The restlessness I've been feeling, it's not fading but shifting into a new electricity. A new desire.

I unhitch my legs and let my body slide down Asher's until my feet hit the ground. Then my hands move to his stomach, searching for a crack in his armor, a way inside.

He notices and obliges, unlatching and removing the heavy leather. My fingers slip up under his shirt, reveling in the velvet hardness of his chest.

Matching my urgency, he slips my dressing gown off my shoulders. Our mouths find each other, mapping new lines of heat.

When we fall into his bed, the pile of down blankets rises in a cloud, a cocoon to contain the storm building between us. Asher's weight pressing me into the softness sparks lightning bolts of desire deep in my belly. He pauses, his mouth against the curve of my jaw.

"Are you sure this is what you want?"

I growl as I kiss him, my hands winding through his thick, soft hair to draw him closer. "I wanted you even when I *did* hate you."

He laughs, the rumble in his chest sending delicate flames of sensation through my body. For a moment, he disappears, and the cool air against my skin is a scream. But when he returns, his bare legs slide against mine, their roughness a delicious contrast.

Our kisses deepen, electrify every nerve ending. I arch closer, my hands gliding down his back under his shirt. With a shift and heave, he pulls it off, his mouth finding mine again. My chemise rides up my thighs, his heat pressed achingly against my core.

He nips at my ear, burning kisses to my shoulder. "Are you on—"

"All the maids are given moonflower," I breathe, pulling him ever closer. "I never stopped taking it."

He sighs, his body sinking into me, and it's like we can both, finally, breathe.

When the storm breaks, we ride it out together.

# THIRTY-EIGHT

MY DREAMS ARE HALF-FORMED AND threatening. Distant voices, an eerie wind, a marble angel with my mother's face crying tears of blood.

And then, suddenly, I'm awake and someone's hand is pressed over my mouth and there's a voice repeating in a whisper, "Don't scream. Don't scream."

My first instinct is to do exactly that.

But I'm so disoriented, so groggy, that I don't immediately struggle. The hand disappears, and in the dim light from the fire, the face peering down at me comes into focus.

Cedric.

Beside me, Asher breathes deeply, evenly. He's still asleep.

I move to roll over and wake him, but Cedric puts a finger to his lips and shakes his head. Then he beckons for me to follow him.

Slowly, unsure, I sit up, untangling from the mound of blankets on Asher's bed. I wrap my arms around myself; I'm still wearing my chemise, but without the warmth of the blankets, the chill of the room seeps into me.

Cedric drops his gaze, to be polite probably, but a blush climbs my cheeks. Oh God. Cedric must know he and I are to be betrothed, and here I am in bed with his brother. Is that why he's here? Because he saw me and wants to know what game I'm playing?

What game *am* I playing?

I hurry to the sitting area, reaching for my things haphazardly. One slipper, my knife and belt, my dressing gown, my other slipper.

"You're not safe here," Cedric murmurs.

*Not safe here?*

Abruptly, he exits Asher's room. Is he sleepwalking? Having a nightmare?

I follow him into the hall and back to his room.

It's cold in here, the banked fire nothing but a single glowing coal. The window's cracked, letting in a frigid blast of late-fall air. Automatically, I hurry to close it. Then I turn my attention to the fire. Kindling, log, a couple of puffs from the gold-plated bellows next to the hearth. Soon, the flames are dancing merrily, and heat is warming my face.

When I turn back to Cedric, he's standing in the middle of the room, watching me.

"Are you okay? Do you need something?" Unease twists in my stomach. Why isn't he saying anything? Why did he want me to leave Asher's room?

Why did he say I'm not safe?

He faces me, his expression stark in the brighter glow of the fire. After an uncomfortable moment, he speaks. "I don't need anything. *You* do. You need to get out of here. Out of the castle. You need to leave. Don't you see? The shadow killed Sorren. It killed my father. It wants to kill you too."

"What shadow, Cedric?" I ask, trying to be gentle. I don't know what he's talking about, if he's having some kind of walking nightmare, or if he's trying to scare me. Whatever's going on, it's unsettling.

He runs his hands through his hair, like he might not be sure either. "I saw it, up on the tower," he says. "A shadow behind Sorren. It pushed him. He fell. The blood—" He shakes his head, like he's trying to dislodge the image. "No, not the blood. The *shadow*. It wants you gone, Ruby, just like Sorren. Just like Father. You can't let it get to you."

"What . . . what are you saying?" My heart is starting to pound, and the last vestiges of sleep have left me fully. A chill shivers down my spine. "Are you saying . . . did you see someone *push* Sorren off the tower?"

Cedric suddenly steps close to me, his eyes glancing around like he thinks someone is watching us. He whispers in my ear, "You're not safe here."

"What about you?" I ask quietly. "Are *you* safe, Cedric?"

His face crumples. "I'm so scared."

Gently, I take his arm. Together we walk into his bedroom, to the bed with the messy twist of sheets, the pillows knocked onto the floor. His sleep was obviously restless. Plagued by nightmares. I help him to sit on the bed. I collect his pillows. I murmur quietly, reassuringly, as he continues to worry about me, about the shadow, about himself.

Next to his bed, there's small bottle sitting on the table. "Is this your sleeping draught?" I ask. He nods, numbly. I urge him to take a couple sips and then persuade him to lie down.

"It's okay," I say. "The shadows can't hurt you."

His eyelids flutter. His head is on his pillow, but tension still runs through his body. I sit on the edge of the bed and pat his arm until his breathing slows.

As he drifts back to sleep, I stare down at him. We're the same age, and he's painfully handsome, just like the rest of his family. He looks remarkably like Asher, with his chestnut hair and green eyes. But that's where the resemblance ends. Cedric has none of Asher's assertiveness. Nor does he share Sorren's quiet maturity or Rowan's charm.

I'm about to stand up when Cedric grabs for my hand. "The shadow is dangerous, Ruby. Don't let it kill you too."

I wait until he's really asleep this time, my heart racing, the thoughts swirling madly through my head.

*Who* is the shadow? Rowan is gone, and Asher—

He couldn't mean Asher . . . could he?

What did Cedric actually see when Sorren fell? And how did he know where I was tonight? Was he spying in the secret passages? What else has he seen?

I shuffle back to his sitting room, the questions twisting in my head like a nest of snakes. I don't know what to make of Cedric's warning, of this shadow—

Asher is standing before the hearth, backlit by the fire, his face bathed in darkness.

"God!" I yelp, my hand going to my throat. "What are you doing?"

"Did Cedric have another nightmare?"

I nod, swallowing nervously. Asher has put his pants back on, and his shirt. It's open at the throat, exposing his collarbone and the small mark I left there.

"Cedric was the one who found Sorren. It was difficult for all of us, but for him . . . he was already so lost in his head most of the time. Now, it's much worse."

"He came into your room. I helped him back to bed."

He glances toward the darkened bedroom. "You should have woken me. I didn't know where you were."

"I'm sorry. But now I need to go," I say. Tonight has been . . . a lot.

I head for the tapestry on the wall near Cedric's fireplace, where I think the secret door must be hidden.

Asher catches my hand. "Wait."

*The shadow is dangerous, Ruby. Don't let it kill you too.*

My heart twists. How can I doubt Asher, after everything? He's saved my life, he's kept the secret of my father, he kissed me like it *meant* something. And still, and yet . . .

I clear my throat. "The guards could check on me, they could discover I'm gone—"

"Ruby." My name on his lips makes me stop. I turn to look at him. In the firelight his green eyes are luminous. "Tomorrow I'm going to end my betrothal to Rosaline."

I study him in the golden light, my heart battering at my ribs like a caged bird. "What are you saying?"

"I'm saying you were right. To hell with duty."

The breath freezes in my lungs. What's happening?

His voice deepens, rough and tender, the way he spoke to me in the dark of his room. The way he kissed me. "You shouldn't marry Cedric. You should marry me."

His words drop into my mind like a stone into a pool of water. The ripples spread.

Hours ago, when I was running my hands through his delicious curls, my body aching for his, I would have celebrated this moment.

But now . . . now all I can see is the haunted look in Cedric's eyes. All I can hear is his voice, urging me to leave. Telling me I'm not safe.

Cedric saw someone with Sorren on the tower. A shadow. He thinks Sorren was pushed. If the king was murdered . . . who's to say Sorren wasn't murdered too?

And who had the most to gain? First from his brother's death, then his father's? And now, a wedding . . . what do I do if it was Asher all along? If his goal was simply to be king, whether by birthright . . . or marriage? No, no. This is ridiculous. He *saved* me.

*But he also knew your attacker.*

It's all too muddled. I'm too tired. I can't see the pieces clearly anymore; I don't know where I stand. What we did tonight, how I felt . . . I can't bear it.

"I—" I have absolutely no idea what to say.

"Are you okay?" Asher asks, cupping my cheek in his palm. The genuine—or genuine-appearing—concern on his face sends a dagger through my heart. How can I be having these doubts?

How can I trust they're unfounded?

"I'm okay." I lean in to kiss his cheek. "Just tired. I need to get back before someone notices I'm missing."

He shows me the hidden latch and walks me back to the king's chambers, holding my hand in the dark passageway.

I wait for a few minutes, until I'm sure he's back in his own room. Then I slip into the passage once again.

I need to see Sara.

There's no one else I can talk to, no one else I can trust. I have to tell her everything. This is no longer a game I can play alone.

I hurry down the passage, feeling with my hands and the toes of my slippers. I reach the servants' quarters and sneak down the hall. I knock quietly on her door. No answer.

Silently I twist the knob and push into her room.

"Sara," I whisper. "Sara, I need to talk to you."

Still, there's no answer.

Sara isn't here.

I whirl and hurry out of the servants' quarters. At any moment, someone could come upon me and wonder what the hell I'm doing down here.

I don't have a good answer, either.

*A queen doesn't need to explain herself.* I try to channel Belle's lessons as I hurry to the secret entrance to the passageway. I pause before the tapestry, trying to remember the location of the latch, when a hand drops onto my shoulder.

I twist, swallowing back a scream.

# THIRTY-NINE

LORD HAYES STANDS BEHIND ME, his large form filling the darkened hallway.

"Your Majesty, what are you doing down here?" he asks quietly. He's also in a dressing gown, ornate and heavy looking. "Where's your guard?"

"I—" I don't have a ready explanation.

I'm so tired. I can't hold on to all of this alone. I probably should have talked to Lord Hayes about my concerns from the beginning. "Tareth, there are secrets in this castle. And if I don't uncover them, I'll be a target forever. I . . . I need help unraveling the lies."

"Your Majesty, this is not a conversation for the hallway. Come on, now." He turns on his slippered heel and heads away from the hidden door.

I follow him, thankful for his lantern, as most of the halls are unlit this time of night. At last, he stops at the threshold of a small sitting room. He closes the door behind us. I move to the warmth of the fire, pulling my dressing gown closer around me. The shivering chill of Cedric's room hasn't left me.

My heart aches remembering the heat Asher and I shared. Did it mean nothing? How can I say he was using me or manipulating me when *I* was the one who pursued him? Even his suggestion that we marry . . . wasn't I the one to initiate that?

It's not as if Cedric named him as the shadow.

I don't know what to think or feel. I don't know what to do.

And I *always* know what to do. I play chess three steps ahead. Why do I feel like I can't even see the board anymore?

"What are your particular concerns, Your Majesty?" Lord Hayes asks.

"I believe the king was murdered," I blurt out, the words popping like a cork from a bottle. We'll start there. It always comes back to the king. "And I'm starting to wonder whether Sorren was too."

To his credit, Lord Hayes doesn't immediately yell that I'm crazy and shuttle me off to Sir Henry for a tonic. Instead, he leans against the small writing desk near the fire, crosses his legs at the ankle, and says, "Tell me everything."

So I do. Well, almost.

I share the mystery of the king's note, his cryptic mention of history, the possibility that someone could have snuck in or left a snake or poison in his room. I don't mention the secret passages or who my father is . . . but I do share the new revelation from Cedric, that someone might have been with Sorren on the tower. That someone might have *pushed* him.

"Cedric said I should leave the castle, that I'm not safe here. I . . ." I think of the snake, the assassin in the crypts.

The way Asher stared at me, his face hidden in shadow.

"Perhaps . . ." Lord Hayes sighs. "Perhaps Prince Cedric has a point."

"I can't marry into the royal family. Any one of them could be the king's murderer, and—oh God—*Sorren*'s murderer. Even

Cedric. He was the one who told me everyone in his family lies. The king himself suspected his family. That's why he chose me."

God, I don't know who to trust. Maybe Cedric just had a bad dream. Maybe he's trying to drive a wedge between me and Asher.

Maybe Asher has been the villain all along.

Lord Hayes looks at me for a long moment. "It explains why Octavius *didn't* choose them. Not why he *did* choose you. Have you come up with any theories as to that?"

I look at him more closely. He's so calm. It's almost like—

"You're not surprised," I say. "This isn't new information. What do you know?"

He sighs a little, gathering his hands at the tie of his belted dressing gown. "I've had my suspicions, I confess. I said nothing because I had no proof, and I hoped I was wrong."

"Sorren too?" I ask, shivering.

"It does seem as if someone has designs on the throne," Lord Hayes says. "And I'm afraid you complicated things further."

"So you *do* think one of Sorren's siblings wants the throne for themselves." Asher, Rowan, Belle, Cedric . . . which one of them could have that level of ambition?

Asher thought *I* killed his father. And Rowan was so determined to *end* the monarchy. How does any of this actually fit?

And what of Narissa, who might have wanted the king dead? Surely she wouldn't have murdered her own child. I remember her after Sorren died. She didn't leave her chambers for a month, and when she did, she was so pale and drawn she looked like a wraith.

Lord Hayes clears his throat.

"What is it?" I ask.

"Your coronation is in a few days. If we can keep you safe until then, the bulk of the danger will be past. I can see now . . . aligning you with the royal family was perhaps a mistake. Once you are queen, you can name a different heir, someone you trust. Change the line of succession completely, so your death will not satisfy their ambitions."

I balk. I hate the thought of fleeing like some pretender to the throne, even if that's what I feel like. "I don't know. I don't think that shows strength. If I leave the castle—"

"I don't think you need to leave." Lord Hayes pushes off from the desk and paces in front of the fire. He rubs his bearded chin. "There is a place where we can hide you that's *within* the castle."

I fight the urge to move, cracking my knuckles instead. After the threats we've already faced, there's something particularly ominous about Lord Hayes plotting to spirit me away *now*. This is when I need to show I'm not afraid, that I can't be cowed by threats and conspiracies. Isn't it?

"Yes, I think this will work," he continues, oblivious to my concern. "I'll announce you are traveling to your hometown to reflect before your coronation. I'll pick somewhere remote. Send Prince Asher with the caravan to help preserve the ruse . . . and assure he doesn't look for you. You will stay here, in safety, until the ceremony."

"I don't like it," I say. "It will look like I'm hiding away, even with such excuses. I think I need to show *more* resolve. I can announce my plan of succession now, before the coronation."

Lord Hayes shakes his head, frustration edging into his expression. "You have to give me time to discover what I can about

Sorren's death. And you need to keep yourself safe. You have no conception of how precarious your position is, Your Majesty."

The more he argues, the less I like the idea of hiding. I'd rather confront Asher again, knife in hand, than sneak off in the night.

"No," I say, more decisively. "We'll question the royal family. We'll imprison *them* if they're a threat. I shouldn't be the one to hide."

Tareth sighs, rubbing a hand over his face. "It's unwise to not take this threat seriously."

"Do you know something I don't?" I ask. He's never pushed back like this before. Maybe there's a reason. "Have there been other threats?"

Just hours ago, he was pressing me to marry Cedric. I've never known Lord Hayes to be indecisive. This doesn't feel right.

At this, Lord Hayes looks up, piercing me with his gaze. "Did you speak with Lord Garrick Donahue when you were in the Reaches?"

A jolt shoots through me. "Why? What does that have to do with this?"

He continues to stare at me. "You tell me. You said the king spoke of history. You asked me about Garrick. Why, Your Majesty?"

A chess piece shifts into place. Lord Hayes and Lord Donahue . . . they knew each other.

"You were there," I say softly. *Click, click, click.* The pieces are moving across the board. "You knew him. You knew what happened. Lord Hayes, can you think of any reason someone might have wanted to frame Lord Donahue?"

Lord Hayes moves to his desk and lights a candle in a heavy pewter candelabra. "Lord Donahue, framed? That's laughable."

But he doesn't laugh.

I don't know what to think, what's happening here. But something is. Something I'm not comfortable with. Suddenly, I don't want to be alone in this room in the middle of the night with this man.

"I'm tired. We can continue this discussion with the rest of the council." I head for the door.

"Your Majesty, wait."

As I turn toward the advisor, there's a flash of movement, a whirl of white and silver. A bolt of pain explodes in my temple, and I fall into the ravenous dark.

# FORTY

THE SHUDDERING CLANK OF METAL on metal shocks me out of my stupor. My brain is a muddle. I blink open my eyes, but at first, I don't understand what I'm seeing. Where am I? Cold stone is beneath me, and the door before me, reinforced with steel, is being locked.

"Tareth!" I cry hoarsely. "What are you doing?"

"Just what we said. Keeping you hidden away until after the coronation."

"After?" My head throbs and I can barely think. *After* isn't right.

He stares down at me through the grates of the small window in the door. He's panting, out of breath. Like he just carried an unconscious woman up a tower's worth of stairs.

*Am I in the Old Tower?*

"Let me out right now. I said I didn't want to hide." Talking makes my stomach roll. With an effort, I sit up. "This isn't how we stop the killer."

"I'm stopping *you* from destroying my kingdom."

I stagger to my feet, and the world swoops around me for a few sickening seconds. It's clear, suddenly, that I misjudged Tareth entirely. "It was you. Not the royal family."

"It has ever been my job to protect Lumaria from all threats, outward *and* within." He almost sounds proud.

I want to knife him in the face.

"You framed Lord Donahue. What he said was true."

Lord Hayes's face suffuses with blood. "I *knew* you spoke with him. I knew you were about to ruin everything."

"Why did you frame him?" I say, my voice shaking. "How does your history with him ruin everything?"

"You expect me to believe he didn't tell you?" he scoffs.

Well, it's clear *he's* not going to tell me. *Damn you, Garrick. You should have told me this great, big dangerous secret. Or at least warned me about Tareth!*

"What will you do now?" I ask, willing the bright spots in my vision to subside. "Slip another snake into my cell? Starve me?"

A cursory glance shows I'm indeed in a cell—a tiny one with nothing on the ground, not even a chamber pot. There's one high window, in which I can see a sliver of lightening sky.

Lord Hayes laughs without humor. "I wasn't expecting to see you this evening, but I'll have the poison to end your life within hours. You will not see another sunset, my dear. And when you fail to reappear on your coronation day, Prince Asher, the rightful heir, will take your place."

He's disgusting. "If you hadn't killed Sorren and the king, the question of my succession would never have come up."

He raises a brow and scoffs. "You think *I* killed them? And you're supposed to be this brilliant mind—the king's little pet project, teaching you chess, allowing the royal tutor to give you lessons . . . Sorren was a tragedy, even if he did know too much."

My hazy, not-feeling-very-brilliant mind twists his words over and over. Wait, is he suggesting he *didn't* kill Sorren and the king?

He's already admitted to framing Garrick and trying to kill me. Why lie about two more crimes?

All the disdain Lord Hayes feels for me has risen in red splotches to his cheeks, and it's obvious he's dying to tell me all about his cleverness, how he's basically creating a power vacuum for himself to fill. Or maybe what he's really desperate for is the chance to tell me I'm not welcome.

A tiny smile tips up the corner of his mouth.

"Yes, I think this is perfect," he says. "You'll disappear, and I'll be here to guide the kingdom, as I've always done."

Before I can respond, he disappears from the window. His footsteps echo, and then they too are gone. I scream, just to be sure. But I know, deep in my bones, that no one is coming to rescue me.

# FORTY-ONE

I STAGGER TO THE DOOR. There's no handle on this side, just a hole for a key and the small, barred window. I grab the bars and try to shake the metal and wood apart, screaming and screaming.

How could Lord Hayes do this?

He supported me, *helped* me.

I shift my attention to the window. The sky has turned from gray to a washed-out blue with golden edges. The sun is rising. Who's stationed at my bedroom door? Garon? Calen? How long until they realize I'm not there? They'll search the castle. They'll find me.

Before Tareth returns with poison? Before he tells everyone I've gone into hiding until my coronation?

My heart slams into my rib cage. My head aches and white streaks still lurk at the edges of my vision.

*Okay, Ruby. Think.*

I look around the small room. Stone walls, small window, bare floor. This isn't a cell set up to house a prisoner. No chamber pot, no straw mattress for sleeping. Not a single thing I can use.

I pull my dressing gown closer around me. It's frigid in here, and we're high enough that I can hear the wind shrieking against the window. My hand pauses at my waist. The dressing gown hangs loosely on me, its belt nowhere to be found. But I feel something . . .

I open the front of the gown to reveal my thin nightgown.

And the knife belt strapped around my waist.

I withdraw the small, sharp blade from its sheath.

I scurry to the door, ignoring the seasick sloshing of my head. I study the lock, the hinges, the place where the bolt joins the door to the wall. If I had a hammer, I could liberate the hinge bolts and open the door that way. But the knife's small, sleek hilt, so perfect for my hand, isn't large or heavy enough to move the bolts.

Next I try to slip the blade into the tiny space between the doorframe and the door itself. If I can push against the deadbolt that way, I might be able to—

The knife doesn't fit in the gap.

My third and only remaining option is to try to pick the lock. Something, admittedly, I once knew how to do, thanks to a somewhat unscrupulous stablehand who taught Rowan, who taught me.

I've no pins in my hair, but the buckle on my knife belt is a similar shape. In a move I'm fairly certain no queen of Lumaria has ever used before, unless Governess Blake skipped a very interesting lesson, I wedge the buckle pin and the tip of the knife into the lock.

It takes longer than I'd like, long enough that my heart is skittering in my chest and a cold sweat has collected on the back of my neck, but the lock finally clicks, echoing in the room.

The door pops open with a clank, and I nearly fall to my knees. In surprise, but also in terror.

The hall is much darker than my cell—there are no windows,

and the light from the cell's window barely makes it through the doorway. Shadows crowd close, dampening my breath, echoing oddly when my blade bumps into the doorframe.

How long do I have before Lord Hayes returns? What if he's on his way even now?

I push away the fear. I am queen of Lumaria.

I have the power here.

But that doesn't mean I want to meet him in this lonely, abandoned hallway. I hurry into the darkness, hands out to feel my way.

It takes an age to find the door to the stairs. I pause, listening.

Nothing.

A torch illuminates the first turn, but the light comes at distant intervals, with swaths of darkness to climb through. The twisting stairs of the Old Tower are worn smooth in the centers and unexpectedly shallow. I have to descend far more slowly than I'd like. But I can't risk falling.

Every few steps, I pause to listen for footsteps.

How long does it take to procure poison? I think of the king lying in state, his lips drawn unnaturally over clenched teeth. His belly bloated. His skin almost purple.

If I don't get down these stairs, it'll be my turn.

I kick off my slippers and let my bare feet connect with cold stone. I move faster now, so fast the spiraling stairs make me dizzy. But dizziness is better than bloat and agony.

Dizzy is better than dead.

Suddenly, my foot misses the stair. I go down hard on my other ankle, the one I twisted at the cemetery a week ago. Pain explodes up my leg. I let out a little cry before I can quell it. But I can't stop, not now.

Limping, I pass doors to other floors, and I pause a half dozen times, wondering whether I should stop, wondering whether it's the floor with the real prisoners and their guards, guards under my command.

But I don't want to slow down. If I'm wrong and it's just a hall of empty storage space, it's that much more time Lord Hayes has to find me.

Finally, *finally*, ankle screaming, I reach the last door. I open it a crack, peering into the hallway. This corridor is better lit, tiny fires snapping in their sconces.

I don't see anyone.

Swallowing back a whimper, I dash down the hall. I have the vague goal to make it to my chambers. My guards will hopefully be there; the door locks; the passageway gives me access to most of the castle.

I hit the corner, and there's Reece, hurrying down the hall toward me. When he sees me, he stops dead. His face drains of color.

"Queen Ruby?"

"What's happening?" I ask.

"I've just been relieved of my post," he says. "Lord Hayes is briefing the council and the royal family. He said you'd been threatened, that you had gone into hiding until your coronation. You shouldn't be out here."

I give him a grim smile. "Reece, I need you to gather as many guards as you can, as quickly as possible. Meet me in the throne room. You're sure Lord Hayes is there already?"

He nods. "He just called the meeting. I saw him myself. He relieved all your personal guards. We begged to go into hiding with you, to protect you. But he said you didn't need us. Garon was irate."

The idea that anyone would be irate on my behalf is reassuring. I tighten my grip on my knife. "I need you to hurry. The throne room, as quickly as you can. Bring anyone you can find who is loyal to me. That's important, Reece. Only men you trust."

He gives me a solemn nod. He might not know exactly what's going on, but I'm sure it's easy enough to see that some political conflict is afoot.

I push my ankle through the pain. Just a little farther.

When I reach the door to the throne room, I slow.

There are two guards framing the door. I've seen them before, countless times, but I can't remember their names.

"I'm going inside," I say, out of breath and trying not to wince. "I need you to come with me. If anyone tries to hurt me, put them down."

The soldier on the right straightens, his eyes widening. The other, older guard just nods. With a deep, steadying breath, I nod, and in sync, they pull open the doors.

". . . credible threat to her life. We have to establish a new line of succession in the event that—" Lord Hayes is speaking to Asher and Belle. Cedric is off to the side with his mother, staring fixedly at the two tall, golden thrones. Lords Stone and Rutherford are also present, as well as a priest, which is unusual. I can't help noting that Asher is standing next to Lady Rosaline. I wonder if he's told her the betrothal is off. I wonder if it still is.

"No, I have not gone into hiding, as you have suggested." My voice rings out over Tareth's lies.

He whirls. It's satisfying, how comically shocked he looks, his eyes bugging out and his face draining of color. Now his lips are opening and closing, like a fish's. "Your—Your Majesty, how—why—"

"Arrest him," I say to the guards on either side of me. "For treason and attempted regicide."

There's a sickening moment when the room is quiet and no one moves. Even the guards are frozen. My heart gives a huge thump. What if they don't listen? What if they turn on me instead?

And then the chaos washes over me in a wave.

The guards rushing forward.

Reece and his reinforcements arriving at my back.

Narissa screaming, Lord Stone shouting, the priest flapping his hands, Belle putting her arms around Cedric. Asher striding in my direction.

And Tareth, still as marble in the center of it all. He stares at me, naked hatred in his eyes. Even when the guards grab his arms, he doesn't look away. He tells me everything in that glare—how much he wants to kill me, how full of rage he is, how determined he is, even now, to stop me. I feel all these things in my gut. But I hold myself rigidly, my spine straight as a javelin.

As he passes me, I raise my dagger. "Make sure you search him for knives."

Suddenly, he lunges right into my face. Close to my ear, so only I can hear him, he snarls, "It will be *my* legacy that endures, not yours. *My* legacy!"

Before I can react, the guards shove him away from me and out the door.

# FORTY-TWO

SOMEONE CALLS FOR SIR HENRY, though it's as much for Narissa, who's swooning, as for me, with the head wound.

Asher lets his fingertips brush the tender spot at my temple, and I wince. "What the hell happened?"

"Lord Hayes tried to kill me. He was behind everything," I say simply. I don't have the energy for the full story. I suddenly don't have the energy for anything. I haven't slept properly in three days, and I've just escaped an abduction. My injured ankle threatens to buckle, but Asher's arm around me keeps me from embarrassing myself. Out of the corner of my eye, I see Lady Rosaline standing awkwardly off to the side, looking like she'd prefer to be anywhere else.

"I need to put real clothes on," I say. "I need to deal with this. Somehow."

"I'll help," he says.

We turn to leave the room, but Belle hurries over before we can escape. "Your Majesty, you're hurt. You should wait for Sir Henry."

I wave a hand. "Send him to my chambers after he revives your mother."

She nods, but she says, "Are you sure?" like she can't help it. I must look really bad.

As Asher and I hobble back to my chambers, Reece shadowing us, I lean into him. I have no more doubts. Cedric's shadow was Lord Hayes, not Asher. For all the darkness of the last few hours, this gives me light.

*Sorren was a tragedy . . . even if he did know too much.*

I wonder what Sorren knew that was so dangerous. The same thing Garrick knew, or something else? Lord Hayes must have a lot of secrets.

I'll make sure the interrogators uncover every single one.

When we reach my door, Asher smiles down at me, and my heart flutters in a distinctly I'd-like-to-rush-you-into-my-big-fluffy-bed kind of way. But my headache and the recent assassination attempt temper the urge.

Asher kisses the tip of my nose. "Get some rest."

I wake hours later to find myself lying halfway across the bed. My gaze flicks to the king's desk. The bed has become mine, but the desk is still his. The silver secret box he left me sits in one corner, hiding his letter to me.

Did King Octavius suspect it was Lord Hayes all along? I assumed he meant a family member, but Tareth, as his long-time advisor, would practically be family. Did he come to suspect Tareth of framing Garrick? And if so, why did he never do anything about it?

Did he want me to find out the truth about the Great Betrayer? To clear the darkness from my legacy, free Garrick and offer him the vindication he deserves? Or maybe it was a warning, to not end up like my father. When the king played chess, he liked to give little warnings, a little tease so I'd know he was setting me up.

*Legacy.*

That word sticks in my brain.

Lord Hayes was talking about legacy. What did he say? Something about his legacy enduring—

A knock on the door pulls me from my thoughts.

"Come in!" I call, expecting Sir Henry. I drag myself to my feet. Ugh. I'm still wearing my dirty dressing gown and nightdress. If ever there was a time for a bath—

The door opens and Sara hurries in. Even better than Sir Henry.

"Sara! Where have you *been*? I tried—" The words die in my throat.

Sara isn't alone.

Lady Rosaline rushes over to me, her arms full of squirming kitten. "We brought Princess back. I'm sure you've been missing her."

"Thank you. You're absolutely right," I reply. Princess tumbles into my arms and leaps right back out before I can snuggle her close. The kitten races around the room, tail in the air, reacquainting herself with her usual haunts.

Rosaline giggles at her antics and suddenly I realize . . . she was the one who took care of Princess. Sara asked *her*.

A larger realization dawns.

"I went to see you last night, Sara," I say, watching her closely. "But you weren't in your room."

She blushes, her gaze shifting to Rosaline, like she can't help it.

"The thing is, she was, um, she was with me," Lady Rosaline bursts in.

"I see." And I do. It's so obvious, the way they sneak looks at each other, their cheeks stained pink.

Rosaline is Sara's fairy tale.

Why didn't she tell me?

Sara reads my face like a book. "I wanted to tell you before. I almost did," she says softly. Pleading for me to understand. "But it wasn't my just my secret, was it?"

Rosaline looks down. "It's my fault. My father is very controlling. If he ever found out, he would find a way to get Sara fired."

"And you thought I would let him?" I ask, more sternly than necessary. Probably.

"Ruby," Sara says under her breath.

Okay, okay. I'll calm down.

"I heard, down in the kitchens . . ." Sara hesitates. "They're saying Prince Asher plans to break the engagement."

"Is it true?" Rosaline asks, almost eagerly.

"Would that be okay with you?" I ask her.

She nods quickly, her gaze flicking to Sara. "Yes. Definitely. It's all I've wished for for years, even before—" She breaks off, but the *even before Sara* is clear. "I tried asking my father once, but he said it didn't matter what I thought. It was an affair of state."

Ah, yes. An affair of state. I roll my eyes.

"It's true. I'm sure Asher is looking for you even now, so he can break the news." I can't help smiling at their shared look of delight. "Now, Lady Rosaline. I must ask you to leave. I need Sara to help me get ready."

"Of course, Your Majesty. Thank you." She curtsies prettily

and blows a kiss at Princess on her way out. But she pauses at the door. "Oh, Sara. Don't forget to tell Ruby about what you saw."

That grabs my attention. "What did you see?"

"Probably nothing of importance," Sara says, "but you were asking if Belle had a lover."

"Does she?"

"Well, I saw her leave Sir Henry's room. It was . . . very late." Sara blushes again. My guess is she saw Belle as she was sneaking up to Rosaline's room.

Belle and Sir Henry? He's so much older than her.

I say, "She could have been getting medicine for Cedric . . . he has nightmares."

But last night *I* was the one who helped Cedric back to bed. Hmm.

Sara shrugs, but her eyes gleam at the prospect of good gossip. "Like I said, it may be nothing."

She's probably right. Still, I file the knowledge away, like the game-playing style of an opponent. Not something that affects my next play, but it might be useful later.

"Thank you for telling me," I say, my gaze pinned to Sara, and hope she understands I mean more than just about Belle.

With a little wave, Rosaline leaves.

Sara starts talking as soon as the door is closed. "Downstairs, they're saying Lord Hayes attacked you. Is it true? Are you okay?"

My finger hovers over the bruise at my temple. "I'm okay. Now. Lord Hayes was behind everything. The assassination attempts, the king's murder. Sorren's too. He was pushed off the tower. He didn't jump."

Slowly, Sara sits down in the nearest chair. Princess immediately leaps into her lap. "Why? Why would Lord Hayes do such terrible things?"

"Well, he wanted to kill me because he didn't feel I deserved the crown. But King Octavius and Prince Sorren . . ."

*You think* I *killed them? And you're supposed to be this brilliant mind . . .*

Did Lord Hayes actually confess to killing them? He definitely said Sorren knew too much.

"I think Lord Hayes knew something, something Sorren found out about," I say. "And it was bad. Worth killing over."

But long after Sara leaves, as I preside over the council, as I eat my first meal in what feels like days, as I try to find sleep in the king's bed, my sore body desperate for it, but my brain restless, I replay the conversation in my head, over and over. His words echo, day and night. *It will be* my *legacy that endures, not yours.* My *legacy!*

I've checked the king, but the game doesn't feel quite over. I have a terrible feeling I'm missing something, and it'll be the play I never saw coming.

When I knock on the secret door to his room, Asher greets me with worry etched into his furrowed brow.

"How are you feeling?" He reaches for me, drawing me into the circle of his arms. For just a moment, I let myself melt into his warmth, the citrusy spice of his scent. Then I pull away.

"I need your help with something."

"Anything," he says without hesitation.

"Will you come with me to Sorren's room?"

He clenches his jaw, suddenly wary, but after a moment gives me a nod.

The main door to Prince Sorren's room is locked, and while I could try to pick it, we do have another option, so we go in through the secret passageway.

Immediately, I notice we're not the only ones who've been here—the dust on the floor is disturbed by footprints leading into the room from the passage. No footprints mark the floor by the main door. Hmm.

"Why are we here?" Asher asks softly. "I have no desire to disturb my brother's things."

I reach back and squeeze his hand. "I know. But it's necessary. I think . . . I think Sorren knew something—maybe the secret Tareth and Garrick have gone to such lengths to hide."

If this doesn't work, I'll go see Garrick after the coronation. And there's always a chance the interrogators will pull it from Tareth. But I'm anxious, impatient. I don't feel like I have the time to spare. Tareth's secret, the truth behind Sorren's death . . . it's the missing piece. I need it to make sense of everything.

Asher makes to step around me, but I stop him. "Wait. Give me just a minute."

The light filtering through the closed curtains is dim, with the tiniest break allowing a single beam of light to play with dust motes in the center of the room. The scent of disuse and stale air hangs heavy, and I have to rub my nose to keep from sneezing.

Slowly, I scan the room. Unlike me, Sorren doesn't have a separate living room and bedroom, but his single chamber is huge. I note the bed in the back corner, neatly made. Not by Sorren . . . a maid was here at least once, just after he died. The table by his bedside holds a candle, flint, and a single slim book. By the cold hearth, two chairs share a low table, upon which rests a chessboard, midgame. I study the state of play—and recognize a gambit my mysterious opponent tried several times with me.

So Sorren was also playing with his father. The king.

In the opposite corner rests a large desk. Its surface is neat, with several stacks of paper and a knife-shaped seal breaker that looks very similar to the one I have in my room. Another sign that Sorren was being raised as the next king.

An armoire against the wall is open, rows of shirts and jackets ghostly in the dim light. I study the dust on the floor, the smudge of footprints.

The desk.

Carefully I follow the path to Sorren's desk.

The signs are subtle, but I haven't spent my life as a maid to not learn how to read a little dirt. The pattern of the dust suggests someone has moved the papers here. I take a quick look, but there's nothing of interest, a conclusion my predecessor obviously also came to.

The drawers have been opened and carefully closed.

Nothing of interest there either. I turn around and lean against the desk. It's clear someone—Tareth?—was searching for something. Did he find it? And if he didn't, where might it be?

"What do you see?" Asher asks. He's still standing by the wall. With the secret door closed, that's all it is . . . a smooth stone wall covered by a tapestry of a knight atop a white steed.

"I see everything a maid sees," I answer quietly.

I continue my perusal. Where is the dust disturbed? What looks out of place? Where might Sorren have hid something?

"What does that mean?" he asks.

My eyes catch on the table by the bed. There's a rug just in front of it, next to the high four-poster bed. The bed's curtains have been drawn back and every pillow placed neatly, but the rug is pushed under the bed, just slightly, instead of lining up along its edge.

Any good maid would straighten it out. Unless she was told not to, or it was moved after the last time the room was cleaned.

There are no footsteps in the dust by the bed.

I glance back at him. "It means I see everything."

I head for the bed and kneel by the rug. Carefully, I pull it back. Beneath, the rough wooden planks of the flooring are clean, protected from the dust that's collected everywhere else for the past six months. I smooth my hands along them, testing each for a wobble.

Asher kneels beside me and does his own inspection.

It only takes us a few minutes to find the right plank. Just under the bed, hidden in shadow and cobweb and rug. Asher works it free, and I reach into the dark space below, drawing out a wooden box.

"What do you think's in it?" Asher asks.

I draw it onto my knees. "Let's find out."

A creak behind us makes me freeze. I look back at the blank wall. The knight's tapestry. And it's almost as if I can *feel* the presence of the person in the passageway.

It can't be Tareth.

My breath catches in my throat.

I'm tempted to force a confrontation right now. But I don't know what this box contains. I don't know the full truth yet.

I stand up, the box in my hands, and lead Asher to the actual door. "Come on," I say clearly. "We'll take it to your chambers."

But when we enter the hallway, that's not the direction I go.

My ankle smarts as I hurry to the servant stairs. Asher stays close and doesn't ask questions. He doesn't say anything at all until we slip unseen into my old room in the cellar, with the tiny window and the tiny cot.

"The door doesn't lock, but you can wedge the chair," I say.

He gets to work, bracing the back of the one chair under the door latch. I light my last candle—and feel an unexpected jolt at the realization I haven't thought about candles in weeks.

"So, what is it? What have you found?"

I unhook the small latch on the wooden box and slowly raise the lid. Inside there's a leather journal, similar to the king's. Indeed, there's an inscription on the first page: *To my son. Record your thoughts and memories. History will be made here.*

I flip to the last entry.

> I can hardly bear to write what I've discovered. They tried to lie, but I know the truth. I <u>feel</u> the truth. Hell, I can see the truth. After all, I have Tareth's eyes.

I can tell the exact moment Asher reads the words. He staggers backward, away from the table, and sits down hard on my cot.

"*What?*" The word explodes out of him.

My eyes skim the rest of the entry, my heart seizing at the end, where Sorren writes, *I'll have to tell them. It will be difficult, but I can't hold this alone. This shadow on our legacy must be brought to light.*

"His legacy," I say softly. "That's what Lord Hayes said to me. That *his* legacy would endure, not mine. Sorren, you, Rowan . . . you're his legacy. The royal family was really *his* family all along."

This was the secret Garrick discovered. The secret worth killing for.

Asher paces the room, his hands clenching into fists. "This can't be right. There must be some mistake. My mother—we'll go to her. We'll talk to her."

I watch him, my heart aching. "We can, if you want."

Asher pauses and stares at me, his eyes burning. "You don't seem at all surprised. Did you know? Why didn't you say?" He runs a hand through his hair, his face drawn and marked by flushed cheeks and a furrow between his brows.

I spent my whole life without a father. Discovering the one you had wasn't yours? That's a pain even I can't imagine.

"I *didn't* know, Asher. I promise, I would have told you. All I knew was that Sorren had discovered a secret, the same secret Garrick thought too dangerous to reveal to me."

I flash back to that moment in the Reaches. The moment when Garrick decided not to tell me. "Garrick looked at you when he said he couldn't tell me. Do you remember? He knew who you were. Maybe he thought that if he told me in front of you, he'd be condemning me to death. Because your true parentage . . . that's a secret to kill over."

Asher drops his head into his hands. "This is too much. I don't understand."

Reluctantly, I go on. "I think . . . Cedric saw someone on the tower with Sorren. A shadow. I think your brother was pushed because of all this. Because he knew the truth."

*A shadow.*

Oh.

Asher groans. "Sorren was murdered too? By Tareth? Who . . . who is also our father?"

The pawns and knights and rooks are moving through my mind, and each one's strategy is becoming clearer. I think I know how the game plays out, but that doesn't make it easy to tell him.

I sigh heavily. "Not exactly."

Asher paces the small room again before stopping just on the other side of the table, the glow of candlelight gilding his face. "What does 'not exactly' mean?"

"Look, there's still so much we don't know," I say, reaching for his arms. Trying to think of a way to comfort him. "But I'm determined to figure this out. Your father—the king—asked me to discover the truth. And I plan to do that."

His hands grip mine reflexively.

"Ruby—"

I pull him gently toward the door. "We have to go. The whole castle will be looking for me. It's nearly sunset already. I can't disappear again."

"You're the queen. You can do anything." He's a mountain, large and immovable. There's a question in his eyes, one I'm not sure how to answer. "Please. I'm not ready to leave this room. How can I live with this in me?"

I lean up and kiss him gently. "Your legacy doesn't belong to King Octavius, or your mother, or Lord Hayes. Your legacy is *yours*. You get to decide what to do with this truth."

He presses his forehead against mine. "Both of our lives were built on lies, weren't they?"

*Everyone lies.*

Cedric was right about that. I think he was right about shadows too.

I hug Asher tightly, my head against his chest, where I can hear the fast, steady beat of his heart. "This—what we have between us—this isn't a lie."

I promise I'll stay with him, here in my room, until the truth becomes something he can bear. I hold him until long after the candle burns out.

# FORTY-THREE

WHEN I AWAKEN, MY ARM'S asleep under the weight of Asher's body, and my mind is clear. I know what I have to do.

The game board is laid before me, all moves, past and future, revealed.

Carefully, slowly, I extricate my numb arm, but I don't get up. For a moment, I stay curled into Asher's chest, warm in our little nest on the floor. The cot was too small for us both. Asher kept whispering that we should be in his big bed with its pile of blankets and pillows. Its velvet and down.

But that would have meant leaving the safety of these plain walls and letting the world inside. So we made do with my small straw mattress and blanket.

"Ruby?" His voice is hoarse with sleep.

"Asher." I kiss his cheeks, his eyelids, light as the wing of a butterfly.

"It's not morning yet." He pulls me tighter against him and burrows his face in my hair. "Come here. Go back to sleep."

I let him hold me for one more moment. One last, perfect moment.

Then, slowly, despite his groans, I pull away. "The world is waiting. And it deserves to know the truth. We all do."

"What are you going to do?" he asks, opening his eyes for the first time. In the dim morning light, they look more gray than green.

"I'm going to play the game," I say, feigning a lightness I don't feel. "It's time to see who wins."

He grips my hand and brings it to his lips, holding on, like he can stop me from leaving. "What if you misjudge? What if you lose?"

"Do you remember when we played chess?" I ask.

He raises a brow, and God, he looks so good, I lean down and kiss him.

"I remember. You didn't win," he says gently, nipping at my bottom lip.

"Yes, I did." I grin. "You just didn't know it yet."

Before I get sucked back into his heat, I climb to my feet and go about tidying my dress.

I catch Sara on my way up through the kitchens.

She gives me a look but doesn't ask questions. I tell her what I need, and she promises to take care of it.

I head to my room to check on Princess. Luckily there's been a shift change with the guard, but I still get a startled look from Calen and Garon when I come walking down the hall.

When I head for the Old Tower, my dagger is strapped to my waist, and I've got Sorren's journal in my hand.

On the battlements, the wind screams.

When Belle arrives, she immediately hugs her arms around herself. "Your Majesty? Your maid said you wanted to meet up here. Whatever for? It's freezing! Shouldn't we get out of the wind?"

I squint into the sun. The day has that diamond quality of late fall, when the sky is bright and clear, and the air is crisp and just this side of cold.

"I wanted to speak with you privately, without anyone to overhear us." I take a step closer to the parapet wall. But not too close. "I hear this is the place to do that. Prince Asher brought me here on several occasions."

"Did he? That's a little morbid." She very pointedly doesn't look to the edge.

"Why? Because Sorren died here?" My tone offends her.

She raises a brow and her chin in that haughty way only she can seem to pull off.

"Let me ask you something," I continue. "Do you really think Sorren killed himself? He was the golden boy, the heir to the throne . . . everyone loved him. He had everything. Why would he jump?"

At last, Belle lets her eyes graze the parapet. "You didn't know my brother. He grew up feeling the weight of every single decision. Was it just? Was it fair? Was it befitting the heir to the throne? When he was kind, our father said he was too soft. When he was hard, our father called him cruel. Perhaps, yes, he had everything. But it was all sitting on his shoulders, weighing him down." She smiles sadly. "I saw it all. We were always together, especially when we were young. Father called me Sorren's little—"

"Shadow, yes," I interrupt. "I remember you mentioning that."

"When he died, I wanted to die too." After a quick flash of emotion, her face hardens into its usual marble.

"I'm sure." With an effort, I keep my voice even. "So, did Prince Sorren ever bring his 'little shadow' up here? For privacy, so you could talk? Or perhaps you followed him up when he was feeling overwhelmed, so you could comfort him."

She stares hard at me, like she's trying to figure out why the hell I'm asking. "I don't know. I guess? I've certainly never come up here by myself. I'm terrified of heights. Why?"

"Were you with Sorren when he fell?" I force the question to sound casual. But my appraisal of her is anything but.

"Of course not." She's trying to hold on to her marble facade, but two pink spots appear on her cheeks. "If I'd been here, I would have stopped him. I would have made him talk to me."

Knight to bishop.

This is when I begin my attack.

"See, I think that's a lie," I say, crossing my arms over my chest. The wind whips my hair free of my braid, but I ignore it, my eyes never leaving Belle. "I think you were here, and this is where he told you the truth about your parentage. He didn't want to hold it all by himself, and who better to tell than his 'little shadow'?"

She shakes her head vehemently as she backs toward the door. "I have no idea what you're talking about."

I hold up Sorren's journal. "I know what happened. I know Sorren told you what he'd discovered, and you pushed him off the ledge. What I don't know is why. Why would you do that? He was taking you into his confidence; he was trusting you—"

She shakes her head. "You don't know anything. I'm finished

with this conversation. You've insulted me in every possible way, Your Majesty, and worse, you've insulted my brother's memory."

She starts for the door.

"Here's the thing, Belle," I say almost gently. I move to block her way. "I *know* Tareth's your real father. And so do you. Otherwise, *that* would have been the source of your shock and denial when I mentioned your parentage. Not whether you were with Sorren when he died."

She freezes. I can see her mind racing, trying to figure out if I'm right, if she really slipped. I push my advantage, moving another piece into play. "Did you and Tareth ever speak of it? Does he know you know? Surely he suspects. He knows Sorren discovered the truth just before he died. Who knows, maybe he's lived with the grief all this time, thinking Sorren couldn't live with the truth of his parents' betrayal. Perhaps he—"

"He was going to tell Father!" she yells, breaking at last. She rips Sorren's journal from my hand and sends it into the screaming wind. It somersaults and dives off the edge of the battlements, fluttering away. "Sorren and his damn honor. He had to push on Mother and Tareth until he knew the truth. He could have just kept his suspicions to himself. The trip to Yanos when we were young, before Cedric was born nine months later . . . he couldn't leave it alone. Especially after he found them together. But he could have! He could have just left it. But he had to push, and then he couldn't keep the stupid secret to himself. If he'd told Father, he would have surely disowned all of us. Sorren wouldn't be king; I would have lost my place in the castle. It would have been a scandal of the highest order. None of us would ever have recovered."

"But—" I begin, a new horror dawning on me. Oh God, she doesn't know . . .

Now that the dam's broken, she isn't listening to me. Tears are streaming down her cheeks. "I was panicked, upset. He tried to hug me, and I pushed him away. I didn't mean—I didn't mean to hurt him. I just . . . I was so upset and so scared. All I did was push him away.

"But then Cedric started talking about shadows, and Father started asking questions. I had to keep my secret. Sir Henry helped . . . We . . . we've grown close over the years. I knew a little help sleeping wouldn't hurt them."

"Until it did," I say softly.

She shakes her head, like she's trying to shake off the truth. "The day Father asked to see Cedric, I knew I had to do something. Father would know I was the shadow. I had to, I had to—"

"Kill him."

She holds herself rigidly straight. She doesn't have to say it. It's clear.

"You were going to help your *actual* father, Tareth, poison me. More blood on your hands."

She holds them up, palms toward me. "I've done what I had to do to protect myself and my family."

"Actually, you didn't," I say, almost gently. "I don't know exactly what Sorren said to you, but my guess is you didn't give him a chance to finish before you pushed him."

Her eyes narrow. They're still streaming with tears, but it might be the wind. My eyes are stinging too. "What are you talking about?"

"Belle, Sorren had *already told the king.*"

In my mind, I tip her king on its side. But the victory is hollow.

She takes a step back, her jaw slackening. Shaking her head, she tries to argue, but I speak over her.

"He wrote about it in his journal. You're right that Sorren was a man of honor. When he caught your mother and Tareth together, he spent months uncovering the full truth. He didn't know whether it was a recent affair or it went deeper, and he didn't want to make any accusations without proof. He went to the king before he spoke to you."

"That's impossible," she says, her hands shaking. "Sorren told me he was honor bound to share the truth. He didn't say he already had!"

"When he told King Octavius, he expected to be disowned. But the king told Sorren he would always be his heir. Being king was 'more about character than blood.' That's what Sorren wrote in his journal. He asked the king if he should tell anyone else the truth, and the king said he could tell who he chose. That the truth mattered less than his love for his children. So Sorren chose to tell you."

Belle's gasping. Her face has gone bone white. She takes another step back, bumping into the parapet. "You're lying. You're lying."

I shake my head. "You killed your brother and the king for nothing. And your real father is imprisoned for trying to kill me to protect you."

Her mouth opens and closes on a soundless scream. Finally, she whispers, "Ruby. Ruby. Please."

I can hardly hear her. I step closer, one hand on my dagger. I almost feel badly for her. She's obviously rocked to her core. "If you take responsibility—"

Her hand darts out like a striking snake. She grips my arm at the same time she throws herself backward, pulling us both off the parapet.

# FORTY-FOUR

IT ALL HAPPENS SO FAST, and yet agonizingly slowly at the same time. The crumbling wall against my hip, Belle's clawlike fingers digging into my arm, the way the wind flings itself against my face as I go over.

I scream, but the breath is ripped out of my mouth.

My fingers scrabble against the stone.

My legs are weightless.

I wait for my life to flash before my eyes, but all I see is Asher.

Asher's face. Asher's whorl of dark hair. His eyes, green as a forest after the rain. Death will feel less lonely with this memory to hold on to.

The memory jerks closer, and my body jerks to a stop.

The wind is yelling my name.

My arm is burning. I am burning.

I'm being torn in two.

Asher—the real Asher—has my wrist in both his hands. Belle is still clawing at my other arm. We're hanging suspended over air. The ground looks so small below.

"Hang on!" Asher yells.

He braces a leg on the part of the wall that's still sturdy and starts to haul us up.

I look down at Belle. She keeps looking below us, and she's breathing like she's running from someone.

"Belle," I say, loud as I can. "Hang on."

Her eyes focus on my face. She gives me a strange, pained smile. Then, to my horror, she lets go.

The sudden change in weight makes Asher stagger backward, taking me with him. The rough stone wall scrapes my thighs, and then I'm up and over and falling in a heap on top of him.

"Ruby, Ruby," he says, over and over again, his hands on my face, in my hair, like he's trying to assure himself I'm real.

My arms and legs are burning but *I'm not falling to my death, I'm not going to die, oh good Lord . . .*

"I'm okay, I'm okay," I say into his neck. "I'm okay."

We lie there for a long time, entangled with one another, kissed by the cool morning sunshine.

"I'm sorry, I'm so sorry. I didn't realize what she was doing . . . I didn't think she'd get so close to the edge." He kisses my forehead, my eyelids.

"I thought she'd run . . . I wanted you here to stop her. I didn't think, I had no idea . . ." Reaction is starting to set in; my hands are trembling in his hair. Slowly, I sit up and shift farther away from the half-destroyed wall.

*I almost died.*

I stare at the broken stone. "I should have had her arrested. I thought she'd be more unsettled if I met her where it happened, more likely to be honest. I thought that it would give us an advantage. I didn't think—I should have considered her safety."

"No," he says vehemently. "We should have considered *yours*."

"Thank you for saving me." I lean into him, out of the hungry wind.

"Thank you for discovering the truth about my family." He warms my lips with a kiss.

I might have never kissed Asher again.

The thought lights a fire in my chest. I kiss him harder. Desperately. Like a woman who's come back to life.

This time, when the soldier on the tower comes to investigate, there is no misinterpretation.

We manage to have Belle's body recovered before it's noticed. I know she wouldn't have wanted to become an eyesore or a curiosity. Asher arranges to tell Cedric and his mother what happened himself, in private, so they can fall apart if they need to. I keep thinking about Rowan, wondering if he could tell when his twin died. I hope not, for his sake. We'll tell him soon enough.

I send Calen and Reece to arrest Sir Henry. It's clear now that he was helping Belle, supplying her with sleeping draughts and the poison she used to slowly kill the king. Their relationship was more than a secret—it was a danger to us all.

Confirmation of the final piece of the puzzle comes to light in Lord Hayes's interrogation. King Octavius was right, in the end. My history was the key to everything. Tareth formally confesses to framing Lord Garrick Donahue, along with sharing the location of the proof. When my father discovered Lord Hayes's affair with Narissa, Tareth himself sold the secrets to Castella that made their attack possible. Lord Hayes planted the evidence on Garrick and persuaded the king to send him off to the Reaches without ever giving him the chance to defend himself. The king wasn't much better, admittedly. He felt so betrayed, he never spoke to his friend again. And so Garrick never had the chance to tell him the truth.

Worst of all, Lord Hayes confessed to having Esme killed before she could convince the king to hear Garrick out.

But now, all these years later, I can finally do something about that.

And Lord Hayes will spend the rest of his life enduring the same punishment he imposed on an innocent man.

# FORTY-FIVE

JUST AFTER DAWN ON THE morning of my coronation, Princess and I visit Sara in the kitchen yard. The sun glitters coldly and ice films the puddles from last night's freezing rain.

"What are you doing here?" she asks with a little horrified squeak. "I said I'd be up at seventh bell. Am I late? Do you need help into your dress now?"

"Oh, we have plenty of time. I had a question I wanted to ask you, and I didn't want to wait. Plus, I miss the morning air." I watch her sweeping up the droppings from underneath the henhouse, her cheeks rosy in the brisk wind.

"Well, go on," she says brightly, squinting back at me.

"Will you be my advisor? There's a spot open at the moment. Shit, Princess! Don't eat that chick!" I lunge for my cat before she can commit murder, entirely missing Sara's reaction.

When I finally turn back to her, she's standing frozen next to the henhouse, the broom on the ground at her feet. Her mouth opens and closes like a fish's.

"You want *me* to be an advisor to the queen?" she asks, her eyes comically wide.

"You seem surprised," I say, grinning. "Do you not remember me saying you were the only person I trusted in the castle?"

She closes her mouth only to open it again. "But are you sure?"

More seriously, I nod. "I need you, Sara. You'll tell me the truth, even when it's hard. You know what it's like to work your hands to the bone. And you know how to collect and analyze gossip, which is really just a way to say you're a wonderful spy. Oh, and if I make you a noblewoman, there's no reason you can't take a noblewoman for a wife. If you want, of course."

Her cheeks flush. I think she's going to do the fish mouth thing again, but instead she says, "In that case . . . I accept, Your Majesty."

"Good," I say, widening my grin.

With a little wink, she curtsies. "Does this mean I don't have to sweep bird shit anymore?"

"Yes. But there *is* a lot of horseshit to deal with." At her mystified look, I just laugh.

The Towered Arches, where the coronation will take place, where every coronation has taken place since the monarchy was established three hundred years ago, aren't so much actual arches as the skeletal ribs of an ancient cathedral. The marble frame stands, but the walls are little more than rubble. Grass grows within the ruins, with a strip of mosaic floor leading from one end to the other, where a massive stone altar sits, chipped and stained, but still standing.

The whole area is packed with people and carriages. Reece, Garon, and Calen help the footmen clear a path to the entrance. Asher will accompany me to the altar—as my official prince consort.

He helps me down from the carriage. The crowd pushes and screams, everyone wanting to get a look at the maid the king made queen. I don't blame them. I'd be ravenously curious myself if the situation were different. But right now, as the object of the frenzy, the intense scrutiny feels like a corset drawn far too tight.

Soldiers line our path. Asher's been dealing with more protests; so far, we've avoided having to mount a violent response, and I'm in talks with several of the antiroyalist leaders, so hopefully we'll find a peaceful solution. I'm excited to see how Sara, as my newest advisor, will contribute to those discussions.

For a moment, I stand in the crisp midafternoon sun, tune out the cheers and jeers, stare at the arches against the bright blue wash of sky, and breathe. Just breathe.

It was a bit of a scandal when we delayed the ceremony by a month, but the extra time was necessary to deal with the fallout of Lord Hayes's arrest and Belle's death.

Asher gives me a gentle nudge, and I am walking. Small, careful, slow steps, like Governess Blake taught me. My back straight and chin up. As Belle said, *Your time of bowing and compromising and considering others is past.*

She may have been a murderer, but she did have good advice on being queen.

"Look," Asher murmurs, tipping his head toward the altar.

In the front row of honored guests, standing up and turned so he can see me approach, is my father. His lean form is encased not in the simple, threadbare uniform of the Reaches, but in a well-fitting burgundy velvet coat, his chin high, his eyes full of pride.

My tears threaten to fall and ruin the makeup Sara and Theia worked so hard on. With an effort, I keep them from spilling out.

Lord Garrick Donahue has officially been cleared of any wrongdoing, with apologies from the crown. I've reinstated him as an advisor and retired Lords Stone and Rutherford. Stone because he couldn't stop asking me to intervene and *force* Asher to marry his daughter, and Rutherford because he's, well, old.

I'll need more than just Garrick and Sara to advise, but for now they're enough, especially as Asher is still my commander and always open to strategy discussions.

Beyond my father, the priest waits, his robes as ornate and over-the-top as my gown. Sara and Lady Rosaline are seated on the other side of the aisle with Prince Cedric. Cedric is grieving Belle hard, but his mind seems clearer as Sir Henry's tinctures leave his system. Asher says he's having fewer nightmares. Asher and I decided it would cause no harm to let Belle keep her secrets and not announce publicly what she did to her brother and the king. But we did tell Cedric, hard as it was, so he could make sense of what he'd seen the day Sorren died and hopefully find some semblance of peace.

Narissa was cleared of any culpability in Lord Hayes's treason, but that didn't make it any easier for her to face her sons or accept what her daughter did. She decided to return to Yanos, the country of her birth. I can't say I was sorry to see her go.

I wish Rowan could be here, but I did get to see him when I traveled to the Reaches to oversee Garrick's release. Rowan isn't exactly thrilled to be imprisoned, but he's holding up better than

I expected. It was difficult to tell him about Belle, but in an odd way, I do think he had a sense that something bad had happened to her. He didn't seem fully surprised. He *was* shocked when I told him about his real father.

In five years, he'll rejoin us at the castle; I plan to have him help us continue to find common ground with the antiroyalists. It'll be a good way to keep an eye on him.

On the altar before the priest rests a giant golden crown.

Asher and I make it to the altar without me tripping, fainting, or being attacked. Which, honestly, feels like a huge win. The priest raises his hands, and the crowd quiets slowly, until the only sound is a trio of lutes playing slow, haunting harmonies. In the distance, a hawk screams.

Asher moves to the side, next to his brother.

"People of Lumaria, we are gathered here today to observe the sacred transfer of power, from the late King Reginald Forsythe Maxwell Octavius, may God bless his soul, to Ruby Esme Donahue, daughter of Lord Garrick and Lady Esme Donahue."

The crowd jeers loudly—word that the Great Betrayer was not, in fact, the reason for the Seven Weeks War is still moving slowly through the kingdom. But it will happen. I'll make it so.

For me, knowing my parents and their history is worth it.

I kneel on a red velvet cushion before the altar as the priest proceeds with his duty, bracing myself for more protests.

But the crowd behaves. And the heavens don't break apart and strike me dead either.

The priest talks until his words have no meaning. I say the vow

Governess Blake helped me memorize, loudly and with conviction, about my commitment to this kingdom, my promise to be just and truthful, and my hope for a brighter future for all. The priest places the crown, heavy as a promise, on my head.

In a daze, in a dream, at last I become the official queen of Lumaria.

# EPILOGUE

THIS LATE AT NIGHT, THE halls are quiet. The library is dim, lit only by a single candle and the embers of the dying fire in the hearth. Princess wriggles in my arms until I let her down, and then she streaks over to the chair where Asher sits, waiting for me.

His dark hair is a mess of curls. His white shirt glows.

"My queen," he says, rough and low.

Slowly, I approach, watching the way the golden candlelight plays across his face. He winces as Princess scales his leg, but his eyes soften as she butts his hand for pets.

"Is she always this . . . aggressive?" he asks.

I grin. "Only if she likes you."

"Then I'm honored."

"So," I say, when I stand before him.

"Shall we play?" he asks, his eyes flicking to the chessboard.

I stare at the pieces, stark white and black, neatly in their places. I play out the game in my head. The moves Asher will make, the ones I'll answer with.

I pick up my queen and turn to face him. He meets my gaze, warm in the firelight. Gently, he places Princess on the floor, despite her squeaks of protest.

I take her place on his lap. Slowly, I draw the queen down his nose. Across his lips.

"We could play," I say softly, moving to replace the chess piece with my mouth. "But it wouldn't be fair."

"And why is that?" he asks, as his hands slide to my hips.

"Because I've already won." The queen falls from my hand as I curl my fingers into his hair. Just before I deepen our kiss, just before I lose myself completely in him, I add, "You just don't know it yet."

"Oh, yes I do," he murmurs, moving under me, breathing into me, lighting my every nerve on fire. "Luckily, this is a game we both get to win."

# ACKNOWLEDGMENTS

THE WRITING OF THIS BOOK was an absolute whirlwind and wouldn't have been possible without the following people:

My fabulous agent, Pam Gruber at High Line Literary Collective, who can always tell when I need straight talk, a strategy session, or a virtual hug. Thank you for always having my back.

The incredible team at Alloy: Lanie Davis and Viana Siniscalchi, thank you for thinking of me and editing the shit out of this book. Romy Golan, thank you for sending the best emails!

Erica Sussman and the whole team at Harper, including Briana Wood, Chris Kwon, Jenna Stempel-Lobell, Erika West, Mary Magrisso, Danielle McClelland, Meghan Pettit, Gweneth Morton, Lindsey Triebel, Maya Myers, and Audrey Diestelkamp: Thank you for believing in me and Ruby. I'm so thrilled and grateful to be working with you. It's an honor.

The Rights People and all my foreign publishers: Y'all are making my dreams come true!

My lovely writer friends, who kept me sane: Kyra Whitton, Ellen Goodlett, Natalie C. Parker, Intisar Khanani, Jax McQueen, Jackson Pearce, Morgan Michael, and C. Cameron Martin. Thank you so much for helping me keep it together.

My non-writer friends, who reminded me that there was life beyond my computer (and who helped me survive it): Danielle,

Tamara, Michelle, Rachel, Hanh, Chenoa, Seth, Florian, Marti, Angie, and Jennifer.

My family. Some of these deadlines were tough, but I always felt your love, support, and encouragement. Thank you for being there for me, even when it was hard. I love you so much.

Ouija and Checkers, who inspired Princess the kitten. Yes, I'm about to get up and feed you. I promise you will not die of starvation in the next three minutes.

And finally, you, the reader. Thank you for taking a chance on Ruby. Thank you for picking up this book at a bookstore, your local library, online, or off a friend's coffee table while they weren't looking (I won't tell). You're the reason I'm here. XO